Sharon Dempsey is a PhD candidate at Queen's University, exploring class and gender in crime fiction. She was a journalist and health writer before turning to writing crime fiction and has written for a variety of publications and newspapers, including the *Irish Times*. Sharon also facilitates creative writing classes for people affected by cancer and other health challenges.

BY THE SAME AUTHOR

Who Took Eden Mulligan?

The Midnight Killing

SHARON DEMPSEY

avon.

Published by AVON
A division of HarperCollins*Publishers*
1 London Bridge Street
London SE1 9GF

www.harpercollins.co.uk

HarperCollins*Publishers*
Macken House, 39/40 Mayor Street Upper,
Dublin 1 D01 C9W8, Ireland

First published in Great Britain by HarperCollins*Publishers* 2022

2

A catalogue copy of this book is available from the British Library.

ISBN: 978-0-00-851876-9 [TPB]
ISBN: 978-0-00-842448-0 [PB]

Typeset in Sabon LT Std by Palimpsest Book Production Limited,
Falkirk, Stirlingshire

Printed and bound in the UK using
100% renewable electricity at CPI Group (UK) Ltd Croydon, CR0 4YY

MIX
Paper | Supporting
responsible forestry
FSC
www.fsc.org
FSC™ C007454

This book is produced from independently certified FSC™ paper
to ensure responsible forest management.

For more information visit: www.harpercollins.co.uk/green

For my mum, Jeannie Copeland, who showed me that magic and joy lurked in all the unexpected places.

PROLOGUE

The girl wakes. When she opens her eyes she sees nothing but a velvet darkness that seems to wrap around her, making her think of the bog. Her mother always warned her to stay clear of the wetlands, saying that they could suck her down to the depths of hell like quicksand. Once, she'd gone looking for tadpoles and when she'd lifted the jam jar out of the pool it was full of gloomy, gloopy water, coloured with peat tannins. She knows this because Mrs Plunket had taught them all about the bog in nature class. She knows that tadpoles turn into froglets, and that the dry patches of bog are covered with ling heather, bell heather, crowberry and blaeberry. She knows a lot of things, but she does not know where she is or how she has got here.

There is a buzzing sound that she can't identify, and after a while she realises that it is coming from inside of her. Her head is thrumming, a low drone of pain that makes itself known through sound. She knows that it is strange but can't figure out why. Nor can she work out

1

why her legs feel as though they have been filled with sludge. They feel numb and as dead as the carcasses hanging in her grandad's butcher shop.

She is lying on her side and can feel a rough surface against her cheek. Instinct tells her not to move, for movement will bring pain. She wants her mammy. Desperately so. She wants her daddy to lift her up in his big, strong arms, and carry her to bed. She wants to feel the warmth of her sister, Ciara, sleeping close beside her. To hear that chortling, piggy noise she makes when she's asleep.

Sometimes she fights with Ciara, pinching her arm or pulling her hair. She's sorry about that now. Wishes she could make up for all the bad things she has ever done. She can't help the tears coming, prickling her eyes and warming her cheeks.

She tries of think of something nice. Whizzing down the lane on her red bike, the dip of the road and the way it makes her tummy feel bubbly. But then she remembers that the bike has been broken. It's twisted and battered, and it will be no good for anything but scrap. A desperate sadness swells up in her chest, squeezing out all of the air. She can't say how or why, but she thinks that she is in danger. That someone has hurt her and will do so again.

No good can come of being in this blackness, this much she knows.

CHAPTER 1

The first time Detective Inspector Danny Stowe saw James McCallum, he was hanging from a tree in the grounds of Osbourne House Grammar school. Corpses never do make good first impressions, he thought. There was no evidence of last-minute regret, no hands still clutching at the neck, no scratch marks suggesting a desperate struggle as the noose's death grip tightened. A slight breeze rustled the leaves above, while a mist of rain fell softly and somewhere nearby a crow cawed, ignorant of the scene unfolding.

Danny stood at the foot of the hill, glad of the warmth from his North Face jacket, and looked up at the hanging tree. It was a big, old horse chestnut tree, the kind that kids would have been scrabbling along the roots of, seeking out conkers, at the end of September. They would have back in the day, anyway. Now he's not so sure, what with mobile phones and video games he hasn't even heard of. He doubted too many of them relied on Mother Nature for entertainment anymore. It was a mighty big

3

tree. Almost all of its leaves had gone. Those that remained were yellowing and brownish, hanging on only until the next heavy breeze stole them away. The trunk was a mossy green and greying brown. Solid and unflinching, the tree had stood as a blind witness to the horror played out under it.

The tech fellas were busy doing their thing. One of them was photographing the scene while another was carrying out a careful examination of the area beneath the tree. On the surface it looked like a straightforward suicide, but Danny had been in the job long enough to never assume. Procedures needed to be carried out, and the man dangling above belonged to some poor family who had yet to be told that their loved one had – most likely – opted out of this life. Selfish bastard. While Danny knew he shouldn't cast judgement, he also knew it is always the ones left behind who suffer the most.

There was low murmur of chat and somewhere close by someone's phone rang.

Beyond the hill where the tree sat, at the end of the sweeping driveway, the red-brick school looked formidable and elitist with that old money architecture of spires, gargoyles, arched windows, and heavy wooden doors. Osbourne House Grammar was the kind of school that had a Latin motto, an old boys' network and a PTA that could raise serious money without trying too hard.

While parts of Belfast smouldered during the Troubles, places like Osbourne House existed as if in a parallel universe. Sure, you could get in with a top grade in the transfer exam, but everyone knows that to make the grade it takes the dedication of an expensive tutor. And once the child was in, it would be all ski trips, swimming galas, hockey games, rowing club, and rugby – none of which comes cheap. It was the type of school people aspired to send their kids to. Not Danny, though. He couldn't see a family in his future. Not now, anyway.

He listened to the drone of the early morning traffic and the soft mumble of the techs going about their business. It was a small mercy that it was half-term. The school had been closed for the Halloween break from the previous Friday. He didn't need hundreds of concerned parents and smart-mouthed little arses trying to get close to the scene with their iPhones primed to snap a picture.

It was a grey, dismal day with more than a hint of cold in the air. The kind of October day Belfast did well. A day that would be better spent back in the office, even if it was a dreary shite hole with artificial lighting and bad heating. Danny turned as he heard a car pull through the school gates. Forensic pathologist Raymond Lyons parked his flashy 5 Series, got out, and nodded a greeting to Danny. 'Some day for it. What have you got for me?'

'Morning, Raymond. Looks like a suicide hanging, but we need to be sure.' They took off together, their strides in sync as they approached the scene.

'Is it a hunch that it's not as it seems or something else?'

'You'll see for yourself. The school caretaker called it in. The old man tried to cut him down but gave up once he realised he was dead. The uniforms got here with the tech fellas about an hour ago and I think the ACC will be making an appearance himself. It's his old school, apparently.'

A uniformed officer stood on guard and nodded as they approached.

'Sergeant,' Danny said in greeting.

'Sir.'

'Anyone other than the caretaker on the premises?' Danny asked, pleased to see the protocols for respecting the integrity of the site were being upheld. It would have been easy for the first responders to trample all over the scene, assuming it was suicide, but Danny didn't like assumptions.

'No, sir. He's waiting in his office up at the school.'

'Right, I'll send someone up to get a statement.'

The hill was steep enough to give the suggestion of being a manmade mound; perhaps a burial site for a village of people long gone. The tree stood like a sentinel at the top, its wide branches spread out against the bruise-grey sky. Once up close, they could see that the man's face was frozen into a grimace, his mouth wide open and his swollen purple tongue protruding in an almost ludicrous, rapacious fashion. There was something unnerving about seeing the dead when they looked around the same age as yourself, Danny thought. He was clean shaven with a flop of greying, russet hair, the kind that would have been fiery ginger as a kid but had tarnished to a duller shade with age.

Only an hour before, Danny had had the call from his new boss, Assistant Chief Constable Alastair Boyne. Some wag at the station had nicknamed him Battle, in honour of the Battle of the Boyne in 1690, and it had stuck.

'You free, big man?' Boyne liked to talk to everyone like they were his new best friend.

'As free as a bird, Battle, if you don't count the pile of paperwork sitting on my desk. What've you got?'

'Take a run down to Osborne House Grammar. They've called in a suicide on the grounds. White male, mid-thirties.'

'Suicide? Why do you need me to go?'

'Something's not right about it. They'll fill you in when you get there.'

Danny had showered and grabbed a coffee before leaving his recently acquired house off the Ravenhill Road. The novelty of living alone had already worn off. Somewhere on the other side of town his ex-wife, Amy, would be starting her day, and he wondered if she still thought about him. Most likely she was too wrapped up in herself to give him a second thought. As churlish as he felt, he had reached peak don't-give-a-fuck and had moved on as much as he could. She didn't exactly deserve his sympathy, but deep down he still felt a connection to her and was left with a sense of bitter disappointment that it hadn't worked out.

He forced his mind back to the job and watched as Lyons went about his task.

'The knot on the noose looks secure and well-executed.' He was speaking as much to himself as to Danny.

Lyons stood staring up at the body, which was about two feet off the ground.

'Make sure your people cut above the knot to preserve any DNA for testing and make sure they photograph and preserve the rope. I'll need to examine the marks around the neck, checking for bruising that is consistent with the rope fibre formation.'

'Anything out of the ordinary suggesting that it isn't a straightforward hanging?' Danny asked.

Lyons shook his head. 'Not yet.'

They stopped under the tree and peered up at where the rope had been tossed over the branch directly above. Part of the rope was frayed where the caretaker had tried to cut it down.

'Have you noticed how the rope was wrapped around another branch, before being tied?' Danny asked.

'That's more your job than mine. What do you make of it?'

'Someone could have used the rope to hoist the body up.'

'That would take a lot of effort. There's easier ways to try to make murder look like a suicide.'

'Yeah and it would require more than one person to lift him,' Danny agreed.

'Probably, though he's not a big fella. He must be around 170 pounds. Maybe five feet nine.'

'But then why would someone go to this much trouble? Surely, heaving him into the Lagan would have been easier.'

Lyons sighed and spoke in his usual didactic manner. 'Again, DI Stowe, that's your job. Mine is more up close and personal with the cadaver itself. Right now, there's not much more I can do. I'll let you know what I find when I get him on the table.'

Danny turned to the chief SOCO, Fiona Madden, who was standing nearby. 'That's us finished here. You can take him down now but be careful with that rope, and make sure to bag and seal the hands. I'm heading back to the station but call me as soon as you've checked his pockets for ID and his phone.'

'No need to tell me how to do my job, Detective,' she replied in a Sligo accent.

Danny resisted rolling his eyes and held his hands up as if in surrender before following Raymond Lyons down the hill. Fiona was known for her prickly exterior but he'd bet that her bark was worse than her bite. As he reached the bottom, he turned back for one last look at the scene, just as they began taking the body down. He couldn't be sure, but he thought he heard a 'huhh' sound as the last of the air trapped in James McCallum's body was dispelled in a watery sigh of death.

CHAPTER 2

Dr Rose Lainey could hardly believe she was still in Belfast. What had intended to be a short-term visit, to attend her mother's funeral, had developed into a six-month secondment, working alongside her old university friend, Detective Inspector Danny Stowe, in the Police Service of Northern Ireland. Her seventeen-year-old self would have shuddered at the notion that she was back here. It was largely Kaitlin's fault. Reconnecting with her sister and getting to know her nieces and nephews had been a more joyful experience than Rose could have ever guessed. Her brothers hadn't been so welcoming, but she hoped that, given time, they could reach some sort of understanding. Returning to London would make that more difficult. By sticking around, she was giving her relationship with them the best possible chance.

Then there was Danny. Seeing him every day and working with him was a bonus and she had to admit working with the police suited her. The dry, quasi-academic life she had been living in London – writing reports on offenders and providing advice on policy for the Home Office – was all well and good, but there was only so long you could do that kind of grind without becoming jaded. Danny had offered her the opportunity to experience police work that allowed her to use the vast knowledge and experience she had acquired in forensic psychology in a new and fascinating way.

Since the Mulligan case had been successfully wrapped up, she needed to decide what her next move would be. Her former boss, Bernard, was expecting her back in London, but Rose could see Belfast had much to offer, and for the first time in a long time, she felt that she had worth to offer too. That was probably down to Danny. He had always brought out the best in her, making her push herself. It had been great seeing how he had developed as a detective, exploring the case in partnership, each bringing their individual set of skills and experience. He had asked her to stick around long enough to get the case over the line with the Public Prosecution Service. Now she was left wondering, what next? Would Danny be in a position to offer her more work? Would he even want her around on a more permanent basis?

Her phone rang and Danny's name flashed up. She smiled. Danny could do that to her, make her feel good without even trying.

'What are you up to?' he asked as soon as she'd answered.

'Sitting around waiting on you.'

'If only. Fancy taking a run out to interview the wife of an apparent suicide?'

'Why are you interested in a suicide?'

'It's not all that it seems. Something isn't right and the boss wants it looked at carefully as the body was found in the grounds of his old school. He wants to ensure we cover all bases.'

ACC Boyne was new to them. He had replaced ACC McCausland and was quick to shout out orders, expecting his detectives to jump to his command while still trying to be one of the team, and engaging in the kind of banter McCausland would have cringed at.

'Sure, pick me up. I'm still at home.'

'I'm right outside.'

'Of course you are.' There it was again, that smile he elicited from her without so much as an ounce of effort. She grabbed her coat, threw her keys in her bag and headed out into the drizzle to meet him.

As soon as she got into Danny's Audi A4, he launched into the job. 'Best not to let the widow know we suspect foul play. It could pan out to be nothing sinister.'

'You said the body was found at a school?'

'Hanging from the branch of a bloody big tree that sits at the top of a hill in the grounds of Osbourne House Grammar.'

'Right, so what makes you suspicious?' she asked.

'The rope for starters – it didn't look right – and then the scene itself. Why break into school grounds to do the deed? Why not go off somewhere remote like Cave Hill or Belvoir forest? Then again, I could be barking up the wrong tree.'

Rose groaned at his weak attempt at a joke.

'So, what do you think we should be looking for with the wife?'

'I want you to read her emotional state and I want to

12

find out if she had any concerns about how her husband had been acting.'

'And if we find that it's not a suicide?'

'Then it's about looking for the usual – motive and opportunity. You have to ask why someone would want it to look like suicide. Staging a death to look like suicide is considered, planned, and executed with a lot of difficulty. So, if it *isn't* a straightforward suicide, that means someone has gone to an awful lot of trouble and we need to find out why.'

Rose reached over and turned up the heater. 'The pathologist is going to be looking for evidence of bruising, blood or DNA from another person. The body will tell its own story.'

'Yeah but we might as well get ahead of the game.'

'Where's his family home?'

'Ballycoan Road. Do you know it?'

She nodded. 'Yeah, it's near the old Belvoir Park Hospital. What do we know about the deceased?'

'His name is James McCallum. His ID was in his wallet, which the SOCOs found along with his phone in a pocket. He was an architect and had his own practice based in Stranmillis. DS Tania Lumen and DS Jack Fitzgerald went around to break the bad news to his wife shortly after ten thirty. She told them she woke up at 6.50 a.m. to find him gone. She thought he'd left early to go to the gym or to get a head start on work.'

Rose knew that no matter how it came – suicide, accidental death, a road traffic accident, or murder – no one was ever prepared for the knock on the door from the police.

'Money trouble? Business about to go tits up?' she asked.

'Possibly. We haven't started to dig yet, but of course that will be one line of enquiry.'

They drove along Milltown Road, past the Belvoir housing estate, and on towards Hospital Road. The house, though tucked away in a lane off the main road, was easy to find.

'Number forty-seven, here we are.' Danny slowed down and pulled into the driveway.

'Nice place,' Rose said.

The house was designed to look like it had been set into the surrounding field without disturbing anything, and trees, shrubs, and bushes seemed to be pressing in on the structure. A Mercedes SUV sat in the driveway, parked neatly to the side as if the owner didn't want anything to obstruct the perfect view of the house. A double height door dominated the entrance way.

'Looks the part of an architect's home,' Rose said, getting out of the car.

'Yeah, certainly does. Like something you'd see on *Grand Designs*.' Danny reached for the doorbell.

The door was opened by a blonde-haired woman who looked to be in her early thirties. Her pretty face was set in a scowl, as if she was furious with the world.

'Yes?'

'Mrs McCallum?'

She nodded, her eyes narrowed in suspicion.

'Forgive the intrusion. I'm DI Danny Stowe and this is Dr Rose Lainey. I rang earlier. Is it okay if we have a word?'

'Sorry, of course, come through. I was expecting my sister.' Emma McCallum was wearing a white cotton shirt with smart dark denim jeans and tan ballet flats. Her dark blonde hair was clipped back from her face,

14

while her freckled skin appeared to be devoid of make-up. She looked shell-shocked and disorientated, as if she'd woken up in the wrong life.

'No need to apologise. We appreciate that this is a difficult time, and you should be wary opening the door, in case the press come calling,' Danny said.

'The press? Jesus, I hope not.'

'Well hopefully they won't, but sometimes, I'm afraid, they turn just up on spec, hoping the family will give them an interview.'

They followed Emma into the hallway. It was wide and bright, painted in a shade of austere concrete grey with a huge cage-effect of light bulbs hanging overhead.

'We can talk in the kitchen. My mother has Grace out in the garden. We are still trying to take it in, and poor Grace can't understand. She's been distraught most of the morning.'

'Grace is your daughter?' Rose asked.

'Yes, she turned eight a few weeks ago. God, it seems like another life now. We'd a big party for her in the garden; everything was perfect. That's why I can't get my head around this. There is no reason for James to kill himself. I keep thinking he wouldn't do that to us, especially not to Grace.' She sighed and wrapped her arms around herself as if she was cold.

They sat at the marble-topped kitchen table and Rose looked around the stylish kitchen. Everything was tidy and looked brand new, making it feel like a show house waiting for prospective buyers.

'Can I get you a coffee?' Emma offered.

'Yes, please, if it's not too much trouble,' Danny said as he took out his notepad.

Rose nodded. 'That would be lovely, thanks.'

Emma busied herself at the coffee machine, inserting little pods while they could hear the gurgling of steamed milk. The view to the garden was picture perfect. The patio area was designed like a courtyard, complete with cobbled paving and oversized planters. A wooden swing-set and a tree house sat to the left and the lawn looked freshly mowed even though it was late October. The garden was full of plants, shrubs, bushes, and trees, all perfectly landscaped. The soft thud of a football being kicked about could be heard, along with the petulant tone of the young girl's voice. It was sad to think that the child would be growing up without her father.

Emma turned to face them. 'I suppose you want me to tell you about James.' She poured coffee into three identical cream pottery mugs and then opened the pantry cupboard in search of biscuits.

'Yes, that would be helpful,' Rose said.

'God, I can hardly believe this has happened. It doesn't feel real yet. Our life will never be the same again. How do you explain to your child that their father is dead and that he died on purpose? That he chose to do this to us? To leave us? It's horrendous. I'm angry with him. That probably sounds awful.' Emma started to cry, but quickly wiped away her tears with the back of her hand. Having recovered herself, she placed the coffee in front of them before sitting opposite and placing her hands around her own mug, as if seeking warmth.

'No, not at all. It's perfectly natural to feel resentment and anger,' Rose said.

'Thanks for this,' Danny said, helping himself to one of the shortbread biscuits.

Rose sat forward. 'We appreciate how awful this is. Suicide can be one of the most difficult deaths to process for loved ones. You'll need support to get through this. There's no instruction manual – no right way or wrong way to grieve this loss – so go easy on yourself. I'm sure the Family Liaison Officer has been in touch.'

She nodded. 'Yes, she was here earlier. She offered to stay but I declined. I need to do this my way. I don't want someone shadowing me, getting in the way and making me feel watched.' Emma stared into her coffee. 'It doesn't make sense. It wasn't as if he was under stress with work or anything. We've a good life.'

Danny took a sip of his coffee and placed the cup down. 'Anything you can tell us might help to build up a picture of James' state of mind. We need to try to understand his motivation.'

She started to cry. 'The truth is there is no reason why James would do this. He had everything to live for.'

Emma took a tissue from inside the sleeve of her shirt. 'I don't know . . . what can I say about him? He was loving, very generous and kind, but sometimes . . .' She paused. 'I don't want to give you the wrong idea. It's difficult to explain without suggesting that James was depressed, but there were times when I'd sense something going on beneath the surface. As if there was part of him locked off from me. Do you know what I mean?'

Rose nodded.

'Of course, we all have parts of ourselves we don't share, but if you knew James, you'd understand how that was so not like him. When those times came, he withdrew. That's the best way of describing it. He removed himself from me.'

'Had James been acting like that lately?' Rose asked gently.

'No, if anything things were better than normal. Really good.' Rose glanced at Danny. They both knew that sometimes, in planning a suicide, the victim experiences a euphoria, a relief that they know their suffering is going to end – that they have planned their death and are prepared to go.

'Sorry if I'm not making much sense. I suppose it's because none of this makes sense to me. None of it feels real. James had everything.' She looked around at the state-of-the-art kitchen with wrap-around windows looking out onto the courtyard with the garden beyond.

'His father died a year ago and he struggled with it. I always felt that James' father had too much influence on him. Stuart was the kind of man used to getting his own way. He was a successful businessman and when he retired, he found it difficult to put his day in so he would often call in to the office to see James. They were close. As far as James was concerned, his father was the first person he turned to for anything in life. When Stuart died James went through a period of grieving, as you would expect, but he seemed better in recent months. I thought that bad spell was behind us.'

'You can never tell how grief affects people. The stresses and strains of life are bad enough without the loss of a loved one to amplify it all,' Danny offered.

'James always worked hard. He could have gone into his father's property business, but he forged his own path. He's a dedicated father – *was* a dedicated father – and he always made me feel so loved. As I said, I'm struggling to accept that he'd do this to us.'

'Where did you two meet?' Rose asked.

'It was through work. I'm an interior designer. We were both on the same project – a house in Crawfordsburn – and we clicked. He wasn't like other guys. More considerate, settled, and sure of himself, in a good way.'

'And James' car? It was here – unmoved – when you woke this morning?' Danny asked.

'Yes, he didn't take the car.'

So they needed to establish how he got to the school, Rose thought.

'How long have you been together?' Danny asked.

'Eleven years in total. Married for nine years. Everything was perfect.'

She looked towards the garden.

Danny turned round on the stool. 'Can I ask how your finances are? Have you any money worries?'

She looked to the side. A subtle glance. 'No, everything is grand. No money worries at all. We've always lived within our means and we both earn good money.'

'One more thing,' Danny said. 'Did James have a connection with Osbourne House Grammar?'

'Yeah, that was the school he went to.' She turned as the glass door opened and Grace entered with her grandmother, a woman who looked to be in her early sixties with shoulder-length grey hair. 'Mummy, it's raining. I don't want to play anymore.' Her cheeks were flushed pink and her curly blonde hair was in a messy ponytail. She stared at Rose and Danny with the same narrowed blue eyes as her mother, as if questioning why they were in her home.

Emma walked over to her, bent down and said, 'That's okay, sweetheart. These people just need to ask

19

me some questions about Daddy.' She turned to Danny and Rose. 'This is my mother, Anne,' Emma said. 'She's keeping Grace occupied while I deal with everything. Go on through to your playroom and I'll follow you up in a minute. I just have to finish off here,' she said to her daughter.

The child walked out of the kitchen, followed by her grandmother.

'What about James' mother? Is she still alive?' Rose asked.

'Yes. She's devastated. She's coming over later with his sister. We'll make the funeral arrangements together.'

'If you think of any questions you might need answered, please call us,' Danny said, handing her his card.

Emma nodded. 'Thanks.'

'And if there is anything else that you think we need to know, or if something occurs to you that you think, looking back on it, was out of the ordinary, then—'

She nodded. 'Yeah, I know. Call you.'

'Right, we'll leave you to it. Thanks for your time,' Danny said.

'And again, we are so sorry for your loss,' Rose added as they walked up the hallway.

Emma nodded, her face contorting as if she was about to cry again.

Back in the car, Rose said, 'Did you catch the way she hesitated when you asked about money trouble?'

'Yeah, we need to look into that. Maybe the perfect life is a façade and James McCallum was struggling with his finances. I'll get DS Gerard Kinley to look at that.' They pulled out onto the leafy Hospital Road, with banks of trees creating an overhead canopy against the rain.

Danny turned onto Milltown Road and fell quiet for a few moments before saying, 'So, Rosie, have you thought any more about staying in Belfast?' His tone was even as he looked straight ahead at the road. 'We don't know what we're dealing with, yet. There's something not quite right about this case and I've a haunch that there is more to this than suicide, and if this pans out the way I think it will, we could definitely use your expertise. I could have a word with Alastair. Make sure he knows we can't afford to lose you.'

'What makes you so sure I want to stay?' she said with a smile.

'Come on, we both know I'm great to work with. Why would you want to give up the opportunity to spend time with me?' He smirked. 'Besides, you're wasted in that prisons job. You can't deny that you enjoyed bringing the Mulligan case to a close.'

Sure, she wanted to stay, but she found she was wary of telling him. She didn't want him to think that she was giving up her London life because of him. He had always been out of reach. A no-go area. She never trusted getting too close, fearing it would destroy the cover she had created once she had left Belfast and her old self behind. Danny had never known Roisin Lavery, the girl she was before she had moved to Liverpool and met him at university there.

'I've a meeting with Boyne this afternoon so one way or another I'll know where I stand work wise. Deciding to move here permanently might be a step too far but we'll see what happens,' Rose offered.

'Sure, but don't rule anything out just yet,' Danny said as he hit the indicator. He was focused on the traffic, but she thought she could detect an earnestness in his voice.

CHAPTER 3

It was after lunch before Danny reported back to ACC Boyne and updated him on his initial findings.

'The pathologist needs to do his bit and then we'll know where we are but, in the meantime, I'll do a bit of digging. It could all be a waste of time and James McCallum will be reduced to another suicide statistic but just in case . . .' He trailed off.

Boyne was wearing one of his flash Hugo Boss suits with a crisp white shirt beneath it. Unlike his predecessor, McCausland, Boyne seemed to want to be admired. Danny could sense he was the type of boss to feel hurt if he wasn't asked to join the team in the pub once in a while. The kind who likes to feel he's one of the boys.

'That's fine. Best make sure we don't miss anything. We don't want to make assumptions and then find it's something more sinister. I've already had the school's Dean on to me. He doesn't like corpses hanging around his school. Bad for publicity, he says.'

'Yes, sir. We'll be thorough.'

'Anything else?'

'Yeah, I wanted to speak to you about Dr Lainey, the forensic psychologist.'

Boyne raised his eyebrows. 'What about her?'

'With the success of the Mulligan case I was thinking that we should hold on to her.'

'Hold on to her?'

'Use her expertise, make her an official part of the team, like.'

Boyne sat back in his chair as if giving it some thought.

'Would you say she's a valuable asset?'

'Without a doubt, sir. The Mulligan case wouldn't have been brought to a successful conclusion without her insights and involvement. I, for one, would be keen to have her stay on. We work well together.'

'That's neither here nor there. Lainey's involvement wouldn't be to partner up with one detective. If she was to stay, we'd use her skills and knowledge across the board, as and when required.'

'Of course, sir.'

'I'll think about it. That will be all, then. Back to it and keep me updated.'

The incident room was quiet for a change and Danny's desk was clear apart from his computer and a few bits of paperwork that needed dealing with. Unless Lyons came back with something out of the ordinary, they would have this one wrapped up before the day was over. Then it would be back to the basement office where Danny was responsible for trawling through historic cold cases. What had at first been a punishment of sorts for messing up the Lennon case, had become a source of great interest for Danny. The allure of trawling through old case notes and potentially shedding new light on long neglected files had got under his skin. In part, it was down to the Mulligan case. The satisfaction of bringing it to a close had inspired him to keep working as part of the Historical Enquiries Unit, if only on an ad hoc basis.

He had to admit, though, that working above ground was more sociable. The basement office, full of box files and dimly lit, wasn't the most inspiring environment, though when a case took hold it was good to have the solitude and the quiet to totally absorb the information. Up here, in the incident room, there were plenty of distractions. Phones going off, the clack of keyboard keys, the banter and chatter of colleagues . . .

He was about to grab a coffee when one of his colleagues stuck her head around the door.

'Sir, there's been a call about your suicide. Fella by the name of Lorcan Burns said he'd had a missed call from James McCallum in the early hours of this morning and then a text message. Seems that instead of a suicide note, he texted his mate.'

'Details?'

'Here you go.' She handed him a printout. 'It's all logged on the system. He said he'll be at home all day if you need to talk to him.'

Danny drove out of the station and headed towards Lorcan Burns' house in Derriaghy Village, on the outskirts of Belfast. Whether or not Lyons came back with nothing amiss, he could show McCallum's intent with the text message. By rights, he should have sent someone junior, but he wasn't exactly swamped. It would be good to get the threads tied up and the case signed off.

The front garden of the terrace house was a neat rectangle of grass edged with hedging and pots holding heather plants. Someone had clearly put time and effort into making it look presentable. Danny rang the doorbell and waited. The door was opened by a casually dressed man about his age, with a freshly shaven face, and dark blond hair in a quiff.

He nodded. 'Police?'

'Yes.' Danny showed him his ID and was welcomed into the narrow hallway.

'Lorcan is in here.'

Danny entered to find the whole of the ground floor had been knocked through into one large space encompassing the kitchen, dining, and living areas with a wall of exposed brick.

'Hi, there. I'm DI Danny Stowe. You called the station about James McCallum?'

'Yes. This is Brody, my partner. I don't mind talking with him here,' Burns said. He spoke in a stuffed-up way, as if he had hay fever or a cold. Danny resisted shaking hands.

They sat down and Danny offered his sympathies. 'Suicide is never easy to deal with. The friends and family are often left with a lot of unanswered questions.'

'Yeah, it's hard to take it in. He was the most settled one of the lot of us. The one who had life sorted, you know? I'm still trying to find my way. I wasn't even sure if I was ever going to meet the right guy until Brody came along.' He smiled as Brody put his hand on his shoulder.

26

'How long have you known James?'

'We met at school.'

'Did James have any other close friends?'

'Well there was Ivy and Emer. The four of us were good mates when we were younger but over the years we've drifted apart. Inevitable, I suppose. But James and I . . . well, we were good mates once.'

Danny watched as Burns looked to Brody for reassurance.

'Now I'm thinking, what if we'd stayed close? Maybe this wouldn't have happened. Maybe James could have confided in me and I could have helped him.'

'No point blaming yourself. These things are never straightforward,' Danny said.

'Once James settled down with Emma it was all baby talk, growing his business and holidays in Centre Parcs. We didn't have so much in common anymore. We all keep in touch on Facebook, as you do – check in on one another from time to time – but life gets in the way.'

'So, this text message, can I see it?'

He unlocked his phone and handed it to Danny, who looked down and read the message aloud. '"I'm really sorry but I can't keep going. The reckoning is coming." Any idea what he is referring to?'

'No. I've thought about it and I can't say there's anything that would make sense. Maybe Emma would know.'

'The "reckoning". That sounds a bit religious. Was James a religious man?'

'I wouldn't say so, no. I thought it was strange.'

'How did you hear about James' death?'

'Emma. She called me this morning and told me not

long after the police had informed her. She was sobbing. I said I'd let the others know.'

'Did you tell her about the text message?'

'No, I didn't. It seemed wrong to share it with her over the phone. She was so upset.'

'Would the friends you mentioned – Ivy and Emer – have regular contact with James?'

He gave a half shrug of his shoulder. 'Like I said, it's all online with Facebook. We don't get time to meet up as much as we'd like to. I doubt they've seen James lately.'

'Would you be able to give me their surnames and contact details? It would be a great help.'

Burns nodded. 'Of course, no problem.' He found a pen and a pad of paper in a drawer and scribbled down the information.

'Thanks,' Danny said, putting the piece of paper inside his notebook. 'Again, I'm sorry for your loss.'

'Yeah, thanks, but I feel for poor Emma and Grace. It's awful for them to have to deal with this. Live with the consequences.' Lorcan looked distressed and Brody took his hand.

Danny nodded. 'Yes, it won't be easy. Look, I'll let you get on with your day. If anything else comes to mind, make sure you give us a call.' Danny handed him his card. 'We'll be in touch if there's anything else we need. Take care.'

CHAPTER 4

The final decision to stay in Belfast had almost been made for Rose. Bernard, her line manager, called from the prison service headquarters in London to tell her of his decision to retire. 'Time to do all those things I've promised Catherine I'd do. Holidays in Tuscany, a trip to visit her brother in Florida, sort out the garden . . .'

'Jesus, Bernard, are you sure you're ready for retirement? Holidays and gardening. It sounds awful.'

He laughed. 'If I'm not ready at sixty-five, I'll never be ready. Better to go now, full pension and good service history, while I'm still fit enough to do what I want with the last years of my life.'

'You make it sound like you're ancient!'

'Not ancient but matured like a good bottle of red. If I've ten good years left in me, I'll be lucky, and I'd rather spend them in more pleasant surroundings than this place. Things haven't got any better since you've been away . . . which brings me to the real reason I'm ringing.

29

Would you be interested in stepping up into my job? You're young but it's possible.'

There it was: the prospect of bedding down and securing her life in London. A life of policy meetings, research papers, management of case workers, and the rest. She thought of the last six months and how she had felt changed by her work with the PSNI. After the Mulligan case she could have returned to London but staying had seemed like the right thing to do. It felt good to be part of a team working towards a clear and certain goal and succeeding in seeing the job done right, though she still thought of Belfast as a temporary sabbatical.

And on a personal level, her relationship with Kaitlin and the rest of her family was at stake. She believed they were worth fighting for. What she had cautiously started rebuilding with them couldn't be nurtured from afar. If she went back to London, she knew that before long they would lose touch again. Kaitlin might make the effort for a while but her brothers, Pearse and Colm, their feelings of resentment towards Rose were too raw. If she wanted to make things right, she knew she needed to stay.

And then there was Danny. The friendship that they had resurrected and which she now prized above all else was worth sticking around for too. After the Mulligan case had been wrapped up, they had fallen into an easy working relationship and had seen two subsequent cases reach a satisfying conclusion.

'It's good to be considered Bernard, but to be honest I've been meaning to call you. I've had an offer to stay on here, with the police. It's an interesting role, one that will allow me to grow and make some real impact.'

Rose had proved her worth with the Mulligan case and though not all forces made use of forensic psychologists, the PSNI wanted to be seen to be forward thinking and prepared to do what it takes to solve crimes. The role of PSNI forensic psychologist offered Rose the chance to work alongside the detectives conducting investigations, providing insights into offending behaviour, developing better interviewing techniques and crime analysis. Danny's support had helped to secure her place for the next year at least.

Earlier in the day, Rose had sat in front of ACC Boyne and felt like she was back in school. She wondered why he had this effect on her. It was something to do with his demeanour, his breadth and height giving him an air of being overly serious though not stern.

'Dr Lainey, good of you to make time to see me. My predecessor, ACC McCausland, signed you up for the Mulligan case, I believe.'

'Yes that's right.'

'And I understand you were instrumental in bring that case to a satisfactory conclusion, am I right?'

'I was part of the team, yes.'

'Now isn't the time to be humble, Dr Lainey.' He looked at her with a smirk playing at his mouth.

Rose smiled. 'No, sir.' She wasn't used to calling anyone sir but for some reason he elicited it from her.

'How do you feel about continuing your work here for a while longer?'

'I'm open to it.'

'Not put off with real police work, then?'

'No. If anything, I welcome the change of pace,' she

replied. Her work in London had involved prisons and the development of programmes to help prevent prisoners from reoffending. It lacked the thrill and excitement she had experienced working for the police over the past few months, but she had yet to work out how much of that was down to the actual police work and how much of it was linked to being with Danny again.

'Good. Well, I want you to consider staying. We can offer a twelve-month placement as consultant forensic psychologist working as part of the Serious Crime Unit, but there's a catch.'

She raised an eyebrow.

'We want you to have a look at how that lot work. To use your expertise to encourage best practice among our force. It's not unheard off within other jurisdictions for a psychologist to have some sort of input with regards to how we can be more efficient and work better.'

'To act like a kind of performance coach?'

'If you like. Help your colleagues to reach into their untapped potential. Make them strive to excel. Morale isn't great and we need to look at ways to improve it.'

Rose was bemused. The idea of assessing and mentoring those who she thought of as colleagues was a strangely alluring and repulsive idea in equal measure. Especially when she thought of Danny.

Boyne smirked. He could see that despite her hesitation she was intrigued. 'Go away and think about it but I expect an answer by close of day.'

'No need, sir. I can tell you now. I know I want to stay, and I think I can do what you're asking.'

'Excellent. Now go and earn your keep. HR will sort the rest out.'

Once out in the corridor, she'd stopped and took a breath. Another year of Belfast, with her family and Danny. Her mother, too. Even though Evelyn was dead, there was unfinished business to be dealt with. It was always there, niggling beneath the surface, the desire to unearth her mother's secrets. She shivered, felt a surge of energy, and reminded herself that fear and danger always came with excitement.

CHAPTER 5

Danny ran through the streets of South Belfast in the freezing evening rain, determined to beat his last ten-kilometre time. Running helped clear his mind of all the shit that had been nagging at him. He worried about his parents on the farm, knowing that the hard, manual work was becoming harder for his father and his fortnightly visits were not enough to provide any kind of meaningful help. He also worried about the recent succession of knife attacks on young women in the city. He wasn't working that case but it still bothered him. He could imagine Rose telling him that he couldn't save all the dead girls singlehandedly, but he had an intense sense of at least needing to try.

He ran along the Annadale embankment, the footpath slick with fallen, sodden leaves, and as cars drove by their headlights periodically caught his eye. The hanging case had been on his desk for twenty-four hours and he was anxious to get the autopsy report back. Until he knew for sure if he was dealing with a murder he couldn't really action anything too dramatic. A rat, wet and bulky, ran out from the gloom of the undergrowth in front of him, making him jump. *Fuck's sake.* He admonished himself for being so easily spooked. The rain had been heavy earlier in the day and the river level was high, flushing the rat out of its habitat.

He thought of Rose and her new role. Typical Battle to go messing everything up. Why couldn't he have let her continue working on important cases the way she had done? She had held her own in the Mulligan case and he had no doubt that she would be an asset to the force. Back in Liverpool, during their uni days, he always handed in his best essays when Rose had been studying alongside him. He'd always tried harder just to impress her. Working on the same team, day after day with long nights thrown in, he had fallen back into that easy friendship they had and found she was pushing him to be his very best again. He had forgotten how much he missed her until she had come back into his life, and he knew there was no point ruining what they had by making a move she may not want. At lunch earlier he had sat down beside her in the cafeteria at the station and placed his tray of food on the table.

'All right, Rose. Rumour has it that Battle has offered you a new role.'

She looked up from her lunch of sourdough bread with avocado and chicken salad.

'Yeah, sort of.'

'Well, what kind of role is it? I assumed you'd be doing the same sort of thing you'd done before on the Mulligan case with me.' He could hear the pettiness in his voice, born out of jealously he had no right to feel as he'd no claim over her, professionally or otherwise. He was always weird when it came to Rose and he could never work out why she affected him so much.

'He didn't give it a title as such but, basically, he wants me to be some sort of human resources performance coach, and I still get to lend a hand on cases as and when I'm needed.'

'What the fuck? As and when you're needed?' He'd assumed Rose would start working with him on the hanging case right away. They made a great team and the idea that she would be kept at the station, dealing with stress management strategies or something along those lines, was madness.

Rose laughed. 'Don't choke on your chips Danny. It could be a good thing. Who's to say I won't be of great value?'

'Jesus, listen to yourself already. "Of great value". You sound like an HR snout. I thought you left the prison service to avoid doing a desk job.'

'Come on, you're not stuck in the dark ages. It isn't so far out there. Other forces have a similar role.'

'What would it entail? Watching our every move and reporting back to HR? Christ, what is this, an episode of *Line of Duty*?' He couldn't help the childish bitterness. He didn't see Rose as someone who'd be happy tied to policy and management restructuring, attending endless meetings outlining grand plans that never actually changed anything for the better. She was worth more than that. The Mulligan case had proved her worth as a great cop and he was reluctant to lose having her in the field. Rose had only just got in the door and he believed she could do well. She hadn't shied away from getting her hands dirty so why this desire to take a different direction?

'No, Danny. That's not how I see it.'

'Well, you wouldn't, would you?' He found himself glaring at her without fully understanding why he was so pissed off. In part, he supposed it was the idea of Rose playing the shrink with him, delving into the inner workings of his mind and assessing him and finding him wanting. He didn't ever want to fall short of her high expectations.

'Whatever, Danny.' She stood, gathered her things, and pushed her chair under the table. 'I'll see you later.'

He was angry with himself for not reacting more professionally. Rose deserved better and he should have kept his personal feelings in check. The truth was that he enjoyed being in her company and working alongside her. Battle had ruined all that by putting her in this quasi-management HR role.

It started to rain and he felt it beat icily against his face, pulling him back to the present. He ran on, willing his body to find its pace and lull his mind into stillness. To block out work, to block out everything.

CHAPTER 6

Rose had felt irritated by Danny's reaction to her new role. She thought he would have been pleased to have her sticking around for a full year. Instead, he had been indignant and dismissive. As far as she was concerned, her position would allow her to use psychology to assist officers to perform better, while safeguarding their own wellbeing. Her training and skills lent themselves to psychological work-based coaching and she liked to think that her input could help the officers perform better and more effectively. Danny's snide remark about her being some sort of higher management grass irritated her, but it was true that she liked the proper investigative police work. She enjoyed the way her senses felt heightened, how she felt that bright energy that comes with doing something worthwhile. The Mulligan case had whet her appetite for police work, and she wasn't ready to give that up, but she needed to have Danny on her side. There was no reason why she couldn't find a happy medium between what Battle expected and what she wanted. She had the skills to be of value as both a performance coach and a forensic psychologist.

Rose closed a file she had open on her computer and sighed. Suicide among young men was on the rise. The statistics were frightening, and Belfast seemed to be ahead of the curve. More men had died by suicide since the ceasefire than as a result of the thirty years of the Troubles. It was an unsettling thought. If James McCallum had killed himself, then his family and friends would be left with questions. From what his widow had said though, it wasn't a stretch for him to be a potential candidate for taking his own life. She had hinted at a darkness beneath the surface. If he had been struggling with depression it would have taken a lot of energy to keep functioning – to operate as a professional in his architectural practice, to be a loving, devoted husband and father . . . It wasn't impossible to live like that though. To portray a persona to convince everyone that you were handling all the various stresses of life. Rose knew better than most that it was possible to show the world a competent, functioning person even while you're struggling to hold it together on the inside.

It had been six months since her mother had died and an undertow of regret had crept in, her initial feeling of numbness soon giving way to something unnerving. Her sleep had been affected, and she found that she would often lose her train of thought as old memories resurfaced, unsettling her. For the first time in a long while, she felt lost. It was a feeling she recognised from when she had first arrived at university in Liverpool. That sense of being alien and the outsider had left her feeling disorientated, alone and out of her depth. Now that the adrenaline rush of the Mulligan case had subsided, she was experiencing those same feelings again.

So much of her life had been configured on the basis of escaping Belfast and her mother. She had created a life away from her family, had happily adopted a new name and Anglicised her accent, wanting to fit in to her new home. Now she realised that she had eradicated part of herself in doing so, and she had lost as much as she'd gained.

The old refrain 'where are you from?' had reared its head a few times at work. People in Northern Ireland liked to place you in a box – us, or them. A geographical location could often provide a shorthand for which side of the fence you were from, and your accent and your school all played a part in defining who you were. It bothered Rose that in shaking off her Belfast roots she had inadvertently denied so much of herself and her working-class background.

From a professional perspective, she was displaying typical signs of grief. While she understood the stages, and the emotions involved, what she didn't understand was why she was feeling them when she had eradicated Evelyn from her life so long ago. Surely she had no right to such feelings?

She sighed and looked down at her case folder. There were photographs of the scene – James McCallum hanging from the gnarled limb of the tree – and she remembered that Danny had said he was concerned about the placement of the rope. She could see what he meant and though she expected Lyons' report to say that James

McCallum had indeed died by his own hand, she felt the pull of needing to know more. Police work, she had discovered, was a game of strategy and enquiry, and it suited her well.

CHAPTER 7

Danny sat beside the white board in the conference room as his team filed in ahead of the two o'clock meeting. He checked the room and saw DS Tania Lumen was back from taking the school caretaker's statement.

'Right, let's get started,' he said as they settled and the rumble of conversation died down.

'Tania, did you catch the school caretaker? What did he have to say?'

'Yes, he's called Alex Bogue, in his fifties, said he usually arrives at seven, opens up the gates and goes about his tasks for the day. The kids are off for the midterm break but some of the teachers go in to prepare for lessons. They also currently have painters decorating the science block and it's part of his job to oversee that maintenance work.'

'And did he arrive at seven a.m. on October 18th?'

'No, he was late. Said his alarm hadn't gone off and he didn't get there until half past seven. The decorators weren't due to arrive until eight thirty, so it wasn't a problem, and he usually doesn't see any teachers, or the head, until just before nine when there's no pupils in the school.'

'Okay. Did he go in through the main entrance?'

'No, that gate remains locked when the school's off for the holidays. He used the side gate and didn't see the deceased as he went into the school, opened up the science block and the head's office. It was there that he caught sight of the body from the window. He rang 999 before he left the building and then ran straight out to the tree, intending to cut the rope and get McCallum down. But he quickly realised it was too late to save him.'

'What about CCTV cameras?'

'There's a secure digital system that covers the front gate and the school itself, but the tree is out of range. I've checked.'

'Okay, thanks. Please get everything written up and on the system as soon as possible.'

'Any more on whether it's suicide or a murder?' Tania asked, straightening the collar of her blouse.

'No. We're still waiting for Lyons' autopsy report.' The delay was making him anxious. A straightforward murder case had parameters, procedures, and systems in place. This lull was doing his head in.

He glanced over at DS Gerard Kinley who was looking at a spreadsheet. Whatever task he was asked to do, Kinley always delivered. He appeared to actually enjoy the grunt work involved in dealing with the HOLMES database, dry data spreadsheets, and whatever tedium they frequently seemed to put his way.

'Gerard, I need you to do a check on the company accounts of James McCallum's architecture practice –

Lanyon Architects. Run your eye over the figures and see if they are in the black and all above board.'

'Sure, no problem. Companies House will have the information.'

'Thanks.'

Danny had reached that stage in life when anyone below the age of mid-twenties looked like they were fresh out of school. Kinley was no exception with his boyish looks and affable charm. It didn't seem so long ago that Danny was the young one on the team, trying hard to make his mark. He had been around Kinley's age when he first met Amy. The job had impressed her – or at least he'd thought it had – and she had seemed keen back then, ready to have a proper grown-up relationship. Maybe they had jumped in too fast, rushed into marriage before either of them had a chance to back out.

Those early days of married life had been good days. He had to remind himself that he had been happy with Amy back then. That they had once loved each other enough to build the promise of a future life together. He felt guilty thinking it but if she hadn't been so tormented with her issues, they might have made it in the long run. Their child would be around one by now, if Amy hadn't made the decision to abort it. A sickening wave of regret caught in his throat and he forced himself back to the present. Thankfully, he could always count on work to provide a distraction.

He clicked on the wireless mouse and brought up a photograph of James McCallum on the projector. It was a corporate headshot taken from his company website. Slick and professional.

'James McCallum was a husband and father. A little

girl will be growing up without him.' He let his words hang, allowing the team to forge a connection with the deceased, hopefully creating a sense of empathy that would fuel a desire to do their best by James and his family.

Without warning he clicked again and brought up a photograph taken at the crime scene. James McCallum's handsome face was transformed into a grotesque mask of pain and horror.

The stillness in the room told Danny he had their undivided attention. He wasn't usually one for using shock tactics, but this case, with its uneasy start and the lack of confirmation as to what they were dealing with, required a sharp jolt to ensure that every one of the team understood what was at stake.

'If someone is responsible for this, we owe it to the McCallum family to ensure we find them.'

Later that day he went in search of Rose. She looked up as he entered the room where she was working. 'Hey, Danny, I was just about to call you.'

She was wearing a cream silk blouse with silver buttons and for some strange reason it made him feel distant from her. He still thought of her as the student he had first known, with Doc Marten boots and baggy jumpers, not this professional version of the girl he'd been best friends with. In a moment of clarity he realised that part of his problem with Battle assigning her to another role was that it placed her out of his reach.

'Oh yeah?'

He sat down on a soft chair placed at an angle to a small coffee table. It had the semblance of a counselling room without the strategically placed box of tissues.

'Yep. I wanted to know if I can add anything to the McCallum case. I don't want you thinking I'm not interested in case work now that I have this new role.'

'Look, I owe you an apology. I overreacted,' he said. She studied his face for a moment and he felt the intensity of her gaze, as if she was deciding something about him.

'Danny, the practice of psychology in a police setting can be a great resource in terms of research and training. Sure, I'll be looking at fitness for duty assessments along with HR, but that doesn't mean to say I'm some sort of internal affairs grass. And besides, I doubt you'd have anything to hide. You're one of the most upfront, reliably straight cops I've ever met. So, I don't get your resistance.'

He took a deep breath and felt his shoulders fall. 'Rosie, it wasn't about you. It's me. The whole divorce thing has messed me up. By the time I called it a day with Amy I'd had it up to here with well-meaning shrinks,' he said as he gestured to a spot above his head.

'Danny, this is me you are talking to, not some professional white coat. I'd never treat you like a patient.'

He smiled at her, but he knew the weariness he felt was etched on his face.

'I know and I'm sorry. You'll do a great job and yes, I do need your input on the McCallum case if it turns out to be a murder. You could have come to the briefing earlier.'

'Wasn't sure I was welcome.'

'Of course you were. Listen, it's good news that you're staying, and that Battle sees fit to expand your role. I apologise again for being a dick. It's been known to happen occasionally.'

She smirked just as his phone screen lit up with an incoming call from Raymond Lyons. He put it on speaker so Rose could hear the conversation.

'Raymond, what have we got?'

'I can tell you what we haven't got. It's not suicide.'

Danny felt the flutter of anticipation. Suicides were tragic but not interesting to a cop. A murder case brought with it the sickening thrill of danger, the injustice of a life being taken by another, and then the swift punch of desire to do something to right the wrong. He wanted action, to start the process of evidence gathering and disseminating tasks to the team.

It was all Danny could do to stay still long enough to finish the call.

CHAPTER 8

Rose was glad Danny had had enough sense and grace to clear the air between them after he'd overreacted. Now that they had the autopsy confirmation that the McCallum case was not suicide they could formally start the murder inquiry. This was not a bog-standard murder case though.

She sensed that for Danny each case was a puzzle, something to be strategically solved like a game of chess. He had an innate sense of justice and a desperate need to see things done right. For her it was more about the mystery, the intrigue. Rose knew her job was to look at the bigger picture, to read those involved, studying their mannerisms, their tells. Part of her training had been in clinical assessments, developing profiles and providing testimony in court. She had developed her skills over the years, and she was suddenly putting all that dry theory into practice, which made her current work with the PSNI rewarding in a way she hadn't expected.

She desperately wanted to assist Danny on the hanging

tree case, as they had started to refer to it. Boyne gave her the go-ahead to join the team and suggested that she spend some time with Fiona Madden, the chief SOCO.

'She'll keep you right regarding crime scene management. It will be useful for you to have some training in what not to do. Last thing we need is an untrained professional getting in the way.' He'd smiled to soften the impact of his words and gave her a half shrug of his broad shoulders.

Rose met Fiona Madden back at the hanging tree to inspect the scene of crime. News that the they were now dealing with a murder case had meant that the SOCO team were back on location to ensure nothing had been missed in their initial sweep.

'Fiona?' Rose called out to the red-haired SOCO. 'I'm Rose Lainey. Thanks for letting me tag along today to see how you work.'

She nodded. 'First rule of SOCO is don't mess with the crime scene. Watch, listen, but don't touch anything. If you contaminate my crime scene, I will kill you.' Her Sligo accent made what she said sound funny rather than threatening.

'Fair enough.'

'You'll need to get suited and booted first.' She jutted her head in the direction of the car park. 'Mine's the blue A-Class Merc. The boot's open and you'll find a spare set of scrubs inside.'

When Rose arrived back at the foot of the tree, Fiona was busy collecting samples from the ground.

'In essence, a SOCO's job comes down to these questions: is the trace evidence at the scene consistent with the death having occurred at this location? Does the body contain any trace evidence that is unusual for this location? Can I find mud on the soles of the victim's shoes, or grass or seeds on the clothing of the deceased? Can I find signs the deceased has been moved? Is the death one that can be attributed to natural causes? Are there any external signs of violence? In other words, what does the scene tell me about the death?'

Rose listened and nodded.

'You have to remember this isn't a drama. This isn't a bit of excitement to heat up your lukewarm life. You don't talk about what you've seen away from the station or the crime scene and you definitely carry nothing away. This is people's real lives we're dealing with.'

Rose watched as she fired off instructions to one of her team. 'Declan, don't forget to check the branches surrounding the rope. You never know what might be lurking up there. Whoever placed the body in the tree would have needed some sort of pulley system or brute force so there might be something left behind.'

She turned back to Rose. 'The other vital part of my job is to ensure the team document everything – and I mean everything – with videography, photography, drawing, and note-taking.'

Rose bent and watched as Fiona scraped soil into a sample container.

'So, you're new to the squad, I take it?' Fiona asked after a while.

'Yeah, relatively. I've been here for a few months. I'm a forensic psychologist by trade.'

'Ah, our occupations are well matched. I take care of the outside and you do the internal,' Fiona said screwing the top on her sample container and labelling it. 'Though

I'm looking for more than just the cause of death. My job is to read the scene, provide objective evidence of cause, timing, and manner of death for verdict by the criminal justice system.'

'No pressure then.'

'The detectives, well, they're the big dicks who swagger in and make pronouncements, but at the end of the day every assumption they make is based on the work that me and my team carry out before they've even got out of bed.'

Rose could see that Fiona took no prisoners. Her discipline and no-nonsense approach may have rubbed some people the wrong way, but Rose liked her.

'The first thing that detectives want to know is did death occur here? We answer that by looking at the position in which the deceased was discovered, as the presence or absence of rigor mortis or stiffness of the body can help determine if the person died where they were found. In this instance, it looks like someone wanted us to think this poor fella had topped himself. An awful lot of trouble to go to in order to get rid of someone.'

'You can think of easier ways?'

'Oh yeah, a hammer and lots of plastic sheeting. That's how I'd do it, if I had to.'

By late afternoon the station was coming to life with the new shift trickling in. ACC Boyne had deemed Rose worthy of an office, but it was actually little more than a cupboard with a window overlooking the flat roof of the canteen below. The sounds of the working day drifted through her open door – footsteps on the stairs, the clack of keyboards, chatter, and coffee cups being filled, the lift doors opening and closing with a soft thud – sounds that she had become familiar with and recognised as the playlist to her new professional life. She certainly didn't miss the journey into her London office, the bodies pressed too tightly together on the Tube, the smell of traffic fumes, and the constant noise. There was a time when those same things had excited her, made her feel a whoosh of enthusiasm for her life, but gradually the novelty had worn off.

Here in Belfast everything felt close by, whether she wanted the city centre, or the surrounding hills, or even a walk along the shoreline. London, by comparison, had been limiting, even constricting. She just hadn't realised it until she left.

Rose's attempts to reacquaint herself with her siblings were a different story. While there were flashes of familiarity, any closeness they'd had when they were younger had long dissipated. All she felt now was a gulf of emotion between them. There seemed to be a lot that was still unsaid and Rose knew from professional experience that the only way through it would be to have it out. The trouble was, she didn't know if she could stomach it.

Her siblings were altered from how she recalled them. Time had passed and they had all changed. The trouble was that Rose hadn't grown with them. Kaitlin, always the wild one – the one who got caught smoking up in an alley way at fourteen and had a constant stream of boyfriends on the go – was now a mother of two. She was settled into her married life with her husband, John, and working as a legal secretary. Rose could still see the odd spark of the carefree Kaitlin she remembered, but most of the time she seemed like there was more going on beneath the surface. It was probably no more than worrying about her kids and dealing with the demands of life, but still, it annoyed Rose to think of her sister carrying worries she didn't know of.

Pearse was multi-layered. He had always been hard to read, even as a little kid, as he would blow hot and cold. Though he had seemed genuinely pleased to see her when she returned, the old recriminations were never far away. There were the jibes he made about her name change – from Roisin Lavery to Rose Lainey – so it obviously bothered him. He also made the odd dig about her working for the police. In his mind the PSNI could never be a fair and just organisation because Catholics would always experience discrimination and maltreatment. It was easier for him to see the police as an enemy and Rose was at risk of being covered by the same cloak.

Colm, the baby of the family, was quick to look to the other two to make up his mind for him. He seemed reluctant to welcome Rose with open arms unless Kaitlin and Pearse deemed it okay. She needed to take it slow with her brothers but that was to be expected. Being part of a family was a hassle she had opted out of for years and though she sometimes found herself resenting them, she still wanted some sort of connection. She knew she was being obtuse.

Rose's childhood had been marred by her father's murder, and growing up with her mother's nationalism had been thorny and traumatic. Looking back, she could see that her family had been a dysfunctional minefield of subterfuge and fear.

But Danny's recent discovery that her mother, Evelyn, had been a police informer, had changed

53

everything. All of the assumptions Rose had made about her mother in the past had been contorted and twisted in the light of this revelation, and she could now see her childhood anew. There was so much that Rose needed to understand, and that meant going back to the beginning of her mother's story to appreciate who she really was.

Kaitlin's name flashed up on Rose's phone. She debated ignoring it, but knew that would only mean she'd feel obliged to call her back later. Better to answer now and use the pretext of work as a reason to keep the conversation short. Her sister had fallen into the habit of phoning Rose nearly every day. It was as if she was desperately trying to catch up on all the time they'd had apart.

'Hi Kaitlin. I'm in work so I can't really talk.'

'I won't keep you. I just want to remind you that we're having a get-together to mark Mummy's birthday this evening. We'd like you to come.' Rose knew she couldn't say no. Strangely, Evelyn had a stronger hold over her daughter in death than she had in life.

'Yeah, okay. I'll do my best,' Rose said. She couldn't prevent the sigh at the end of the sentence. What was it with this need for family get-togethers? While she appreciated having reconnected and being part of their lives, it still felt alien to Rose, to be in regular contact with her family. Old habits were hard to shake off. The plan was to meet for dinner at their old family home. Kaitlin was going to bring a pot of curry and they'd make some rice while they were there. The boys were going to supply the wine.

'It will be good to see you,' Kaitlin said. 'We can have

a proper catch-up. I want to hear all about what you've been doing.'

'Look, sorry, I have to go but I'll see you tonight. Seven o'clock?'

'Yeah, seven. Looking forward to it.'

Rose hung up. Kaitlin hadn't asked her to bring anything, the subtext being that she was still the outsider and had to renegotiate her way back in. The trouble was, she wasn't so sure if she wanted to be fully accepted into the clan again. Maybe she'd been right to keep her distance all these years.

CHAPTER 9

Rose parked her car and switched the engine off. The street was dead. Back when she was young there was always something going on, kids playing on bicycles or kicking a football, neighbours chatting. Dogs would often roam freely, chasing cars and barking at nothing in particular. Rose could remember a time when this part of Belfast was swarming with activity. Now absent of children, the streets were instead congested with cars. The Markets area was so close to the centre of town that some drivers from other parts of the city paid a monthly stipend to residents so they could park outside the red-brick terrace houses, and walk to their city centre offices; the arrangement offered a lucrative deal for the residents.

Most of the houses on the street housed older residents, some having lived there since Rose's time. She noticed the flicker of a curtain at the window across the street, a shadow passing silent judgement, just like the old days. That was Mrs Farley's house, if she remembered correctly.

She was probably wondering what Rose was doing sitting in her car. It was the type of place where neighbours were suspicious of outsiders and old habits of mistrust still lingered. The truth was Rose needed to steel herself before going in. It was hard to step over the threshold of her old family home. The smells and the sounds of years gone by still loitered in her mind, too close to the surface for her liking. She had found herself drawn to the past more frequently lately. Her mother's death had hit a switch in her brain that suddenly illuminated parts of her childhood that she had deliberately dimmed. Memories of her mother cooking breakfast at the gas stove, later shouting up the stairs, 'Get out of that bed before I have to come up and drag you out.' The thunder of the boys running down the stairs, the squabbling, and the laughter. The sounds of family life layered over the constant background noise of the television.

Rose turned off the engine, checked her reflection in the rear-view mirror, and then reached for her bag. The past was a place of shadows and fear and Rose needed to find a way through it, to cast out the half-truths and misconstrued facts, to try and build something new from what she'd find there.

Pearse opened the door to her. 'You made it.'

'Seems so.' Pearse had lines on his face that had no right to be there. Rose wondered what worries had laid themselves down on him, making him look older than he should. When they were kids, she'd felt responsible for him and Colm. She'd hoped and believed that they had been sheltered from the worst of the troubles that befell their family back then, but there was no denying that the death of their father had affected them all. It was only now that she realised she'd been naive and stupid to think that she could shield Pearse and Colm from any of it.

'We're all here,' Pearse said as she followed him into the living room.

'Alright?' Colm said. No small talk.

'Is that Roisin?' Kaitlin called from the kitchen.

'Aye, she's here,' Pearse called back.

Rose took the chance to help Kaitlin in the kitchen. She felt more comfortable with her sister than with her brothers. Maybe it was because Kaitlin was relying on her and they spoke more often. They needed to pack up the family home and put it on the market and the first step in the process was to make the arrangements and take whatever mementoes they wanted.

Rose couldn't think of a single thing she'd want to keep.

There were reminders of Evelyn everywhere; from the history books to the silver cutlery bought at Ross's Auction House for under twenty quid. Rose could remember Evelyn coming home with them, delighted with herself. She'd made Rose and Kaitlin sit at the very same table that still sat in the kitchen today and polish them with a special cloth until the tarnish had been buffed away, leaving them sparkling.

The evening had a forced, jovial feel to it. Everyone was trying too hard, laughing too long, and being overly polite. It didn't feel natural, the conversation more like the surface topics of dinner party guests, not siblings who were sat around the same table they'd grown up at. It took Rose a while to work out what was wrong – it was too civilised. Too polite. The Laverys didn't do polite. Most families didn't, she thought, not close ones anyway. It should be banter and craic, not this piss poor attempt at being grown-ups.

'More wine?'

'Yes, please. That's lovely. Thank you.'

'Cheers!'

'Cheers!'

'Does anyone want the last of the naan bread?'

'You go ahead.'

'Are you sure? We can share it.'

On it went. Happy bloody families. Rose knew it wouldn't last forever.

They were gathered to honour Evelyn's birthday. Their mother hadn't been buried long – only six months – so Rose felt it was a strange undertaking to raise a glass to her. The cross between remembrance and celebration felt uneasy.

'Do you remember the way she used to refuse to separate the whites in the washing?' Kaitlin said, laughing.

'Jesus, yes! My school shirts were every shade from grey to pale blue and pink. She claimed that if they were clean, we shouldn't complain,' Rose said. 'And that any woman who had time to do separate washes didn't have enough going on in her life. It was a feminist's duty to not care about laundry, she claimed.'

They all laughed.

Pearse sat with his elbows on the table, leaning over his glass of red wine. 'I remember the way she used to send me to the shop for messages and then ask me to tell her who I'd seen, what they'd said. "Tell me all your news," she'd say. Made me feel like the man of the house going out into the world to report back.'

Rose felt her lips form a tight line. Pearse had a deep, rumbling Belfast voice, the kind she recalled from her childhood. He sounded both hard and masculine, yet also comforting and protective. He was the type of guy that it would be easy to be jovial with down the pub, feeding him lines that you knew he'd pick up and run with until he delivered a withering punchline, to which they'd all laugh. There was a wit and humour to him that she recognised from when they were young. He was always the one to make their mother laugh.

It had been Rose who had checked his homework and had made sure that he had his lunch packed into his Danger Mouse lunch box. Little things that their mother should have done. Rose liked to think she had picked up Evelyn's slack and compensated without complaint, but there were times when she wanted to say she was just a child, too. That she needed and wanted someone to check on her school uniform, to pack her sandwiches in grease-proof paper and write a little note to 'be good, be happy', just like Grainne Burke's mother did.

'Aye, she was something else,' Colm said. He was quieter than Pearse. He hung back from the conversation, allowed others to dominate, but was always engaged, with his head cocked to the side, listening intently.

'So, Roisin, are you ever going to tell us what made you stay away all these years?' Pearse asked.

How could she put into words all the recriminations that she felt in that question? How could she explain that she had judged their mother all this time, believing her to have been involved in paramilitary activities, and only recently learned the truth?

She shrugged, choosing the simple answer for now. 'I

got caught up in my work across the water. After a while I felt that I had no home to return to.'

'That's bullshit, Roisin. You always had a place here. Don't dare say otherwise.' Colm spoke sharply and his words cut to the bone, deeper than if they'd come from Pearse.

'That's how it felt, Colm.'

'No. That's how you have chosen to see it. That wasn't the reality.'

Rose looked down. He was right, to a degree. She had painted Belfast and her mother in colours not of their choosing.

CHAPTER 10

The body lay waiting on the steel table, covered with a paper sheet. A cold mass of flesh, sinew, and bone waiting to be read like a deck of tarot cards. Lyons was standing, suited up in the blue, long-sleeved surgical gown complete with shoe covers, cap, and wrap-around plastic face shield hanging round his neck. A young woman, with dark hair pulled back from her face, stood beside him, dressed in the same regulation gown.

'Detective Stowe, nice of you to arrive on time,' Lyons said.

'Did you think I wouldn't?'

'Your lot like to think your time is more important than mine.'

Danny didn't bother replying. It wasn't up to him to convince Lyons they were on the same side.

'I've a student in today. I assume you have no objections?'

'None at all.' He nodded towards the student. 'Hi there, I'm DI Danny Stowe.'

'Maria McDermott, third year medic.'

Danny nodded. The Royal Victoria Hospital was a teaching hospital, so students were to be expected. The main hospital for victims of shootings and bombings during the Troubles, it was also once the best plastic surgery unit in Europe, with necessity requiring innovative techniques to repair and rebuild that which Semtex and guns had destroyed.

'Right, shall we make a start?' Lyons said. The autopsy had already been performed, but in cases of complexity or special interest it was usual to have the pathologist talk through the results with the body in situ.

Lyons turned to Maria. 'We start with an examination of the body and evidence collected at the scene, and then proceed to the physical examination, laboratory tests, and assessment.'

The student looked like she was keen to make a good impression.

'What would you say the aim of the autopsy is?' Lyons asked her.

'Well, the primary aim is to provide objective evidence of cause, timing, and manner of death for decree by the criminal justice system,' she said, as if she had memorised the answer from a text book.

Danny walked over to the body and stood to the side, waiting for Lyons to begin. He was obviously enjoying showing his expertise off to the young medic. When he had first met Lyons on the Mulligan case he had come across as standoffish and superior, but he now recognised his arrogance as something else. Danny guessed that Lyons was probably just socially awkward. He had that air of intractable obstinance that made you feel an instant dislike, but his inscrutable façade cloaked a likeable

5r6h

persona that took time to uncover. Danny admired anyone who was good at their job and he was confident that Lyons would miss nothing.

Danny was itching to get started but he allowed Lyons to have his moment.

Lyons continued speaking to Maria. 'With this case, I was in attendance at the death scene. The purpose of being present allowed me to view the body in the context of its surroundings, but I am better able to interpret certain findings at the autopsy, such as a patterned imprint across the neck from the rope. The forensic medical expert is also able to advise the investigative agency about the nature of the death.'

He turned to Danny. 'In short, your investigation structure, the manpower required, and the securing of vital evidence is ultimately directed by the findings of the pathologist.'

Danny resisted rolling his eyes. Lyons was enjoying this way too much.

'So, what have you got for me?' Danny asked.

Lyons took a deep breath and launched in. 'External examination is as follows: White male of thirty-five years, moderately built and weighing in at one hundred and seventy-six pounds. Five foot eight in height. Post-mortem lividity static. No signs of decomposition. Facial features puffy and cyanosed.' As he moved around the body, he pointed to various parts with his oversized Q-tip. Danny looked at the cadaver, seeing the y-shaped incision carefully stitched closed.

The student stood quietly with her notepad in her hand, taking it all in with interest. Lyons would get to the point soon, telling Danny what the cause of death was, but until then they had to go through the process, the pathologist demonstrating his findings to his student step by step.

This wasn't a particularly difficult cadaver to look at, but it was still unpleasant. Danny wasn't one of those cops who felt that it was a matter of pride to turn up with a belly full of breakfast and not as much as glance away as the pathologist talked them through the horrors of death. It wasn't the killing itself that bothered Danny. Instead it was the process of decomposition that began almost as soon as the last breath was taken. That slow, all-encompassing putrefaction that proved humans are nothing beyond a complex system of cells and biology. He had heard colleagues talk of the birth of their first child as miraculous, the wonder of bringing new life forth into the world making them feel a new sense of awe and wonder that maybe there was more to life. Funny how every single time he witnessed a cadaver and smelled that sickening odour of death, he sensed the utmost futility of believing in anything beyond the here and now. If birth made a believer out of some, then death created its own infidels.

'Usually we don't have much input with the clothes and scene of crime evidence but in this case we did ask to do our own examination. The type and position of the knot plays an important role in the mechanism of death and autopsy findings in a hanging, so the cord rope was of particular interest to me.'

Lyons led them over to the table running along the back wall of the lab with a bounce in his step.

'With the rope, I started by looking at the direction of the fibres. Then I moved on to the loop and the knots.'

Danny looked at the blue nylon cord laid out before them.

'Now, a reef knot is formed by tying a left-handed knot and then a right-handed knot or vice versa. There's a rhyme, "right over left, left over right, makes a knot both tidy and tight."'

Danny nodded, waiting to see where all of this was going. The student seemed to be drawing the knot formation in her notebook.

'One other thing – in most cases of suicide by right-handed victims, the knot is situated on the right side.' Danny looked at the knot, sitting to the right of the noose. He made a note to check if James was left or right-handed.

'This type of knot is known as a granny knot. Every boy scout from here to Donaghadee knows how to construct a granny knot. Now the thing is, the granny knot is usually considered a lesser knot compared to, say, a reef knot.'

Danny found his fingers moving towards his collar, loosening it; a reflexive gesture as he contemplated a noose tightening around the neck.

'Let's move on to the good stuff,' Lyons said, returning to the body. 'In deaths due to full-suspension hanging with feet not touching the ground, we usually find the parchment abrasion – the ligature mark.' He pointed at the mark around the victim's neck. 'The length of nylon rope had a diameter of 1.5 cm and has caused a ligature mark of 1.3 cm width.'

Maria walked to the head of the steel table to get a closer look.

'During the autopsy exam you often see bruising over the lower legs and forearms. These are thought to be due to terminal seizure type movements while suspended. We've no evidence of this here, though there is some bruising around the jawline.' He pointed to the markings. 'And if you look here, you can see some further blemishes on and under the skin. Sorry, I'm going on a bit but it's all necessary.'

'Look, he has a tattoo!' Maria said.

'Yes, a small tattoo on the left hip,' Lyons said.

'Don't you think that's strange?' she asked.

'A tattoo? Hardly. Every man under thirty seems to have one these days.'

'No, I mean, it's strange to have it in such a hidden place. Most guys get them to show them off, not hide them. Why get one at all if he doesn't want anyone to see it?'

Lyons looked put out that the student had dared to offer an opinion.

Danny looked at where she was pointing. It was a small symbol with the words '*Taw bro-in orr-um*' around it.

'What is that? Irish?' Danny asked.

'Yeah, I think it means brother or something to do with being a brother,' Maria said.

Danny took a quick picture of the symbol on his phone.

'Well, for whatever reason, he had it done in an area not likely to be seen by anyone but his wife. Now, if we can get back to the examination?' Lyons said.

Maria nodded and looked chastened.

'Moving on.' He paused and looked at Danny. 'Significant to note is the fact that there are signs of asphyxia – petechiae in and on the eyes, face, and around the mouth.'

Lyons pressed his hands together as if in prayer. 'Now, we know that the spine is affected during a hanging, but here is where it gets interesting . . . A voluminous subdural haematoma with brain swelling was found.' He looked at Danny as if expecting a reaction.

'And that means . . .' Danny said.

'This rope was not your murder weapon.'

'Any idea of what was?'

Lyons tutted as if his big reveal had been ruined and ignored Danny's question. 'It also means that the victim was unconscious when the rope was placed around his neck, and potentially already dead at the time of the hanging.'

'So, whoever killed him did so at another location and then staged it so that it looked like suicide by hanging.'

'Almost certainly. But that isn't all we found. We also identified some markings on the neck that suggest a ligature of sorts was used to carry out the strangulation and it wasn't the rope found at the scene.'

'Any idea what it was?'

'The width of the ligature and the markings are suggestive of something like a leather belt.'

CHAPTER 11

Rose had found herself driving aimlessly after the dinner with her family. The city always looked more attractive at night. There was a romance to the streetlights and the Victorian red-brick buildings that daylight achromatised. She parked on the Annadale embankment and decided to walk along the river towards the looming Lyric Theatre.

She hoped a late-night walk would clear her head and help her sleep better. For the past week she'd been feeling uneasy, with a sense of dread that was hard to shake. Rationally, she knew that it was nothing more than the lingering hangover of a bad dream that haunted her mind, but still the sensation of something menacing nipped at her.

The dream had involved Sean Torrent, her mother's former . . . what? Friend, lover, comrade, compatriot? She didn't know what to think of him. In the dream she had been with him in a room devoid of windows and doors. Neither wanting to be there, both of them had prowled around one another, fearful of giving the other an advantage.

She shuddered and wrapped her coat tighter around herself. The chill in the air made her walk faster, and before she knew it, she had looped around the river, passing over the Ormeau Bridge, and ended up back at her car. A weariness crawled over her and made her long for bed and a comatose sleep, the kind that only comes through sheer exhaustion.

Earlier that day she had chased up James McCallum's GP. The doctor's receptionist had asked Rose to wait while she informed Dr Cusack of her arrival. The waiting room was full of older people, young mothers with sick toddlers, and a teenage schoolgirl staring at her phone screen. Rose took a seat and busied herself scanning through the notes she had saved to her phone from the interview with James' wife Emma. There was something about Emma that made Rose feel uneasy. She was too perfect. The gorgeous home was an extension of her professional life, she understood that, but was she a little too polished and together to be mourning her recently dead husband?

'Dr Cusack will see you now,' the receptionist called over.

Rose headed down the corridor and was greeted enthusiastically by a white-haired man who beamed at her.

'Come on ahead. What can I do for you?'

'I'm here in connection to one of your patients, James McCallum. He was found hanged and I would like to ask a few questions and request access to his medical records.' Rose offered her identification card.

'Tragic. I'd heard about the hanging. The practice

received a call from one of your PSNI colleagues. Awful business altogether. It's the families left behind that suffer.'

Rose nodded. 'Had you had any concerns about James?'

'James had been in a few weeks ago. I checked the records in advance of you coming. It seems that he had asked for sleeping tablets.'

'And did he seem okay?'

'I'm afraid I wasn't the one who saw him. The locum, Dr Donnelly, was on and from the notes I can see she offered James a short course of Zolpidem. I would expect James had been pretty insistent for a locum to prescribe sleeping tablets on the first visit.'

'Did he have any history of depression?'

'Mild episodes that were treated with short courses of anti-depressant medication, but not since last year.'

'Did he say what the cause of the depression was?'

'Modern life. Too much work and not enough rest. Nothing specific.'

It was convenient for the killer that James' state of mind played into the suicide narrative. Whatever had actually troubled James, it was clear he hadn't shared it with his doctor. The stresses and strains of modern life was a whitewash. Something else had been disturbing his sleep, troubling him and make him act out of sorts. His wife had hinted at something going on that she wasn't part of. Some part of his life had evidently been kept from her, and Rose wanted to know why.

She needed to be clear as to how James was acting in the run-up to his death. Was he aware that someone may have wanted to kill him? At this point in the investigation they couldn't be sure of anything but the odds were good that he knew the person or persons responsible for his murder.

At work the next day she went looking for Danny.

'So, where are we with the case?' she asked, settling into the chair next to him.

'It's early days so we still don't know how James got from the house to the school or the primary kill site. Did he get taxi? Did someone drive him there? The family are being told this morning that we are dealing with a murder, so we need to go back to the wife and see how she's taking it and press her for more information. Plus, I want to find out more about the rope that was used to hang him. Meet me in the team incident room at two and we can take it from there.'

After lunch, Rose grabbed her folder of notes and headed to the first-floor incident room. She took a seat near the back and was looking out the window when Danny strode in, business-like and in charge. Sometimes it took her by surprise that he was no longer the nineteen-year-old student that she knew so well. A thought flitted through her mind – did he also have trouble making the adjustment with her? She liked watching Danny command a room, seeing the looks of respect on his colleagues' faces and the authority with which he held their attention.

He stood, hands on hips waiting for everyone to arrive, settle down and pay attention. When the last of the team straggled through the door he cleared his throat to gain their attention, and the scraping of chairs against the floor and the murmur of conversation came to an abrupt end.

Danny began. 'As you are probably all now aware, the death of James McCallum, found at Osbourne House Grammar at the weekend, has been proven to be murder, not suicide. State pathology has provided us with the full autopsy report confirming this.'

They all sat up straighter and looked intently at Danny.

He clicked on the wireless remote in his hand and a picture of James McCallum in death flashed up on the screen. His eyes were glazed, staring blankly, the skin pallid with the tell-tale bruising around the jawline. 'Our victim is James McCallum, aged thirty-five. An architect, he was married to Emma, an interior designer, and they had one child – a daughter. He was strangled with what the pathologist believes could be a leather belt and later moved to the school grounds where the hanging was staged.' He paused.

'So far, all we have to go on is a text message sent by the victim to Lorcan Burns – an old school friend – in the early hours of the day his body was found.' Danny clicked the remote again and the message appeared on the screen.

I'm really sorry but I can't keep going. The reckoning is coming.

'The message was sent from James' phone, which was retrieved by SOCO from his trouser pocket, but we can't assume that he was the one to send it. This raises the questions of: if James didn't send it, then who did? And was it sent to make it look like James was struggling and was contemplating suicide? That's what we need to suss out.'

'Do we have any idea what the message refers to?' asked DS Tania Lumen.

'No, we don't yet know what it is referencing. It could be something in his past or something that was happening in his life in the present. Burns claims he doesn't know what it meant. Actually, Tania, when we're done here, could you take a run out to Lorcan Burns and pick up his phone? It might be worth having a look at it.'

'Sure,' Tania replied.

'Sir,' DS Fitzgerald said from the back of the room, 'were there any prints found on James McCallum's phone?'

'Good question. No.'

A low murmuring travelled around the room.

'So, the phone was cleaned of all prints?' Fitzgerald asked.

'Yes, so it seems. We need to ask why and who else could have handled that phone,' Danny said. He looked around the room. 'Mal, I want you to track down any old acquaintances who might have known James and Lorcan back in the day when they were at school. Find out what they were like. If they had – or have – any enemies.'

'Sir, don't you think we'd be better off looking at James McCallum's life now rather than his school days?' DS Malachy Magee asked.

'Yes, by all means we need a full picture of his life in the present but he was found in the grounds of his old school, having sent a message to an old school friend, so there might be a link. Gerard, you're already looking at the financials involved in the architect business. Anything turn up yet?'

DS Kinley looked up. 'Sir, I'm still waiting on Companies House to come back to me. I'll chase it up today.'

'Okay, good. We also need to ask: was there another

woman on the scene? Or could the wife have had anything dodgy going on? Jack, can you look at Mrs McCallum's background?'

'Yep, no problem,' Fitzgerald said.

'Should we request a trace on Mrs McCallum's phone?' Tania asked.

Danny shook his head. 'We don't currently have enough to convince the boss to sign off on it. At this point I'm more interested in CCTV from the surrounding area. If he didn't put himself up that tree, someone had to transport him. It wouldn't have been an easy task either, so we are possibly looking for more than one suspect. So, Mal, can you also chase up the school's CCTV footage?'

'Ahh bit of a problem there, boss. It appears that the CCTV wasn't on in the school itself, on the night in question. The decorators had knocked the system off, something to do with painting around the circuit board,' Mal said.

'Damn. The tree and hill weren't in range of the cameras, but we'd hoped to clock any vehicle coming or going from the school grounds. Now we'll have to go through all the footage taken from the surrounding area.' He continued, 'We've at least one partial footprint from beneath the tree, so we'll need to have that looked at. And we'll need to visit the caretaker again to get impressions of the shoes he was wearing when he found the body to rule him out.'

Tania raised her hand. 'What about the victim's clothes? Did anything come up from the forensic review?'

Danny shifted his weight. 'Yeah, and it could be significant, SOCO came back late last night with some animal hair on McCallum's clothes. Our hope is that it will give us some sort of lead on the primary murder scene. We also have a fragment of orange fibre – some sort of plastic-based material. They are doing some follow-up research on it now.'

Danny looked towards Rose. 'Dr Lainey, I appreciate that we are at an early stage of our enquires, but can you make any assumptions about the killer from the crime scene and the nature of the hanging?'

Rose drew herself up in her seat. 'I think what you are asking me is, what kind of person goes to such lengths to kill someone and then undertake the misdirection of evidence? The hanging would have been extremely difficult to physically stage.'

Danny nodded. 'Anything you've got will help us.'

Rose stood and walked to the front of the room. 'At this point, from what we know and have seen, we can reasonably assume that the killer has intimate knowledge of the victim, and his weakness – the fact he's prone to dark moods. We've confirmed with the wife that he had experienced periods of mild depression, and that during those times he withdrew from her and seemed distant.

'Cases like this one are rare, so the forensic evidence obtained is of crucial importance. The victim was found in the grounds of his old school suspended by a rope around his neck.

'I have heard of another case similar to this one, where a forty-eight-year-old man was hanged by his wife, assisted by her lover. The autopsy findings in that case were largely in keeping with that of a suicidal suspension but the small contusion on the victim's lower inner lip, along with abrasions on the lower part of the legs – which

were due to the struggle and terminal asphyxial movements – revealed that the cause of death was not suicide,
as first suspected. As with that case, the primary staging
involved misdirection to make it look like the victim has
taken his own life. The amount of care put into the
staging suggests this is not a random murder and I think
we can safely theorise that the death scene, the victim,
and killer are all intrinsically bound together.'

She paused for a beat, enjoying the power of having
the room's undivided attention. 'The nature of the staged
suicide, and the killing itself, tells us that the murderer
is ruthless, controlled and disciplined. This was well
thought out and executed almost to a professional level.'

'What do you mean by a professional? Like a hit man?'
asked Mal.

'No, I mean professional in that our killer knows about
the body and death and how to present the body to
make us think that it was a suicide.'

'So, you think that the killer or killers were definitely
close to James?' Danny asked.

'Yes. Whoever was involved knew James McCallum
well enough to know he had a history of depression. The
murderer may have felt that by staging it like a suicide,
the death would fit with how James had been presenting
to those around him and few questions would be asked.'

'Why choose the school grounds?' DS Fitzgerald asked.

Danny moved forward. 'At this stage we can't hypoth-
esise as to why, but the school setting does seem
significant and again suggests the killer knew James well.'

'We also need to take into account that the school
setting provided some cover for the killer. They most
likely knew that the CCTV cameras did not cover the

area around the hanging tree and that the back gates were easily accessed and would allow a vehicle to get close to the hanging site,' Rose offered.

Danny walked across the room and leaned against the radiator. 'So, it appears as though our killer knew the victim and had enough knowledge about the pathology of suicide to think he or she could get away with the murder.'

'Yeah, our killer is most certainly in the know,' Rose agreed.

CHAPTER 12

Danny spread the crime scene photographs on the table and his team leaned in to get a closer look. The close ups of the corpse had all the gruesomeness of death etched onto the contorted features. His washed out T-shirt and faded jeans made him look younger than his thirty-five years, and the rope from which McCallum hung was pictured in individual frames, each providing information about the process that led to his death.

'Look at the formation of the knots here . . .' Danny pointed to the photograph of the branch where the rope had been slung over to gain purchase and allow the murderer to pull the body up. 'This is what gave us our first indication that we were dealing with a murder not a suicide.'

'Boss, it wouldn't be easy to string someone up from a tree. Like, it would take a lot of strength, surely,' Mal Magee said.

'True, that's why this afternoon we are going to stage our own re-enactment and see what it would take to do

79

it. James McCallum wasn't particularly big – five foot eight and 176 pounds. Anyone measure up to that?'

'Nah, that's a light weight. None of the lads would be that short either,' DS Fitzgerald said.

'I come closest,' DS Tania Lumen said. They turned to appraise her.

'Yep, you'll do fine,' Danny said. 'Let's head to the gym and try to run through how the killer or killers managed to pull this off.'

'You want me to stage a hanging?' Hugh Robinson asked. The PSNI fitness trainer looked incredulous.

'Yep. I need to see how someone could string someone up from a tree to hang them, or at least to make it look like they've been hanged.'

Hugh shook his head. 'I don't know if the gym insurance covers death by accidental hanging.'

'Aww get over yourself and give it a go. It's all in the line of duty.' Danny grinned.

Robinson stood back with his hands on his hips, his enhanced biceps on show, and looked Tania up and down. 'You up for this?'

'As the boss man says, the case requires it. Just don't let me drop when the noose goes around my neck.'

'You've brought a rope, I see.'

'And a harness for Tania. Came prepared,' Danny said, grinning and handing it over. He then squatted down and rolled out a diagram of the crime scene on the gym floor. They crowded around and looked at a drawing of the hill, complete with height and distance measurements along with the tree and the body.

'Right, so look here. To get the body positioned at the

height it was found they would have needed to be at least twenty metres away pulling with all their might. That would place them on the gradient of the hill. I have to say, I didn't expect to be doing physics as a cop.'

The group laughed as Robinson looked around the gym and settled on the beam at the back. Walking over to stand beneath it, he then threw the rope up and over the beam, and tested it against his bulk.

'Should be okay to take your weight, Tania. Now what?'

'Now we work out how to lift Tania into position and dangle her from the beam,' Danny said.

Using a printout of the original knot formation they worked at the knots and spent a while getting it right.

'Okay. I think we have it now. Tania, if you care to do the honours,' Danny said.

Tania stepped forward and put on the harness before Danny attached it to the rope.

'Any last words?' Mal joked.

She sighed. 'Go on. Do your best lads, but if you accidentally hang me, I'm definitely coming back to haunt you all.'

Danny and Mal lifted Tania off the ground with relative ease and raised her up towards the beam.

'Not the hardest thing to do, but would it be so straight forward if she was already dead? And do you absolutely have to have two people involved to do the lifting?' Danny asked.

'Mmm, not sure,' Hugh said.

Mal let go and Danny pulled on the rope to try to lift Tania singlehandedly. Her feet left the ground but not enough to be raised to the height they had found James McCallum's body at.

'So, in theory, as long as the killer weighed more than James McCallum, it could have been done by one person,' Mal said.

Hugh moved towards Tania. 'Let's get her down. I don't care if she's in a harness, you lot are making me nervous.'

When Tania was safely out of the rope, they sat down on a bench to think the process through.

'We need to figure out what equipment the killer could have used,' Tania said.

'What do you mean?' asked Danny.

'Well he or she could have had a pulley system. Something to make the process easier.'

'She's right,' Hugh said. 'If you have a single wheel and some rope, a pulley helps you reverse the direction of your lifting force. If you want to lift something that weighs a hundred kilos, you have to pull down with a force equivalent to one hundred kilos. And if you want to raise the weight one metre into the air, you have to pull the loose end of the rope a total distance of one metre at the other end.'

'That orange cord fragment that was found on the tree. Maybe that will tell us something about how it was done,' Mal said.

Danny stood. 'Yeah, you could be right. I'll chase up Fiona Madden to see if she's found out more on it yet.'

CHAPTER 13

Danny left the station for the night and drove home considering his options for dinner – takeaway, or a stir-fry using whatever ingredients lay languishing in his fridge. When he parked the car and made his way to his front door his mind was on teriyaki noodles, so it took a moment for him to compose his features when he found Amy standing on the doorstep.

'Amy, what are you doing here?' He couldn't help sounding pissed off. No one tells you how to navigate breakups. The longing for her had dissipated and he sure as hell didn't want to trigger any latent feelings. She didn't belong in his life now and he resented the intrusion.

'I wanted to see you, Danny,' her voice faltered, 'to talk.' Her hair was longer and she wore make-up that emphasised her eyes.

He hesitated, then put his key in the lock and opened the door. Though he didn't invite her in, she followed anyway.

'Nice place.'

He shrugged. 'It's fine for now.' He watched as she looked around the living room, taking in the soulless interior and the not so tidy set-up. He scrambled to lift a sweatshirt that lay cast off on the sofa and the empty coffee mug that sat on the low side table.

'Do you want something to drink?' he offered. There was a coolness and an awkwardness between them. A sense of needing to treat each other with the politeness afforded to strangers.

'Black tea would be good, thanks.'

'Sure, I'll be back in a minute.' He went to the kitchen and boiled the kettle. He was about to shout that he'd no biscuits in, when he caught himself. She never ate biscuits anyway.

He returned with their teas and deliberately sat on the chair beside the window, as far from her as possible. It seemed stupid that he didn't know if he could trust himself if she reached out to him. The ease with which he could potentially fall into her arms frightened him.

Amy looked different. At first, he couldn't put his finger on it, but then, as she picked up her mug of steaming tea, he realised. She looked healthy and well. She'd put on some weight and the painful skeletal appearance he had grown used to had softened, making her more beautiful than ever. Anorexia had stolen so much from her. From them both.

'I'm doing better, Danny.'

'Yeah, I can see. You look good.'

She smiled. 'How have you been?' Her voice was light and normal, as if they were just two old friends catching up. The pain and hurt of their years together suddenly seemed distant, as if it had happened to two other people and not to them. Danny had once watched a visiting artist at school apply a pale blue wash to a page and then build up the layers of tone and shade until the painting became something entirely different. That was how he felt now, as if Amy was re-creating their life into something unrecognisable with all the edges softened and blurred.

'Busy. Work stuff, you know?'

She nodded. 'I miss you. This. Us.' There was a sadness in her voice that pulled at him, made him feel the ache of wanting to make everything better for her. It was an old habit that was hard to break.

Instead he shook his head. 'There's no going back, Amy.'

'I know what I did was wrong. I should have talked to you first to make you understand.' There was a hint of panic in her voice.

He shook his head. 'Make me understand? What, that you didn't want our baby? That you went behind my back to get an abortion in England?'

She started to cry. 'Danny, my head was wrecked. I was sick. You know how I was. I wasn't well then but I'm doing better now.' She reached for his hand. 'We could try again. It would be different this time.'

Some part of him wanted to take her in his arms; to kiss her and tell her that he would fix it all. He thought of the promises they'd made each other – to be there through the good times and the bad.

But deep down he knew there was no going back. He didn't think he could ever get over what she'd done, no matter what her reasons were. It would always be there between them, festering and threatening to soil everything.

Danny stood up. 'I'm sorry, Amy, but we can't go back to how it was. Besides, you seem to be doing all right on your own.'

Outsiders tend to think that if you work on the murder squad you're a lone wolf who inevitably drinks too much and exists on a diet of adrenaline and fried food. The truth is that most good detectives have a support network – their family. A wife or husband taking the time to make sure you leave the job at the door is one of the most effective ways of ensuring you don't lose yourself to the job. Once upon a time, Amy was Danny's support, his reason for washing away the stench of death at the end of the day. In time, though, he'd discovered that while he was always looking out for her, she hadn't been looking out for him. When he'd needed her, she wasn't willing or able to meet him halfway, so now that she had come crawling back, asking for a second chance, he couldn't help but feel an icy splinter of resentment. He made bad decisions when his head was elsewhere worrying about Amy. He couldn't blame her for what had happened on the Lennon case – a major fuck-up on his part – but he sure as hell knew that if he hadn't been having such a hard time in his personal life, he wouldn't have lost his cool and smashed that perp's head against the wall in a blind fury.

No, Amy hadn't been there for him. And he wasn't going to repeat his past mistakes now. The conversation moved on to their families before eventually fading away to an awkward silence.

'So, I suppose I better head on,' she said.

They said their goodbyes and she reached to hug him. 'Take care of yourself, Amy.'

'You too, Danny.'

He closed the door and found he'd no appetite for dinner after all. A stiff drink would do instead.

CHAPTER 14

The next morning, Danny hit the station gym to sweat out the remains of the previous night's whiskey. Drinking on a work night wasn't a good look. He didn't want his team smelling the sourness of self-pity on him. Amy was part of his past and he needed to move on. The momentum of the case would offer him a place to go, a refuge from the nagging of his own mind when he doubted the validity of his decision. Deep down though, he knew if he had any unease in showing her the door, it was born out of a sadness that it hadn't worked out. Life could be a bitch at times. Relationships don't work out for all sorts of reasons, but he didn't think Amy was his only chance at finding love.

Drying himself off after a shower, he forced his thoughts to return to the job.

He didn't feel it was fair to keep James' mother in the dark any longer.

* * *

Rhea McCallum was sitting at the living room window of her detached home in Broomhill Park when they pulled into the driveway. She opened the door before they had a chance to ring the doorbell.

'You're from the police,' she stated.

'Yes, I'm DI Danny Stowe and this is Dr Rose Lainey. We are very sorry for your loss, Mrs McCallum. May we come in?'

'Yes, of course. I was expecting you. Go on ahead.'

She led them into the wood-panelled hallway and through to a formal sitting room.

'How are you, Mrs McCallum?' Rose asked.

'I can't take it in, that James would have killed himself. It doesn't seem right that he would leave Gracie. I keep saying it's just not possible that he took his own life.' Her pale lips were pulled into a tight line and the shadows beneath her eyes suggested she hadn't slept. She twisted a tissue in her hands. 'James had everything to live for. He adored his daughter. I can't fathom any reason why he would do this to himself.'

Danny nodded. 'Mrs McCallum, please, can you sit down?'

'Oh for god's sake. I've had the worst news possible, what difference does it make now?' She stood at the fireplace and glared at them. Her hair was short and styled into curls which seemed incongruously girly for her age. She looked like the type of woman who maintained a rigorous routine of hairdressing appointments and facials.

Danny noticed a framed photograph on the mantelpiece of James with his blonde-haired daughter. It must have been recent, for the girl looked exactly the same as when they had met her just a few days ago.

'I appreciate that.' He paused. 'Mrs McCallum, there's no easy way to say this but we're here to tell you that we suspect James didn't kill himself.'

Rhea McCallum's hand shot to her mouth. 'Oh my god, I knew it. He's been murdered.'

'Suicide is a very difficult death to accept but finding someone has deliberately killed your loved one is . . .' Danny trailed off. 'Well, I can't imagine how painful this must be for you to hear.'

She walked across the room and sat down on the edge of the chair opposite them, staring straight ahead.

'It didn't feel possible that he would take his own life. I knew he wouldn't do that to Grace or me. But this – the idea that someone has killed him . . .' She began to cry softly, using the crumpled-up tissue in her hand to wipe her nose.

Rose leaned forward. 'In cases like this where we have suspicion that something is amiss, it can be useful to have what we call a "psychological autopsy." This means that I would look closely at James' life and try to establish what was going on day to day, as well as looking at those around him to try to establish any avenues that may lead us towards the killer.'

Rhea nodded. 'You need to dig deep into his affairs.'

'Yes, and sometimes families don't like what we unearth. It can be upsetting to have your loved one's life raked over,' Rose said.

'Believe me when I say James has nothing to hide. He was the best son and an absolutely devoted father to Grace.' She began to cry again. 'I'm sorry. This is so awful. I don't know how to control my emotions.'

'Please, don't worry. No one would expect you to,' Rose said gently.

Rhea sighed and reverted to twisting the damp tissue in her hands. 'James was the type of person who was acutely aware of others. He cared about them and went out of his way to help people.'

'Is there any reason you can think of – anything at all – that would make you think someone might want to harm James?' Danny asked.

Rhea McCallum lengthened her back, leaned forward and looked straight at him. 'Well, I know where you need to start. Begin with Emma, his wife.'

CHAPTER 15

Rose looked up from her computer as DI Robert Conroy walked into her office.

'Hey, got a minute?' He sauntered in, all bounce and swagger, and closed the door behind himself. She'd spoken to him a few times but didn't know much about him. He was a large man, solid and broad with a strong jaw and greying hair which he wore short. He was always immaculately turned out. The suit – navy pinstripe – looked dry-clean-fresh, as if he had barely worn it, and his pale blue shirt had a starchy quality that spoke of careful ironing. Someone had taken time and care to make sure he looked his best.

'Sure, what can I help you with?'

He sat down on the armchair placed by the coffee table, his large frame making the chair seem too small, like something designed for a child to play house with. Rose got up from her desk and sat in the other armchair facing him. HR had deemed her new role as being worthy of comfy furniture to help put her clients at ease. 'Clients', that was how she thought of them. 'Patients' wasn't right and 'colleagues' would diminish the careful professional distance both she and they needed.

'I'm not doing too good,' Robert said. His voice was gravelly, like he smoked forty a day and washed his mouth out with whiskey.

'First of all, I want you to know that whatever you say in here is between us, though if I fear you are a danger to yourself or others then I am obliged to take further action. Anything else is confidential.'

He nodded and gave a sort of half shrug.

'So,' she started, 'how has this sense of not doing well manifested?'

He sighed and then inhaled deeply, as if readying himself. 'I've not been myself. Not as excited about getting up in the morning, if you know what I mean.'

'Would you say you feel down? Depressed?'

'Maybe.'

'Overall, how would you describe your mood?'

'Sort of flat. Like everything's a bit grey.'

'The fact that you're aware of something not being right is good. It means I can help you to start putting strategies in place to help. What's your most overwhelming concern at this moment?'

He gave a half smile. 'It might sound stupid, but I feel like I'm losing my edge, you know? I like to pride myself in being good at my job. If I can't give one hundred per cent here, then what's the point?'

Rose nodded. 'That's not stupid. We can all feel a sense of not performing at our best from time to time, and the fact that you are aware of it reinforces to me that you are conscientious. That's what makes you a good cop.'

'It's like my nerve has gone, which is mad when you consider that the Troubles are over and the threat from Dissidents isn't what it used to be. But you never know, do you? Any day now, they could stick a pipe bomb under my car. A pizza delivery boy could deliver more than a twenty-inch pepperoni and mushroom.'

'Listen, Rob, this job isn't easy, nor is it without risks. Has this sense of being anxious affected how you deal with other people? Or made you change your behaviour?'

He nodded. 'Yeah, I check under my car three, maybe four times, before I get into it. I've moved my bed so I'm facing the door in case anyone comes in to get me. I'm jittery. The wife says if I don't talk to someone like you, she'll kill me herself.' He gave Rose a wry smile. 'She loves me really, but I guess I'm hard to live with at the minute.'

'What about sleeping, exercising, and eating?'

He nodded again. 'Yep, I'm still doing the usual circuits and lifting weights at the gym. Eating all right. Sleep, not so much. I struggle to get over before three a.m. and at the weekends I'm downing a brave few whiskeys to get some shut eye.'

'So, it's really about the job?'

'Yeah. The pressure, you know. It's hard. Maybe I need anti-depressants and sleeping tablets or something. Like a quick fix to get me back on track.'

'You don't necessarily need medication. Often, we just lose the sense of who we are for a time. The person we want to be. The outside crowds in on our thoughts and we don't get to recalibrate when we need to.'

He leaned towards her, as if willing her to make him feel better.

94

'I don't want to go off on the sick with stress. That shit would stay on my record, impede me making any kind of proper career progression. Despite everything, I love this job. I believe in it.'

'Then you need to commit to a process of talking about how you are feeling. To work your way through whatever is holding you back. Can you do that?'

'I guess. I can try, at least.'

'These feelings of anxiety and fear could be born out of a greater feeling underlying it all.'

'Like what?'

'There could be many factors at play. It could even go back as far as your childhood.'

He looked totally in now, as if she had revealed something about him that he knew was there all along but had been just out of reach

'I can help you but you're the one that needs to do the work. Are you in?'

'All in.'

CHAPTER 16

For a detective, each case is a chance to right some of the wrongs of the world. To make a difference. A crime scene is a killer's calling card, and if you're lucky it leads you straight to him. Or her. In his experience though, nine times out of ten it was a man, so Danny didn't mind making generalisations. The problem with this case was that they didn't have any clues pointing to the primary crime scene. But then again, an absence of data was information too . . .

Half an hour later he'd tracked Fiona Madden down to the lab.

'What about ya, Fiona?'

'I'm due out to the field in ten minutes, so whatever it is, make it quick.' She didn't bother looking up from her computer screen.

'I won't keep you long. The hanging tree fella, I'm trying to wrap my head around the findings.'

'It will all be in the report. What's wrong, Detective, frightened I'll use big words you won't understand?'

'Very funny. I understand that the body was clean. No fibres beyond the hair found on his clothes. Yet, it was moved from the original scene of the killing. Surely that alone would create some sort of evidence trail?'

She leaned back from the computer and gave Danny her full attention for the first time since he'd arrived.

'The absence of material evidence tells you quite a lot. Whoever did this knew enough about keeping the body clean of evidence. They went out of their way to ensure they tidied up after themselves,' she said with a meaningful look.

'What, you think it could be someone on the force?'

'"Not only his fingerprints or his footprints, but his hair, the fibres from his clothes, the glass he breaks, the tool mark he leaves, the paint he scratches, the blood or semen he deposits or collects – all these and more bear mute witness against him. This is evidence that does not forget. Paul Kirk Crime Investigation, 1953." I read that in first year and memorised it, knowing some day in the future a detective dick like yourself would need to hear it. Physical evidence doesn't lie but we can fuck it up in our interpretation.'

'So we have unknown DNA, but none that matches his wife or his business partner. No latent prints, or fibre, tool mark, or other conducted forensic evaluation except for the animal hair.'

'Yep, you've no smoking gun. You'll have to work hard to solve this one – the lab rats aren't going to do it for you this time. The only thing I can say is that we did find traces of oxygen producing detergent. In luminal tests we rely on the ability of blood to take up oxygen. The haemoglobin reacts with hydrogen peroxide and gives a positive

97

test result. Something like Vanish shifts more than a grass stain since it causes the blood to degrade, but we found no blood or wounds in this instance.'

'So, they cleaned up well and knew enough about police procedure to know an oxygen-based cleaning detergent will do a good job of wiping away all traces.'

She shrugged. 'I give you the findings. The rest is up to you to sort out.'

CHAPTER 17

Rose sat at her computer screen reading about the historical belief in suicide notes as establishing suicide as cause of death. Notes, whether handwritten, typed – or in the case of James McCallum, texted – serve as external evidence for determining suicide as the manner of death.

Outside, the light of the day had drained, leaving a gloomy darkness. Rose googled the *Belfast Telegraph* website and read the headline: *Murder by Hanging* with the strapline *Scene of death in Osborne House Grammar*. They had missed the point; the death had been by strangulation, but they weren't going to let that get in the way of a good headline. No reporters had been at the scene, which was a small mercy, and until yesterday, they had managed to keep the details out of the media due to the initial presentation as suicide, but now that they had a murder investigation on their hands, a statement had been released. Rose knew that media intrusion was always difficult for families to cope with. The story was accompanied by an archive photograph of the school, and one of James, which Rose recognised as having been lifted from his professional LinkedIn page.

Just then, Danny arrived at the door of her basement office. 'Alright, Lainey. What are you working on at this time? Have you no home to go to?'

'I could ask you the same,' she said with a smile. They were two of a kind now, both married to the job. 'I've been looking at research surrounding suicide notes. Did you know some countries require a suicide note to record a death as suicide? Even as recently as the 1970s that was the case for coroners in the US.'

'No, I didn't. But the text. Kind of convenient, don't you think? We can't exactly get a handwriting expert in to verify it.'

'Yeah, that text needs to be fully investigated, and Lorcan Burns, too. What did you make of him?'

'Seemed like a nice fella. Pretty cut up about his mate's death but you never know.'

Rose nodded.

Danny leaned against the radiator. 'I wish Malachy Magee put in the same hours as you. The wee shite buggered off home just as I went looking for an update on James McCallum's social circle.'

'Oh, I wouldn't worry. I saw him earlier and he told me he hadn't gotten very far. Apparently, James was tight with the friends from his school days – Lorcan Burns and the two girls, Ivy and Emer – and they would meet up every so often. Ivy is a GP and is single, and Emer, who works in PR, is married. And we already know Lorcan lives with his partner. There also doesn't seem to be any romantic connection outside of James' marriage that we can trace, so whatever Rhea McCallum hinted at, the marriage wasn't failing on James' side.'

'Any reason why he kept the friendships going but excluded his wife when they met up?' Danny asked.

'No. Nothing. Married people don't have to have the same friends though, do they?'

'No, of course not. But it's unusual to exclude the spouses at every social get-together. I would've imagined that they would have met as a complete unit every so often with the husband, wife, and boyfriend included. Might be worth querying.' He sat on the edge of her desk, looking at the news story on her computer screen. 'I sometimes wonder what it would be like to have a normal job,' Danny said.

'What, one that doesn't throw up corpses?'

'Exactly. Look around upstairs and you'll see there isn't a single person who doesn't feel the urgency to get this case cracked. It's a compulsion we all feel, a sense of desperate need to make sure we do our job right. Except for Magee, of course. He's off getting his dinner with the wife and putting the kids to bed.'

'Unlike, say, someone sitting in a call centre who doesn't give a rat's arse? Yeah, might be nice not to care once in a while, but trust me, I've been there and done it with my previous work. The quiet life isn't all that great.'

'Yeah, it would give me too much time to be in my own head worrying about shite that's not important.'

'Exactly. Boredom is overrated.' She gave him a wry smile and he got up off her desk and headed for the door.

'Don't work too late. I think we should go have another

word with Emma McCallum and James' mother tomorrow. That animosity has to come from something.'

Rose agreed. While she didn't think at this stage that Emma had a hand in James' death, she couldn't rule it out.

'I'll see you first thing,' she called after him.

Rose turned back to her desk and looked at the photograph of James McCallum. On the surface he looked like a man who had his life sorted. The good-looking wife, the swish house, the architectural practice where he designed award-winning buildings, and a beautiful young daughter. He looked attractive with his intense dark eyes, a good strong jawline, and the reddish hair threaded with grey. She clicked through to his company's website and read the text on the screen aloud.

'Lanyon Architecture specialises in contemporary, sustainable, and environmentally conscious projects. We are an award-winning company, offering modernist designs with respect for tradition.'

Beneath the strapline on the page there was a photograph of James standing next to his business partner, Martin Kilburn. Kilburn looked slick with his navy suit, bright white shirt, and a pale pink tie. His thick, fair hair gave him the appearance of someone younger than his years. He was posing with his hand placed on James' shoulder while they both looked at a model building. The photograph was staged to give an impression of professionalism and success.

Rose wanted to know what lay behind the successful image of James McCallum. Sometimes the most controlled façade hid chaos and trauma. Was there something sinister going on beneath the cool exterior? 'What were you hiding, James?' she asked.

Maybe Martin Kilburn could provide some answers.

CHAPTER 18

Rose stood with the back of her legs against the radiator, glad of the heat. She was working on building up a profile of the killer. From the staging of the death she could deduce that the killer was a fabricator, someone capable of lying easily, and creative enough to think up the suicide scenario. It was also clear that the killer was a planner. Someone who was considered and exact in their preparations. The positioning of the body would have required serious effort and possibly assistance from someone else.

Her phoned beeped with the arrival of a text message. Her sister, Kaitlin, checking in to see if she was doing okay. Rose half smiled. She was so used to being on her own, without anyone to worry about her. It would take some adjusting to having this familial intrusion in her life. She sent a quick reply – *All good. Will try to catch up at the weekend. Hope you're fine too. R. x* – and returned to her work.

Why had Lorcan Burns not called James' phone when

he got the message? And why hadn't he phoned James' wife before phoning the police? Would it not have been better to call Emma, hoping to speak to James or ask about his whereabouts, and to try to establish what the message meant? It wasn't clear that he intended to commit suicide from the message, only implied.

While they had no positive forensic evidence of Lorcan Burns being involved, the circumstantial evidence surrounding the text made Rose question his motivation.

There was something about the killing that bothered Rose. She was used to reading research and data concerning killing scenes. This one was clean, planned, and almost too well-executed. The criminal self is evident in every crime scene in one way or another. Though the school grounds hadn't been the primary murder scene, Rose could ascertain a narrative from the careful execution of the staging that told of a killer with a particular, painstaking ability to curate a specific tableau.

She flicked through her notes and noticed that she had jotted down words that suggested female killers' motives as opposed to those of their male counterparts. Words like: strict, precise, meticulous. It was true that female killers tended to avoid stabbing or using guns. They prefer a clean, tidy kill. That's why the old fashioned modus operandi of murder by poisoning suited female killers. It was contained and clean. But what would the motivation be? Money? If Emma McCallum wanted out of her marriage, she could have left easily. Rose didn't think she would have resorted to murdering her husband.

Whoever they were looking for was most likely highly conscientious instead of impulsive and irresponsible, with self-discipline and a drive to achieve. Rose was beginning to feel like she was looking for someone who was callous and self-serving, yet could operate in society without ever attracting attention.

People can do all sorts of things out of desperation – greed and jealousy were powerful motivators – but she couldn't imagine that fraud, embezzling, or theft had led to this murder. No, she had a feeling that this had to be something darker. Whatever the motive, it was murky and sinister and would take time to excavate.

CHAPTER 19

After lunch, Danny gathered the team to discuss their findings to date. It was time to stir them up, get them enthused and primed to do their best work. He looked around as they settled themselves into chairs, some familiar faces from his previous cases and a few who were new to him. ACC Boyne had made the call as to who was working this case and Danny had had little say in it. Mal Magee was there, so that was one pair of safe hands. Tania Lumen and Jack Fitzgerald were also reliable. DS Gerard Kinley was good with numbers, so he was a welcome addition when it came to looking at the detail of Lanyon Architects' business. And then there was Rose. She would provide insights that the rest of them couldn't begin to imagine. Her training, experience, and skill would take the dry facts and reports and turn them into a psychological profile of depth and real meaning. He recognised her worth went deeper than case profiling though. She could see and identify parts of him that he didn't care to cast light on, but in doing so helped him to perform at his best, just as she would for the rest of the team. Rose was special and he would fight tooth and nail to keep her.

'All right, settle down and we'll get started,' he said.

'Dr Lyons, the forensic pathologist, has determined that James McCallum was murdered and that the hanging occurred while he was either unconscious or already dead. We have also established that the killer chose the hanging to masquerade as suicide. So let's focus on those closest to James McCallum. Who knew him well enough to know that he had a history of depression? This knowledge may have influenced the killer's decision to make it look like a suicide, thinking that the state of James' mental health was enough to make us accept what was presented at the scene.'

Danny turned to DS Magee. 'Mal, you were looking at his social circle. What have you come up with?'

Mal got to his feet. 'James didn't have much of a social life outside of his family. It seems that his school mates,' he looked down at this notepad, 'Ivy Duffy, Emer Ward, and Lorcan Burns, were his closest friends, though they didn't see each other often. His wife, Emma, said they were inseparable at school, but all went their separate ways after A Levels. She said James liked to keep that part of his life separate, that if he made arrangements with the friends, then spouses weren't included.'

'Maybe there's something in his past that he doesn't want to share with his wife? Did he have a relationship with one of the girls?' Rose asked.

'Worth checking that out,' Danny said.

Rose nodded.

'The mother suggested that there was something going

on in James' marriage. She told us to look at the wife, Emma. Tania, you were following that up, correct?'

'Yes, Emma McCallum, she's thirty-four, an interior designer, and she works freelance but has carried out work in conjunction with James' firm. On the surface she's the perfect wife and mother but I got the feeling that she was hiding something. I was the assigned Family Liaison Officer on the day we found Mr McCallum's body and she didn't want me hanging around. The one morning I did sit with her, a few days later, she had four calls from a number she instantly rejected. I had the impression that she didn't want to take the calls while I was in the house.'

'Right, keep an eye on her and see what you can find out from her work colleagues. Maybe someone in Lanyon Architects can throw some light on her.' He turned to Rose then. 'Dr Lainey, you're working alongside me to try to establish a profile of our killer. At present, what can you tell us about who we might be looking for?'

Rose got up from her chair, walked to the front of the room and stood beside him. 'It's early days yet but at present, considering the difficulties involved in staging a hanging, lifting the body and securing the rope from the tree we know the killer – or killers – took everything they needed with them to execute this and that means they were prepared. What's more, they have gone to extraordinary effort to leave nothing behind, no traces to help us. Finally, the knots suggest someone who knows how to tie them effectively.' She stopped and looked around the room. 'I would put the killer at higher than average intelligence and suggest that the relationship with James is close. I can make that assertion because they wanted a clean death – not one involving blood or overt violence. I believe that we may have more than one killer and there is a strong possibility that one of them is female.'

Danny nodded. 'We aren't dealing with some random psycho. This is someone with reason. Justification in their warped mind. And I don't think it's a simple grudge against James McCallum. This has taken thought and planning. On the outside, James McCallum's life was picture perfect but I'd bet something under the surface was off. We need to find out what it was.'

He looked around at the faces of his team. They were eager to make their mark and be the one who delivered what they needed to solve the case. Danny could feel their keenness radiating off them like energy. He recognised it because he felt it too. As killings went, this one was clean and as ungory as they come, but there was something about the unblinking strategy behind it. The cool approach somehow elicited greater fear and more of a drive to discover the motive.

Yep, Danny thought, there was definitely something unsettling about this one.

CHAPTER 20

There are plenty of ways to begin a story, and many more to end one, but the bits in between are what really count, thought Danny. His story with Rose began in Liverpool. Two fresh-faced students away from home for the first time, negotiating the world and figuring out who they wanted to become. He had fallen for her pretty quickly. It wasn't just the familiarity of the accent, or the notion that she would understand his humour and way of looking at things when those around him felt so different. No, it was more to do with her control and contained manner. Never giving too much away. There was an intrigue and a mystery about her. The dark hair and the ocean-green eyes had enticed him, but it was her steely intelligence and wit that held him there.

Over the years he had thought of her with wistfulness, wondering if he had ever been in with a fair chance or if she'd have knocked him back without a thought. Since Rose's arrival back in Belfast he had spent a lot of time thinking about the past and their friendship. It was inevitable that his mind would play through all the old times at uni. In part, it was because of his divorce. The breakdown of his marriage to Amy had left him feeling vulnerable, his moods fluctuating from loneliness to optimism that the future might hold the promise of something better. While he was no longer pining after what he'd had with Amy, her visit had unsettled him. For a while there he had hoped everything would go back to the way it had been, but now life without her seemed easier, less stressful. But he had loved her once and it was inevitable that he would wonder if he was foolish to give up on that so readily.

Their wedding anniversary was approaching. Amy had wanted an autumn wedding, and it had been as perfect as a wedding day can be. It was a simple affair compared to some; fifty guests, a church service followed by lunch at Malone House and a wedding band playing all the old favourites. They'd left at midnight and had spent their honeymoon in Italy. He shook his head as if to dislodge the memories and dragged his attention back to the job.

The forensics report on the rope had come back and he needed to study the detail before the afternoon's team meeting. He spread out photographs of the hanging scene and studied them. They had yet to find anything to indicate the location of the primary murder scene.

He phoned Fiona Madden to discuss her findings.

'So, Fiona, can you tell animal hair from human hair?' Danny asked.

'I can get in touch with a veterinary forensic specialist. She may be able to give a suggestion as to breed type but it wouldn't be definitive. I suppose they might be able to say a recovered hair was visually consistent with samples from a similar dog if comparison hairs were obtained, but it would not be a definitive identification.'

'Right, set it up for me and see what your contact has to say.'

It would mean more waiting, but there was nothing he could do about that. In the meantime, he referred back to the photographs and videography of the death scene. There was something about a noose around a neck that made him queasy. Danny sighed. He needed to get out of the basement and chase some leads.

The team had exhausted all current lines of enquiry. The angle of the school's CCTV camera didn't cover the hill and the tree, and the entrance had been left wide open to allow easy access for the decorators to come and go. The two remaining friends, Emer and Ivy, were the obvious next port of call.

Emer Ward swung long legs out of her black Volvo, grabbed her expensive-looking leather handbag, and slammed the door before locking it with her key fob. Danny recognised her from her company website and she looked every bit the public relations strategist that she was.

'Ms Ward, DI Danny Stowe, I was wondering if I could have a word with you about your friend, James McCallum?'

She turned around slowly, as if she needed a second to compose herself before facing him.

'Yes, Lorcan said you might want to speak to me. How can I help you?' She smiled warmly, and Danny could see up close she was a beautiful woman. Her skin was smooth and virtually unlined, her make-up subtle and expertly applied.

'Shall we go into your office?'

She led Danny through the glass doors of the Chichester Street offices. Immediately the drone of midday city centre traffic quietened as they walked into the plush, carpeted reception area.

Emer turned to the receptionist sat behind a marble desk. 'I'll be using the meeting room for a little while. Can you tell Jonathan that I'll be a bit late for our next appointment? Thanks.'

The receptionist nodded and picked up the phone as Danny followed Emer into the meeting room and took a seat.

'I'm busy so I won't have long but how can I help you?'

Her business-like approach didn't surprise Danny. He had dealt with people like Emer before. People who, when they were in their place of work, found it difficult to be anything but brusque and efficient.

'We are investigating a murder, Ms Ward, so anything you can tell us about your friend might be of help.'

'Well, I don't know if I can tell you anything that Lorcan hasn't already said. We all loved James and we're shocked that this has happened.'

Danny nodded. 'When was the last time you spoke to James?'

'A week or so ago. He called me to have a chat.'

'And would that be usual for him to do? To call you for a catch-up?'

'Well it wouldn't be *un*usual.'

'Can you check your phone to see when exactly the call was?'

She hesitated and then reached for her phone and scrolled through her call list.

'It was Saturday. He called me at two o'clock in the afternoon.'

He made a note of the date and time.

'So, you all met at school. Were you all the cool crowd?'

'Hardly.'

Danny watched her as she looked away, a slight flicker of something in her eyes.

'More like the odd crowd, if you must know. The four of us felt lucky to have found each other. None of us really fitted in anywhere until our little gang came together.' She placed her hands on her lap. 'I was never popular in junior school but after third year, when we had chosen our GCSEs, the form groups changed, and the four of us became friends.'

'And you all hung about outside of school, too?'

'Yes. We'd meet up at the weekend.'

'You were close,' Danny said. 'Must be hard to hear how James died.'

'Yes, it was. Is. I can't understand why anyone would do such a thing. There's no reason why someone would want to harm James. He was a gentle person. Never as much as said a bad word against anyone.'

He jotted that down in his notepad.

'Your business is public relations, is that right? What's that involve then?'

'Mainly high-end executive clients. I focus on reputation management and communication strategies for companies. We deal with banks, law firms, investment funds, that kind of thing. I'm officially on maternity leave at present but I have been finding it hard to stay away.'

Danny whistled. 'All that's well beyond me. Must be tough keeping it going.'

She said nothing.

115

'And you know Emma McCallum too?'

'Yes, of course.'

'Would you have regular contact with her as well as James?'

'No, not really. We were never friends independently from James.'

'What about yourself, are you married?'

'Yes, and I've two children.'

Danny noticed that she flinched ever so slightly at the mention of her family.

'Just getting the full picture. Police work's all about people and their relationships. Making the dots join up.'

She pressed her lips together in a tight line and sat up straighter, as if to assert her authority.

'I'm afraid I'll need to get back to work, Detective. Is there anything else?'

'One more thing – where were you on the of evening of Saturday the 17th of October?'

'I was at home.'

'And were you alone?'

'No, I was with my family and my husband will confirm that. I can assure you I had nothing to do with James' death.'

Danny thanked her for her time. 'Sorry to have interrupted your day. I'll be in touch if there's anything else I need.'

CHAPTER 21

Rose checked her phone and saw she'd a text from Fiona Madden. She wanted to share some of her findings of the fibre fragment found on the tree and asked if Rose would like to call into the lab. They had been waiting for the report to come back and the fact that Fiona wanted to discuss it meant that there must be something of particular interest.

Within minutes, Rose was on her way to Old Shore Road in Carrickfergus, where the Forensic Science offices and laboratories were situated in an industrial complex looking out onto Belfast Lough. There had been riots the previous night in that area. Disgruntled Loyalists, angry at the Brexit consequence of the Irish sea border, had stirred up young people to rage against the police. As she drove she listened to the local radio station discussing the criminal gangsters commandeering young people under the guise of defending their right to be part of the United Kingdom. The irony of the fact that the same Loyalists had voted for Brexit in the first place seemed to be lost on them. Before she could hear the end of the ranting she turned into the car park.

Fiona Madden was dressed more casually than the last time Rose had seen her in the grounds of Osbourne House Grammar, when she'd been wearing her white plastic jumpsuit. Now she was dressed in faded jeans with a yellow Levi's T-shirt and a fluffy grey cardigan. Her red curly hair was loose around her shoulders and she was wearing a little make-up.

'You got here quickly. Come on through and I'll get you a coffee.'

Rose followed Fiona into a meeting room where a tea and coffee station was set up. She accepted the cup of hot coffee and took a seat at the table.

'Well, what have you got for me?' Rose asked.

Fiona settled into her chair and opened a folder that she had placed on the table.

'These images are of the fibre sample retrieved from the branch of the tree.'

Rose looked at the magnified images, waiting for Fiona to explain their significance.

'So, what you are looking at is a magnified image of kernmantle rope. Kern means "core" in German and mantel means "sheath". This type of rope is constructed with its interior core protected by a woven exterior sheath designed to optimise strength, durability, and flexibility. The core fibres provide the tensile strength the rope, while the sheath protects the core from abrasion during use.'

'Okay, where's this going?'

'Well, if it had been standard nylon I would have said look for someone who's into yachting. A few decades ago, nylon would have been used in all kinds of outdoor type activities. But kernmantle rope is often used in rescue equipment, since it can absorb the force of a falling object. It has a good shock loading capacity and is used for arresting a fall.'

Rose listened as Fiona talked about magnification and the processes she had used to learn what she had about the fibre fragment.

'And where does all of this lead us?' Rose asked.

'As you know, an investigation always starts with a visual examination. Then further techniques, such as optical and scanning electron microscopy, are used to provide additional information for a more detailed understanding. Examples from several fibre ropes were used for comparison and we were able to narrow it down to this.' She removed an image from the folder and placed it in front of Rose.

'You are looking at a rope with a continuous filament polyester cover braided over nylon core, and superior chemical and abrasion resistance. It's also torque balanced to eliminate spin.'

'And who would most likely use this type of rope?' Rose asked.

'Well, it could be used in rescue situations, as I mentioned, or even employed by a tree surgeon.'

'Interesting. That's great Fiona. Thanks.'

'One more thing. Some of the soil samples retrieved from the foot of the tree showed sand particles.'

'Content transference?' Rose said.

'Yes, exactly.'

Rose nodded. 'So it's possible that someone under that tree had been to a beach fairly recently?'

'Yep, sand doesn't tend to hang on to the sole of a shoe for long as it's usually easily dislodged. So I'd take a punt and say they'd been to the beach within twenty-four hours of the murder.'

CHAPTER 22

Danny drove down the Ormeau Road, considering the case and his plans for the day ahead. Emer Ward's alibi had been supported by her husband and Danny had no reason to doubt him. The body had been released to the family and the funeral was taking place later in the week. Danny suggested that he and Rose should go to pay their respects. It would be a chance to see James' friends together and to gauge how they interacted. Until then, he wanted another word with the family, and he expected the Companies House financial information to have come back. Maybe they'd get the break they needed within the details of James McCallum's business. He wasn't ruling anything out at this point, and was already planning on taking a closer look at Martin Kilburn.

He ran into Rose as he arrived at the station.

'I've phoned ahead, Rhea McCallum is excepting us at ten,' she said.

'Good, I'll catch up with the team and meet you in

five minutes.' He grabbed his second cup of coffee, bitter and hot, and went to the open plan main office.

'Listen up.' They all looked up from their computers and stopped what they were doing.

'This is day eight of the investigation. The body has been released to the family and the funeral is in a few days. I want our people in the church. Go pay your respects and keep an eye open for anything untoward. Anyone weeping and wailing like the chief mourner, I want to know. Anyone lurking at the edges, keeping an eye on the proceedings from a distance, I want it recorded. Until then, keep at it and see if you can bring me something worth looking at by the close of today.'

There were mumbles of 'Yes, sirs'.

'DS Kinley, I need the financials by this afternoon – both the Lanyon Architect Practice and any information you can get me on the family household bills.'

'Companies House came back to me yesterday. I'll have finished going through it in the next couple of hours.'

'Good. And the rest of you,' he looked at a couple of officers, new and keen to be thrown a bone, 'see what you can gather about McCallum's time at school.'

Rhea McCallum didn't look so pulled together this time. Her previously styled hair lay flat on her head and without make-up she was pale and drawn.

'Mrs McCallum, thanks for seeing us again. I know this is a hard time,' Danny offered.

The woman looked broken as she stood in the hallway, pulling an oversized cardigan around herself as if she was cold. 'Come on in. The funeral is happening on Thursday. I don't know how we'll get through it.'

Rose put her hand on the woman's shoulder. 'It will be hard, but Grace will help you and you will help her.'

Rhea nodded but she looked defeated, as if all the fight had gone out of her.

They went into the living room where the curtains had been drawn, making the room feel cold and gloomy. Rhea reached over and switched on a lamp.

'I can't bear the thought of seeing anyone, so I've been sitting in the dark, hiding.'

'What about your daughter-in-law? Would it not be better to go to her house so you can all be together?'

'I'll always think of it as James' house, not hers. He designed it, you know.'

'It's a beautiful home,' Rose said.

'It was . . . until she destroyed it.'

'What do you mean?' Danny asked.

'Emma destroyed their marriage.' She began to cry. 'I'm not one for hanging my dirty laundry in public, but I think you should know. Emma was having an affair with James' business partner – Martin Kilburn.'

'Did James know about this?'

'Yes, I think he did.' She sniffed loudly and then blew her nose.

Rose leaned forward. 'How did you know this?'

She rubbed her nose with a tissue. 'I was looking after Grace one day a few months ago and arrived back at the house an hour earlier than Emma expected me. When I rang the doorbell, it took her an inordinate time to come to the door. When we eventually went in Martin Kilburn was sitting in the kitchen. He made some excuse that he had called thinking he'd find James at home.'

123

'Mrs McCallum, surely that wouldn't be enough to make you suspect an affair?' Danny said reasonably.

'They had it written all over their faces, and besides, I noticed his car wasn't parked in the driveway. It was probably further up the road. Why not park it in the driveway, unless they didn't want neighbours to be suspicious?'

'If there was an affair going on, what made you think James knew?'

'Because James started to fall apart not long after. He wasn't himself at all. A mother knows if something is troubling her son. The last time he came here to see me, he looked wretched. He had lost weight and there were dark circles beneath his eyes. I could tell he hadn't been sleeping. He seemed anxious and jittery.'

'Did you discuss your fears with either Emma or James?'

'No, I didn't. I regret that now.' She started to cry again. 'I kept my suspicions to myself, thinking it wasn't my place to say anything. I figured that James would work it out for himself and end the marriage in his own time. God, how stupid I was!' She shook her head as if she was angry at herself. 'Part of me hoped that they would weather whatever difficulties they had in their marriage and stay together for Gracie's sake. I never thought something like this would happen.' Rhea stood, walked to the fireplace, and reached for a framed photograph of James and Grace sitting on a low wall with a storm-grey sea behind them.

'I keep thinking of that dentist and his floozy up in Castlerock. They murdered their spouses, didn't they? What's to say Emma wasn't inspired to do the same?'

CHAPTER 23

Danny woke and found that the muscles in his neck and shoulders felt tight and stiff, as if he had done ten rounds in the ring. He stretched, luxuriating in the warmth of the bed and the extra space afforded him by virtue of living alone. Before the divorce, Danny often woke before Amy. He'd lie there with her beside him, listening to her soft breaths rising and falling as she slept. It was an indulgence and annoyance to study her without her knowing, to check her for signs of impending problems. The fragility of her mind always reflected in her physical health so he'd find himself checking the knots of bone on her spine and trying to decide whether she had gained weight or lost it.

Now he turned over and sighed. Amy was no longer his to worry about and while in some ways that was a relief, in other ways he missed that sense of knowing she depended on him. Rose had told him he had saviour issues, that he was finding his own worth in trying to solve Amy's problems. Rose could be a pain in the arse with her psychological insights, but he had to admit there was some truth in it.

In the old days, when they were in uni studying psychology and criminology, they would use their newfound knowledge to try to analyse and define one another. She had declared that Danny was the 'defender', with a strong sense of loyalty and a desire to protect. When she looked at him with those green eyes, he felt sure she could read him and would know that it was her whom he sought to be loyal and devoted to. He assessed her in turn, and decided she was the fairly rare 'logician' personality type, which makes up only three per cent of the population.

'Good,' she had said, laughing. 'I don't want to be average or common.'

'You pride yourself on your inventiveness and creativity. Yep, I'd agree with that. You've a unique perspective and vigorous intellect,' he read from his battered textbook. 'Usually known as the philosopher, the architect, or the dreamy professor, logicians have been responsible for many scientific discoveries throughout history.' He knew they were the least likely personality type to trust anyone completely and that bothered him. Rose rarely appeared open and carefree, and he knew her well enough to know that it wasn't an act. If he ever got too close or brought up something about back home, she shut down immediately, became cagey and withdrawn for days. Later, when he was on his own, he returned to the textbook and read more. Rose wasn't the type of person who relied on others. She was fierce in her independence, and he knew she would never look to him for emotional support despite them spending nearly every day together. Problems for Rose were a series of obstacles to be solved. 'Logician personalities are likely to reassess their own thoughts and theories, worrying that they've missed a critical piece of the puzzle. Overcoming this self-doubt stands as the greatest challenge logicians are likely to face.' Those words had stayed with him and he knew that to get close to Rose would mean having to unlock some of her reserve and self-doubt.

He climbed out of bed and headed for the shower, all the while mulling over the case. The kids had gone back to school after the Halloween half-term break and the pressure to catch the killer or killers had intensified. All evidence of the macabre finding of James McCallum's body had been eradicated, but he was sure the stories would be passed between the pupils, with added gory details. It didn't help that it had occurred just before the Halloween period. He never understood the need for creating scary stories. As far as he could see, real life was frightening enough all on its own.

The press hadn't helped with their clickbait ghoulish headlines reposted on social media, leading to insinuations and speculation about the police inquiry. He'd made the mistake of looking at Facebook to find that there was a whole conspiracy theory around paramilitary involvement, drugs, and even a suggestion that James McCallum had been a paedophile. He couldn't help himself from reading the thread of comments. The more ludicrous the allegation the more comments it seemed to attract.

Why else kill him in the school grounds?
Somebody knows something.
I heard that he had been having an affair.

Yeah could have been a girl from Osborne House.
He's clearly messed with the wrong one.
Got what was coming to him. Scum drug dealer.
The family deserve answers.

He was used to people giving off about the police, demanding action when the whole team was already working day and night, so wasn't surprised to see push for a result.

He was drying himself when his phone rang. It was the station. Something must be up if they were looking for him this early.

'Stowe here.'

'Sir, it's Tania. You better come straight in. It's Lorcan Burns.'

'What about him?'

'He's received a beating.'

'Where is he?'

'In the Royal. It got called in to the duty sergeant at Lisburn Station last night and we've only just got word. Looks like someone was sending him a message.'

CHAPTER 24

Rose was ready within ten minutes of Danny's call and on their way to the hospital he filled her in on the scant details he knew.

'Lorcan is injured but it's nothing he won't recover from eventually, and they're keeping him in for observation as he took a whack to the head.'

'What did they use?'

'Sewer rods and a hammer.'

Rose shuddered. 'Jesus. Why would Lorcan Burns have been targeted?'

'That's what we need to find out.' She could see the tension in the white knuckle grip of Danny's hands on the steering wheel. It was clear that whatever had brought trouble to Lorcan Burns could be in some way connected to James McCallum's murder.

They parked the car and headed to the fifth floor where Lorcan Burns was being treated. A nurse directed them to bay B and they found him looking forlorn and sorry for himself. In one fluid motion, Danny swished the curtain around the bed, seeking a semblance of privacy by shutting out the bustle of the hospital ward.

Rose looked at the blackening and dried blood encrusting Lorcan Burns' left eye as he lay on the hospital bed. Whoever had done this intended to frighten him, yet he looked embarrassed, ashamed even, rather than scared. Brody was sitting on a chair as close to the bed as he could get, his face a tight contortion of concern.

'Lorcan, we came as soon as we heard. How are you doing?' Danny said, his voice low.

Rose stepped forward. 'I'm Dr Rose Lainey. We haven't met. I have been working with DI Stowe on James McCallum's case.'

'How do you think he's doing?' Brody shot back, ignoring Rose. He sat forward and glared at them, his eyes red-rimmed.

'Brody, it's okay,' Lorcan said. 'They're only doing their job.'

'Have you any idea who did this?' Danny asked.

'None. They jumped him from behind,' Brody said.

'He's right. I'd no way of knowing who they were. They wore masks.'

'What kind of masks?' Rose asked.

'Balaclavas, and I'm pretty sure they were all dressed in black hoodies.'

'How many were there?'

'Three. I was on my way out of the gym – Fitness Fast in Derriaghy.'

'What time was this at?'

'Just after nine.'

'Did they say anything?' Danny asked.

Lorcan paused for a brief second and shook his head.

'They jumped me as I was about to get into my car. It was all over so fast.'

'They didn't give you any indication as to why you were targeted?' Rose said.

'Nothing. They just started whacking me with the sewer rods. One of them had a hammer.' He lifted his hands towards his head where a row of black stitches had knitted his skin together at the temple.

'He's lucky they didn't kill him,' Brody said, placing his hand over Lorcan's.

'A couple of other guys from the gym came running out, shouting at them. They backed off but not before doing this.' He raised his other hand and showed them the bandages.

'He's got three broken fingers. Plus cuts and bruises all over,' Brody said.

'What happened when the guys from the gym came out?'

'A car drove up real fast, out of nowhere, and they jumped in and fled.'

'Did you see the car? The registration?'

'I was on the ground spitting out blood. No, I didn't see the fucking car.'

'We'll follow up with the gym. See if they have CCTV,' Danny said. 'And we'll need the names of the fellas who came to your aid and chased them off.'

'Lorcan, do you think this could this have anything to do with James' murder?' Rose asked gently.

'No, absolutely not. Why would you ask that? It was just some randoms who don't even know me.'

Brody leaned forward. 'I wouldn't be surprised if it was a homophobic attack. You wouldn't believe the crap that we've put up with over the years.'

Rose knew that while a lot of the world had moved on, there were unfortunately some in Northern Ireland who were still staunchly homophobic.

'We can promise you both that this will be thoroughly investigated,' Danny said. 'But if there is any reason to think this has something to do with James McCallum, you need to tell us. If it has, then your life could be in danger. We can't protect you if we don't know the full story.'

CHAPTER 25

'Listen up.' Danny shouted slightly louder than necessary to get his team's attention.

'Last night, Lorcan Burns was jumped coming out of a gym in Derriaghy. He was beaten badly enough, with a hammer and sewer rods, to wind up in hospital. I want to know who has it in for him. What message were they sending with the beating?'

Rose watched as Danny prowled around the room, intent on motivating the team.

'This could well be related to our ongoing murder inquiry so I need your full attention. Forget birthday parties, visiting your mother, and slacking off early. Lumen and Magee,' Danny said.

'Yes, sir?' they both said.

'Get over to the gym – Fitness Fast in Derriaghy. Chase up the CCTV footage and interview the gym goers who intervened. I want every detail.'

'On it,' Tania said.

'Gerard, I want you to look into Lorcan Burns and

his partner Brody Sullivan. Find out if they have any enemies. What's Burns been involved in? Who does he see outside of work?'

Gerard nodded while writing the questions down on his notepad.

'Brody suggested that it could be a homophobic attack.'

He looked over to DS Jamie King. 'Can you follow up that angle for me, Jamie? See if there has been anything similar recently carried out on the gay community in that area.'

'No problem, sir.'

'I don't believe that this has been without purpose and planning. A car was primed and ready for a quick getaway. If we find out why the attack happened and who organised it, then just maybe we might be closer to catching James McCallum's killer.'

They ate their sandwiches in Rose's basement office, discussing the details of the case.

'This has certainly put a new spin on things,' Danny said through a mouthful of his salmon on rye sandwich.

'Mmm. Makes you wonder if Lorcan Burns knows something. Is he being silenced?'

Danny took a swig of hot tea. 'Did you see how defensive the partner was?'

Rose shrugged. 'He just seemed concerned to me. I didn't pick up anything more than that.'

'Maybe so, but we need to check him out.' He was glad he had Rose to bounce ideas off of. He trusted her judgement – maybe even as well as he trusted his own. The endless gathering of information, the late nights spent chasing possible leads, and the ongoing conversations with those close to James McCallum had all failed to give them anything concrete. Now, with James' friend in a hospital bed, the pressure to get answers, and fast, was becoming unbearable. He felt a hot flush of frustration. Danny didn't like being kept in the dark. He especially didn't like feeling that he was letting the victim down.

'Have you any theories percolating?' she asked.

Danny scrunched up the packaging his sandwich had come in and fired it into the wastepaper bin before leaning back on his chair. 'I'm only thinking out loud here. What if James McCallum had been involved in something – say money laundering, drugs, or who knows what – and the business dealings had come to a nasty end? Maybe whoever he had been working with suspected or knew that he had turned to his friend Lorcan Burns for help and they dealt out a hiding to keep him quiet. A warning shot, if you like.'

'Do you think Lorcan could be in real danger?'

'It's possible. If they are keeping tabs on him, they won't want him talking to us. He should get discharged tomorrow so we should park a squad car outside his house. It will keep him covered – give him some protection – if someone has it in for him, and also make him sweat a bit knowing we're watching.'

CHAPTER 26

Rose struggled to find somewhere to park on Stranmillis Road. Usually Danny drove but she had grabbed the pool car keys before he had reached them.

'It's a male-dominant trait to assume you are driving every time, Dan, so get over yourself and get into the passenger seat.'

He rolled his eyes. 'Feeling threatened by my testosterone, Rosie?'

'As if. The only thing you're a threat to is the canteen spaghetti bolognese.'

'Well, it is my favourite. Nice of you to notice.'

It was a busy road, populated by restaurants, cafes, an art gallery, and offices but eventually she found a space in St Ives Street and they walked to the Lanyon Architect office.

The office was painted bright white, with lighting artfully placed to make the space feel bigger than it was. The receptionist, a young woman wearing a red and white striped T-shirt with tight, black trousers, greeted them as they walked in the door.

'Dr Rose Lainey and DI Danny Stowe. Martin Kilburn is expecting us,' Rose said.

'No problem, take a seat and I'll let him know you're here.'

She picked up a phone and rang through to an office out of sight and a few minutes later Martin Kilburn descended the open staircase.

He was slightly built, of average height, good looking with blond hair cut short, and was dressed in the business casual uniform of navy trousers with a white Ralph Lauren polo shirt.

'Hello there. Come on through to our meeting room.' He was breezily casual.

Rose and Danny followed him into a room at the back of the office, which was set up with a conference table and chairs. A model building sat on display at the centre of the table.

'Please, take a seat. Can I get you a coffee or a tea?'

'No, thanks. I'm fine,' Rose said, sitting down. Danny declined too.

'So, Martin, we just need to ask a few questions about James. I imagine you two were close, having worked here together?' Danny said.

'Yeah, I've known James for around five years. We started out in the same firm after our training.'

'You must have got on well, to decide to go into business together,' Rose said.

He shrugged. 'We needed each other to make it work.'

'And how is the business doing?' Danny asked.

'Great. We've just finished a particularly busy period and we were due to make a good profit this quarter.'

'How was James the last time you saw him?' Rose asked.

'Absolutely fine. There didn't appear to be anything out of the ordinary.'

'Did he seem tense or worried about anything?'

'No. Tired, maybe, but we had been working hard and life's busy, as I'm sure you know.'

'And James' wife, Mrs McCallum? Do you know her well?' Danny asked the question neutrally.

He hesitated. 'Look, I don't know what you have heard, but Emma and I, well, we're just good friends.'

'Friends? Isn't that a bit strange to be good pals with your business partner's wife?'

He shot Danny a look. 'You can think it looks strange all you like, but it's the truth. We're friends. Nothing more. We haven't done anything wrong, so I don't see what business it is of yours.'

Danny held up his hands in mock surrender. 'Listen, mate, our job isn't to judge. We need to look into every aspect of the victim's life.'

Kilburn nodded. 'I understand, but James' death has nothing to do with me . . . or with Emma, for that matter. She's devastated. Can you imagine how hard it is for her trying to console wee Grace?'

'We appreciate that this is a very difficult time for all concerned, but if you have any ideas that might throw some light on why James was killed, we need you to speak up now,' Rose said.

Kilburn shook his head. 'I'm sorry but I can't help you.'

'Okay. We do need to know though, where were you on evening of Saturday the 17th of October?' Danny asked.

'I was at a corporate dinner. A black tie affair at the Clandeboyne Estate for the Institute of Chartered Architects. James was supposed to be there too but he phoned me earlier in the day to say he couldn't make it, that something had come up and he couldn't go.'

'And you didn't question him on what he had to do?' Rose asked.

'No. James was not the type of person to go into detail. Besides, he was never comfortable at social events like that. He didn't drink and I think he struggled a bit with the whole networking part of those kind of things. I just thought he was fobbing me off because he didn't fancy going.'

'Didn't it bother you that he was letting you down?' Danny asked.

'No. We each brought our own strengths to the business. James was a brilliant architect. He'd lose himself in a project and work at it until he had it just right. I'm more the front of house face of the business.'

'What about clients? Did James have any difficult jobs that may have led to any antagonism?'

'No. We're not dealing with crooks. Most of our work is prestigious residential projects. We've also done the odd church and a school.'

They were interrupted by the receptionist opening the conference room door. 'Martin, your next meeting is here.'

'We're just finishing up. I'll be there in a second.'

Rose and Danny stood. 'If you think of anything that might be of help, please give us a shout,' Danny said, handing over his card. 'Anything at all.'

* * *

139

Out on the street, they were about to get into the car when they heard a voice shout, 'Excuse me!'

They both turned to find the receptionist behind them.

'I just want to say that James was a lovely man, a great architect, and a very kind boss. I know that probably doesn't help you at all but I thought it worth saying.' She looked back towards her office. 'I'm not saying Martin is difficult, as such, but James was the nicer of the two. He treated people well, you know? Martin is more ruthless, sharper. He has a steeliness that keeps this place going.'

'You don't like Martin Kilburn then?' Danny said.

'It's more a matter of trust. I can't say I'd like to be dependent on his good nature, if it came down to it. Martin is competitive to the extreme and wouldn't hesitate to throw a rival under a bus. James and him are like chalk and cheese. Were, I should say.' Her eyes filled with tears.

'Do you know James' wife, Emma?' Rose asked.

She nodded. 'A little. She's been in the office a few times and has worked on some of the domestic projects.'

'Any reason to think she and Martin were close? Perhaps involved?' Rose asked.

'God no. I couldn't see that happening. James loved Emma and Gracie.'

Back in the car, Danny reached to put his seat belt on. 'Did you believe him? That they haven't been shagging?'

'Yeah, I think I did. He was too emphatic, too sure of himself. I would say though that if they haven't got together, it was heading in that direction. They were obviously close, but it hadn't gone over the line yet.'

'Even so, James' death has cleared the way.'

'Yeah, it sure has,' Rose said. 'We know that it likely took more than one person to hang James from that tree. Could Emma have enticed Martin to help her?'

'It's certainly a possibility. We can't ignore the fact that Martin stands to gain from James' death, both in a financial sense and on a personal level.'

'I can't see him being the murderer though. Falling in love with his partner's wife isn't the stuff murder cases are made of. The motive isn't strong enough. It has to go deeper than that. Murkier,' Rose mused.

'We should be able to rule him out pretty easily, if his alibi checks out.'

Rose hit the indicator then turned left at the roundabout and drove past the Lyric Theatre and along the river Lagan.

'Yeah, let's watch him though. See how he reacts to our visit. I wonder if he'll be visiting Emma McCallum to compare notes.'

CHAPTER 27

There was a chill in the air that necessitated the heater in the car being turned up. The noise of it drowned out everything else and for a moment Rose longed for her bed. She'd been extra tired these last few months. It was as if the intense concentration and alertness the Mulligan case had demanded had prevented any emotion stirring up, and once her part in it had finished and the CPS had taken over, she had hit a wall and the dull ache of grief and longing had arrived with force. The carefully constructed façade she had worked so hard to maintain since she had first left home at eighteen now felt fragile and tremulous. She was homesick, bereft of everything she had known as a young child. Her mother's death had stolen from her the possibility of ever making amends – she would never have that coming together and understanding that she now realised she had desired all along. Her body felt sluggish and heavy, as if the weight of grief was dragging her down.

She turned down the heater fan and switched on the

radio to find Van Morrison's 'Into the Mystic' playing, and suddenly something cracked open inside her. At first, she wasn't sure why or where it came from but in her mind she was back in Bond Street, sitting at the table doing homework, when there was a knock at the door. He didn't wait for an answer though, just walked on into the narrow hallway like he owned the place.

'Where's your mammy?' he asked, looking at Rose. She had been studying Seamus Heaney and her head was full of country words like 'shuck', and 'ditch', and 'clods'.

'She's at work,' Rose said, her voice high and unsure.

'Well, tell her Sean's looking for her. She'll know what it's about.'

There was something in the way he looked at her, the swift tongue darting out to lick his lips as his eyes lingered over her a second too long, that unnerved her. Then, just as suddenly, he was gone, and Rose went back to doing her schoolwork and watching the clock until Evelyn returned.

For years Rose had believed her mother to be Sean Torrent's lackey. Someone who was ordered around and who willingly jumped to perform whatever was requested of her, no matter how dark and dangerous. While most of the women involved in Republican paramilitary groups remained on the fringes, involved in civil rights protests and in fundraising, there were some whose devotion to the cause saw them participating in planting bombs and shooting people. How far Evelyn would have gone, Rose never knew, but she had made assumptions.

In her imagination then, Evelyn had been moving weapons, transporting fugitives over the border. Now her imagination was going in a different direction. Danny's

Sharon Dempsey

information that Evelyn had been an informer threw up all other sorts of scenarios. How would it have worked? Had Evelyn been compromised in some way, arrested and offered a deal that had led her to being a dangerous pawn in the war on paramilitarism? Rose pushed images of gun-wielding patriots out of her head. Belfast was different now and although Rose had been at odds with her mother – for what felt like her whole life – she needed to address this new information and let her mother re-emerge from the mists of her regret.

The next thing she knew she was driving to the Short Strand, looking at the street names until she came to 32 Mountforde Drive. The home of Sean Torrent.

144

CHAPTER 28

Sean Torrent looked surprised to see Rose when he opened the door.

'Jesus, what the fuck do you want now?' The last time she'd seen him had been in a dive of a pub where she'd tracked him down to question him about the Mulligan case.

'I just want to talk. No funny business. I'm here as Evelyn's daughter, nothing more.'

He stood back and let her inside. 'I'd rather you didn't arrive at my door at ten o'clock at night, giving the neighbours something to talk about, especially if they get wind of the fact that you're a cop.'

'Sorry, I would've called ahead and arranged to meet somewhere neutral but I was in the area and just . . .' She trailed off. 'Besides, I don't have your number.'

'You may sit down.' He reached over and took the remote control from the arm of the chair Rose sat on and turned the volume down. He'd been watching the Stephen Nolan show.

'So, want do you want?'

'I want to know what my mother was up to.'

He took a packet of cigarettes out of his pocket, lit up, sat back into the chair, and exhaled.

'I don't know what you want me to tell you. Evelyn was a patriot. A loyal soldier of Mother Ireland. She understood what it meant to be oppressed – by the patriarchy, by the Brits – and she wasn't prepared to be a bystander in history and not do the right thing. Or maybe that's what she'd want me to tell you. Your generation can't understand. The war has been won for you. You had no struggle. Look at you – sold out to the PSNI. Jesus, your mother would be turning in her grave.'

Rose held his gaze. He looked older than the last time she'd seen him, as if he was finally nothing more than an old man who'd had his day. Spent and useless. Whenever she thought back to her childhood, Sean Torrent was always there, lurking at the edges.

'What was she like?' Rose surprised herself by asking, her voice quiet.

He blew out a plume of smoke and smiled. 'Before everything, Evelyn was a feminist. God, she loved to put any man in his place that didn't treat her as an equal. One night we were down in the club having a drink and she told me, "Men round here are used to the women looking after the house and the children, but we've so much more to offer." She claimed her nationalism gave her a feminist awakening. That the two were entwined. She'd read all of these pamphlets and magazines printed by these women's groups and was well versed in the statistics and the theories. She wasn't content to play the martyred widow when your da was killed. No, Evelyn had other ideas.

146

'She'd seen her older brother get lifted during internment, your father shot dead. Did you not think how that would've affected her? Was she supposed to take it and not react? Every day must have felt like an assault on her. Soldiers patrolling the streets, the harassment dealt out by them and the police without provocation.'

She was taken aback by his openness. Once he started talking it was as if he'd been waiting for an opportunity to shoot the breeze with someone. She assumed he was lonely and she was a convenient audience while he reminisced.

'That doesn't excuse her involvement with you and the IRA.' She needed to know if Torrent knew of her mother's covert activities, if he suspected her of passing information on to the security forces, but she couldn't ask him outright.

'Jesus, you're awful naive. Can you not put yourself in her shoes for a minute?'

Rose said nothing.

There were so many things unsaid between them: how he would turn up at the house, day or night, and Evelyn jumped to attention, how he could intimidate Rose and her siblings with just his presence in the doorframe.

'She was a rebel at heart. Smart and quick, with looks that would turn heads. You look a lot like she did. She stayed faithful to your da, you know. Never once went with another man after he died. Plenty tried though, myself included.' He gave a wry chuckle.

She listened as he talked of parties back in the day, when he and Evelyn were young. How the local social club operated during the darkest of days, a wire cage built as a defence against petrol bombs, and a camera operated system that buzzed you in only if you were deemed safe.

'Once you got in, well, it was another world. The beat of the music, the laughter, the smell of the booze and cigarette smoke. It was our sanctuary. Outside the streets could have been teeming with petrol bombs and plastic bullets, but in the club, well, all that mattered was whose round it was and if your girl was likely to give you a ride at the end of the night. Your ma was the heart and soul of any party. She'd be there talking all about her women's lib movement, trying to get others to sign up for the newsletter she was producing, talking about human rights and self-determination.

'I remember one night when she was in full flow and Mickey Devlin, knowing no better, told her a United Ireland would automatically mean freedom for all. Well she took him to task and before he knew it the poor fella was getting a lecture on how the Republican move- ment could be as patriarchal as any British institution.' He laughed again. 'Plenty believed the Republican agenda was all that mattered. Your ma, though, she didn't see it like that. She pushed to make women's issues a priority for the organisation.'

Rose sat for a moment, considering how to say what she'd come here to say. 'Did you ever suspect that she might not have been completely honest with you?'

He narrowed his flinty eyes. 'How do you mean?'

'Could she have been working with a different agenda?' Rose watched as he flinched.

'Fuck no. Evelyn was never a tout.' He shook his head. 'The Provos would have known if she was an informer.'

Rose knew of the stigma associated with informing.

Even a suggestion of passing on information to the security forces could be enough to find a bullet in the back of your head. Women like Evelyn risked everything. Rose wanted to know why.

'How can you be so sure?'

'Because they'd have killed her. The very same people she mixed with would have had no qualms about taking her out if she'd touted on them.' He sat back in his chair as if that was the matter finished.

'What if I told you I knew different?' She watched as the colour shifted in his face, a warm flush of blood rising in his cheeks.

'Evelyn did no such thing. I could prove it to you with stories of what she did do, but I think some things are best left in the past. And if you know what's best for you and your family, you'll act like a good wee girl and leave well alone.'

Rose didn't know what she had expected to get out of Sean Torrent but his fond reminiscence wasn't it. She thought of Evelyn at her own age. She'd had three kids by then and their lives were so different. Did Evelyn understand the risks she was taking with her life back then? With her children's lives?

Rose drove through the city centre crying silent tears as the bright lights blinked all around her.

CHAPTER 29

Danny liked to conduct initial interviews away from the station as he believed he got the most out of people if they were relaxed and at ease. The time for formality, recording devices, and protocol would come later. They still had too much that needed clarifying first. For now, all theories were still conjecture. At some stage he hoped they would be gifted a break from the gods above, but until that happened, the grunt work of policing was all they had.

Next on his list was paying Ivy Duffy a visit. He'd brought Rose along to provide support and insights that he might miss.

'Happy to get away from flow charts and pay reviews, Lainey?'

She rolled her eyes. 'Danny, stop messing with me. You know the job is more than HR logistics, and if you're not careful I'll take you in for a bit of one-on-one time. Dig down and see what lurks in your psyche.'

Danny grinned. 'Not a chance. What you see is what you get. I'm a simple soul.'

They were approaching Holywood, a town on the north down coast, four miles from Belfast, where Ivy Duffy lived. It was a place known for being populated by those with money and had the high-end, gentrified air of the well-to-do. The kind of town that managed to cloak itself in middle-class denial during the Troubles, watching from afar as Belfast and Derry suffered.

As they turned into Tudor Oaks Road, Danny could see the attraction of living there. The road was leafy and wide with only a ten-minute walk to the seafront. The houses were all individual in design and a mix of modern bungalows and older Arts and Crafts style, though they all shared the similar look of money well spent. Ivy Duffy lived in the last house of the cul-de-sac, at number 46.

'Here we are,' Danny said as they pulled into the driveway of the former coach house. The house wasn't big, but it was picture-book-pretty with a view over a cliff walk leading to Belfast Lough. Some sort of flowering red leafed creeper had adorned the exterior walls and in the weak autumn sunlight its intense colour seemed to glow.

'She's expecting us,' Danny said as they got out of the car.

'How do you want to play it?' asked Rose.

'I'll take the lead and you watch for anything that might suggest she's hiding something.'

Rose and Danny watched as Ivy Duffy pulled into her driveway and got out of her silver Lexus. She was wearing gym gear and had a towel placed around her neck.

'There she is, let's go,' Danny said.

'Ivy Duffy?' Danny asked as they approached her.

'Shit! You scared the life out of me.' She turned around and glared at them.

'Sorry, we didn't mean to frighten you. I'm DI Stowe, and this is Dr Rose Lainey. Can we have a word with you about James McCallum?'

Rose noticed that Ivy switched from being spooked to appearing completely in control in a split second. She took a deep breath and walked away from her car towards her red-brick house. Her dark hair was damp, falling in curly ringlets, and she smelled faintly of eucalyptus.

'Been to the gym?' Rose asked.

'A hot yoga class.' Her face was flushed, and she'd a thin layer of perspiration coating her face.

'Is it okay if we come in for a chat?'

She hesitated and then nodded before opening her stained-glass windowed front door.

They followed her into the hallway and she invited them through to her study.

Rose looked around the room. An old mahogany desk was covered with a scattering of papers and mail, and against the far wall a bookcase stood framed by muted wallpaper with a display of trailing roses. 'It's a beautiful house. I have always liked these old places. Full of history,' Rose said.

'I like it. It was my family home growing up,' she replied.

'You're not working today, then?' Danny asked.

'No, I have Wednesdays off and cover out of hours in the evening.'

He nodded.

'So, Detective, what can I do for you?' She looked at Danny with a coolness that suggested she was calm under pressure. Unshakeable, that was the word Rose would use to describe her. Someone who was practical and not given to extremes of emotion.

'We're investigating James' death and we're trying to piece together what we can about his life. Naturally, that includes his friendships.'

'I've known James since school. We used to hang out occasionally. Beyond that, there isn't much more to say.'

'When was the last time you saw James?' Rose asked.

She considered the question before answering. 'Probably sometime in August. I'm not certain of the date. I didn't expect to be asked months later.' There it was again – the niggle of irritation.

'And when did you last speak to him?'

'I rang him a couple of weeks ago. It was a Thursday, I think.'

'What was the nature of the call?' Danny asked.

She shrugged. 'Normal catching up stuff. Nothing specific. I asked him how Emma and Grace were.' They watched as she glanced out towards the view. The sea was a darkening mass, reflections of the pale afternoon light turning with each surge of waves.

Danny leaned forward. 'How did he seem to you when you spoke to him?'

'Fine. Nothing untoward.' She was sat poker straight, as if braced.

'You had no worries about him? He didn't confide in you about money troubles or, perhaps . . . troubles in his marriage?'

'God no. James was a private person. He wouldn't have shared anything like that with me.'

'Did James ever speak to you in a professional capacity?' Rose asked.

'What, you mean in a medical capacity about his mental health issues?' She narrowed her eyes.

'Yes, did he ever share any of his concerns with you?' Rose asked.

'No, he didn't. I know he had periods of being depressed and that he struggled with stress and anxiety, but we didn't talk about it. Most men don't like to admit that they suffer from depression.'

Rose gave her a curt nod of the head. 'Fair enough. But you were friends for a long time. Any issues that you think we should know about?'

'Listen, if there was, do you not think I would have contacted you before you door-stepped me? James was my friend. I am devastated that he's dead. If I could help you find out who did this to him, I would have made it my business to contact you. But I don't, so I didn't. Now if that is all, I need to have a shower.' She stood up.

'Before we leave could you tell us where you were on the night of October 17th and the early hours of the 18th?' Rose said.

'Working. I was on call-out duty.'

'And you have someone who can vouch for that? We have to check these things. Otherwise, what's the point in asking?' Danny spoke as if their conversation was merely friendly banter.

'You can check with the on-call duty rota.'

'And when you are a duty doctor on-call, where are you based? It wouldn't be your normal surgery, would it?'

'No, it's the doctor on-call service at Knockbreda Health Centre.'

154

'And at what time did you begin your shift?' Danny asked.

'I arrived shortly before six o'clock. I am on duty from six thirty but I had paperwork I had to catch up on before my first patient.'

'So you would have been working through until when?' Rose said.

'I can't be sure. Probably sometime around midnight.'

'Fine. And we can check that out?' Danny said.

'Of course. I'll be sure to forward the details on to the Health Trust if you need to contact them,' Ivy said, dismissing them.

'We'll be in touch,' Danny said, moving towards the doorway. 'We may need to speak to you again at a later stage. Here's my card if you should think of anything that might be relevant.'

She accepted the card and set it on the table before leading them to her front door. The view of the sea from the path was obscured by another house but Danny could still sense it, like a malevolent presence waiting to pounce.

CHAPTER 30

Rose had noticed how time took on a new quality while working with the PSNI. She worked longer hours, keeping up with the murder investigation and providing professional support to those who requested it, but the days were flying in. She'd barely time to register how different her life was these days.

Now she was sitting in an update meeting with Danny and his team. The CCTV from the gym had shown a dark-coloured Audi the night Lorcan Burns was attacked, but the plates were false.

'The eyewitness accounts corroborated what Burns told us, namely that he was jumped by three hooded and masked men, and then beaten,' Jack Fitzgerald told the group. 'But look at this.' He hit play on the remote control and they watched the screen as the car drove into the car park. Three men got out with their weapons and the car drove off out of sight. Next, they watched as Lorcan Burns was approached at his car. Instead of the beating beginning immediately, they saw the men speak to Burns. The exchange wasn't long but it was clear that something was definitely said before they began the attack.

Malachy let out a low whistle.

'Lorcan Burns told us that they didn't say anything to him, and that he was jumped from behind,' Danny said. 'So why did he lie?'

'This has to be related to the McCallum case. Maybe Lorcan Burns isn't as innocent as he looks,' Tania offered.

'And there was no sign of any similar attacks? No homophobic attacks reported over the last few weeks?' Rose asked.

'No, nothing reported,' Jack answered. 'It could be something else that Lorcan is mixed up in. But what?'

'Jack is right.' Danny stood. 'We have to consider all angles but there is also the possibility that the assault on Lorcan Burns is directly related to James McCallum's murder.'

'You think he's been warned off?' Rose asked.

'That's what my gut is telling me,' Danny replied.

'Lorcan clearly knows something. He's been holding back on us,' Rose said.

The room fell silent as they each pondered the new development. It seemed as though they were entering the darkest waters of the case, the murk and silt on the surface as impenetrable as ever.

CHAPTER 31

Danny woke early and decided he had time to go for a run around Minnowburn. This part of the city was beautiful, a tranquil oasis of woodland and river, frequented by dogwalkers and runners. A cyclist cut past him causing him to curse quietly under his breath. The damp earthly scent from the riverbank filled his nostrils. The hangover of a bad night's sleep had left him feeling drained. He'd be reaching for the coffee on the hour just to get through the day ahead of him. One of these days he'd get the exercise and eating right and maybe he'd feel better all round. He'd a notion that his body would thank him for it.

As his feet pounded the muddy path he thought about the case. James McCallum was the type of victim the media liked – successful professional, with everything to live for. Journalists like nothing more than a story their readers can relate to, and say 'there but for the grace of god go I.' Thankfully, Lorcan Burns' beating hadn't been linked to the McCallum case by the media, but there was still time for some eager beaver of a reporter to put two and two together and come up with a hell of a lot more than four.

DS Kinley had finally come back with the financial information the day before, his face wide and excited, telling Danny that he'd found something of interest before he'd even spoken a word.

'Right, hit me with it, what have you got?' Danny said, resting his back against the wall.

'Emma McCallum opened a new bank account six weeks before her husband's death.'

Danny whistled. 'That's not a good look. What was she up to?'

'Could be simply a practical thing and bad timing but we certainly need to look at it.'

'What about the business?'

'Lanyon Architecture accounts don't look too healthy, and they failed to file their accounts on time last year. Apparently said there were issues around paying debtors on time and poor capital management, whatever that means.'

'Nothing fraudulent though?'

'Nope. Just your general eye off the ball type stuff.'

'Which would go towards the general picture of James not being in the right frame of mind. Something was bothering him and it could have been money trouble. I wonder who knew outside of his wife and his business partner?'

'Boss, there's more. Martin Kilburn had been looking to borrow for some housing project. He had plans to purchase land in East Belfast and build an apartment complex that he'd designed. He was doing it on his own. Not involving James.'

159

'That *is* interesting. So, he had big ambitions.' The housing market crash had come and gone and now people like Martin Kilburn were happy to stick their hands in the fire again.

'Did you come across anything to link Kilburn to Emma McCallum financially?'

'Nope. Nothing.'

There was definitely something to work with though. Martin and Emma may not have crossed the line but they had history and a romantic link. Give it a few more weeks or months and James' life would have possibly imploded.

By the time Danny arrived at work after his run he was determined to do further digging on Martin Kilburn and Emma McCallum. He knew that he shouldn't put too much faith in Rhea McCallum's musings that her daughter-in-law was having an affair, but for some reason he didn't trust either of them.

Later in the afternoon Danny was trawling through the system checking all the necessary information had been logged. He liked to think he could trust the team to pull their weight but at the end of the day he was responsible for overseeing everything was recorded as it should be. Working with cold cases had made him extra aware of the need to record all details that are thrown up by an investigation. Nowadays, he asked himself if his case came up for review down the line, would he and his team be said to have done a good job? He owed it to the victims and their families to ensure he did everything in his power to conduct a thorough investigation every single time.

'Hey, boss,' Malachy called from across the open plan office. 'I've just heard back from IT. I need to talk to you.'

Danny indicated with a jerk of his head for Mal to meet him in the private office.

'What's come up?'

'They've found a curious folder on James McCallum's laptop that has been encrypted. I think it needs to be followed up.'

'Curious how? Dodgy porn? Searches for suicide methods?' Danny asked.

'No, weirder. He'd made hundreds of searches in reference to the disappearance of a child in Mistle, a small town in Donegal, back in the summer of 2001, and had a folder named "Darkling Thrush" containing information pertaining to the missing girl.'

'Fuck, that is weird. What was he searching that for?'

'Maybe he was a true crime fan? There's plenty of them out there listening to podcasts on all sorts. My sister listens to them all – *Serial*, *West Cork*, *Case File* – on the school run. She thinks she's better qualified than me to solve crimes.' Mal snorted in derision.

Danny couldn't see the attraction of true crime as a form of entertainment. He had experienced enough of the reality of crime to know that there was nothing diverting or enjoyable about it.

'The first file I opened details the case of eight-year-old Maeve Lunn, who disappeared on the afternoon of August 17th, 2001. She'd left home on her bicycle at approximately 1.15 p.m. to go the local shop to buy sweets for herself and her siblings. The town was unusually quiet that day as a local boy, Darragh Conlig, was playing in the all-Ireland Gaelic football final at Croke

Park. Most people were at home watching the game on RTE or had gathered in the local pub, O'Malley's, to watch it there.'

'So, what happened?' Danny asked.

'Maeve never made it to the shop – a journey that should have taken her no more than fifteen minutes – and she was never seen again.'

'Let's get a proper handle on this. We're going to have to follow it up.' Danny was already mapping his next move out in his head. 'Get the files sent over to me.'

A short while later, Danny had the folders open on his computer. He clicked on the icon for the 'Darkling Thrush' folder and saw hundreds of files open up. 'The Missing Mistle Girl'; 'The Girl who Never Came Home'; 'Calls for an Inquiry into Missing Maeve'; 'A Mother's Sorrow: Missing Girl'; 'Bring Maeve Home'.

Danny looked up. This was weird as fuck. He felt that creeping sensation across his scalp. Something wasn't right about it. What reason could James McCallum have to be interested in Maeve's case? Was he simply into unsolved true crimes, as Mal had suggested? Or was there something more sinister behind it? Danny did a quick calculation in his head – James would have been eighteen when Maeve went missing. He'd have to make contact with An Garda Síochána and see what they could tell him.

He clicked on another file on the screen and a headline flashed up: *The Stolen Girl, Maeve Lunn.*

A shy girl, Maeve, eight, was never one to stray far from the family home. Her primary school teacher, Ms Coyle, remembers her as a helpful child who

162

preferred assisting her teacher in tidying up the class-room to running around the playground at recess.

'Maeve was a joy to have in my class. She wasn't the most academic pupil, but she tried hard and always handed her homework in on time. I don't think any of us will ever get over her disappearance. Children don't just vanish into thin air. Someone has to know something.'

The general feeling in the town of Mistle was that something untoward had happened to Maeve on that fateful day. Had someone stolen her away? There was even talk of fairies being implicated.

One of Mistle's older residents, Peggy Rainey, said the fairy folk were known for taking children to the underworld to punish townspeople. 'Maeve wasn't the first child to be stolen by the wee folk and I've no doubt she won't be the last.'

Danny opened another file. More newspaper features on the lost child.

Her family tirelessly searched day and night with the help of local neighbours, but despite many searches over bogland and fields, Maeve Lunn was never seen again. Life has never been the same for the Lunn family who hope against hope that Maeve is still alive and will be returned to them one day.

Maeve's mother, Eileen, still prays that her daughter will find her way back to her. 'I will never lose faith in Maeve and the hope that she will come home. I have to believe, otherwise I'd never be able to cope.'

What was it about the missing Mistle girl that interested James so much?

Danny felt the stirrings of intrigue. His gut was telling him there had to be something more to James' interest in the Lunn case and he wouldn't rest until he found out what it was.

CHAPTER 32

The white board in the conference room was covered with information pertaining to the case: a photograph of James McCallum, a map of the school where he was found, and frames taken from the CCTV camera footage in the area. Rose stood back and stared at the display. It was like an alternative Pinterest board, macabre and sinister. At the side of the board they had a list of possible suspects: Martin Kilburn, Emma McCallum, Lorcan Burns. It was sad to think that those closest to James were now in a line-up of people who may have committed his murder.

She was aware of the chatter of conversations going on behind her. Everyone was anxious to know why Danny had called the impromptu meeting. Rose had heard something had been found on James McCallum's computer, but she didn't yet know what it was.

Danny was running late. Her phone buzzed and she checked it, finding a text from Kaitlin: *Need to see you. Let me know when you're free. X*

165

They had intended to put their mother's house up for sale, so she was sure that Kaitlin was keen to organise the clear-out. Rose dreaded it. The idea of rummaging through her mother's belongings made her feel uneasy. So much of her mother's life felt unknown and full of secrecy. There was already plenty for her to unpack emotionally and as far as she was concerned, the longer she put it off, the better.

'There you are. Sorry I'm late,' Danny said, rushing in through the door. He strode across the room with a bundle of papers under his arm. 'Rosie, we are hitting the road.'

She gave him a look that suggested he had gone mad. 'Where are we going?'

'Ever hear of place called Mistle?'

'Mistle in Donegal?'

'Yeah, that's the one. I'll fill you in with the rest of the team.'

Intrigued, Rose took a seat as Danny cleared his throat, silencing the room.

'Right you lot, it seems James McCallum had a special interest in a town called Mistle, in Donegal, and the disappearance of an eight-year-old girl called Maeve Lunn. Mal Magee has been working with our friends in IT and they have found a number of encrypted files on James' computer all relating to the case. I've phoned through to the Gardaí up in Mistle and they told me that the girl has never been found and they failed to identify any clear suspects at the time of her disappearance.'

There was a sharp intake of breath.

'We could be chasing a ghost of a lead, but we need to ask why James was so interested in the case.'

'Do we know if James has any connection to Mistle?' Tania asked.

'I checked it out with his mother. Rhea McCallum couldn't recall at first but she said James and his friends – Lorcan Burns, Ivy Duffy, and Emer Ward – all holidayed in Mistle following their A Level exams during the summer of 2001. Lorcan Burns' family had a holiday home there.'

'Jesus, and when did the girl go missing?' Rose asked.

'Maeve was last seen on the 17th of August . . . 2001. James McCallum was in Mistle at the same time as Maeve Lunn's disappearance,' Danny said.

A hush fell over the room as they took in this new information.

'Whoa. You think James had something to do with it?' Jack Fitzgerald asked.

Danny shrugged. 'Who knows, but we've got to follow it up.' He moved forward and removed a photograph from his folder of papers, placing it on the white board and securing it with a magnet. Maeve Lunn stared out at them. Her head was tilted as she smiled, and she had a head of unruly red hair.

Rose looked at the print of the freckle-faced girl. It was a posed school photograph, the embarrassing kind that would have sat on a mantelpiece until she was old enough to tell her mother to put it away. 'Cute kid,' Rose said. 'I can't imagine what it's like for your child to go to the shop and never return.'

Danny turned to Rose. 'Neither can I. That's why we need a trip to Mistle, but first we need to speak to Ivy Duffy and Emer Ward again. Maybe pay Lorcan Burns a visit too. Let's get all of our ducks in a row.'

CHAPTER 33

James McCallum's funeral was held in Drumbeg Baptist Church. The family were gathered in the pews at the front while an organ played hymnal music.

The low mournful strains of the music grew louder, reverberating through the crowd, and everyone hushed their murmurs in preparation for the ceremony. The coffin had been placed at the front of the church with an arrangement of white lilies on top. Rose always associated the scent of lilies with funerals. She couldn't help remembering her mother's funeral and how she had come home for it from London, uncertain if her family would welcome her back.

Up ahead, Rose could see Emma McCallum sitting next to Rhea McCallum, all evidence of tension between them set aside for the time being. Grace sat on the other side of Emma, and Rose thought how tragic it was for her to lose her father at such a young age. She understood what that was like and how the rest of her life would be shaped by his death. When Rose's father had been

168

killed by a loyalist gunman, she had been nine years old, much too young to have to experience the impact of such violence. While she hadn't been there when it had happened, the talk at the wake and in the weeks after had been about the brutality of it and how he had bled out for fifteen minutes before the ambulance had arrived. Now she wondered at the apparent disregard for the children such talk displayed. There had been no attempt to protect them from the horror, and for months afterwards she feared going to sleep, terrified that dreams of her father would come.

She looked around the gathering now and was struck by how austere and simple the church was. No Virgin Mary statues with sorrowful eyes, no crown of thorns biting into the head of a life-sized statue of Jesus, looking on beatifically from a cross.

Danny had said to meet him there and she could see him sitting next to Tania Lumen in the pew in front of her. The police's presence at the funeral had to be low key so they could be watchful without attracting attention. The chances were that the killer – or killers – was in the congregation.

The service murmured on until it came to a sudden end and the organist started to play 'How Great Thou Art', while a soloist sang. The body of people began moving out, pew following pew, until they were in the graveyard adjoining the church. Rose walked past Martin Kilburn, noting that he looked strained, with his eyes cast down. She turned to look at him again and saw that he was hanging back from the crowd, as if he felt like he was imposing to be so close to the family. Emma McCallum was crying softly and comforting her daughter while her mother-in-law stared straight ahead, watching the pastor as he prayed over the open grave.

'Alright, Rosie,' Danny said quietly as he arrived at her side.

'Yeah. Sad day for them.'

He nodded. The crowd began dispersing and they held back, watching as Emma McCallum approached them.

'Why are you here?' she demanded. She looked as if a gust of wind could blow her over.

'We're here to pay our respects,' Danny replied.

'This is a day for family and friends, not the police. You should be doing your job, not loitering in a grave-yard.' Her voice was weak and thin, like she had no air left in her lungs, and she was trembling.

Rose reached forward and placed a hand on her arm. 'We're very sorry.'

'You knew that it was murder when you first came to see me, didn't you?'

'We had our suspicions, but we couldn't say anything until the autopsy had been completed,' Danny offered.

'I don't like being treated like a suspect. My husband is dead, and I want to know who did it.' Her eyes were blazing, tears threatening to spill.

Her mother appeared at her side. 'Emma, come on, Grace is looking for you. We need to go,' she said, gently guiding Emma away.

CHAPTER 34

Danny figured that Lorcan Burns had sweated long enough with the squad car parked at his door. It was time to pay him a visit. By rights, he should bring Burns into the station, but he believed in playing nice . . . to begin with. Most people respond better to being treated with the respect they believe they deserve, so until Danny had anything firm to move Lorcan to the top of his list of suspects, he'd take the gentle approach.

Lorcan was dressed in sweatpants and a wine-coloured cable-knit jumper that looked like something your granny would buy you for Christmas. The bruises on his face had faded to a greenish ochre but the stitches at his temple were still evident.

'Lorcan, how are you doing?'

'Getting there.' He looked down at his slippered feet and muttered something that could've been 'Come in.' Danny followed him into the living room. The partner Brody was nowhere to be seen. Probably at work. The television was on, playing some Netflix series that his colleagues at the station had been talking about but which Danny had yet to get round to seeing.

Danny sat down on the sofa without waiting to be asked while Lorcan took the chair in the corner of the room.

'Mind if I record our conversation?' Danny asked. 'Keeps me right.' He placed his phone on the coffee table and hit the voice memo icon without waiting for Lorcan to reply.

'Did you get the guys who did this?' Lorcan asked.

'Not yet. We did get our hands on the CCTV footage from the gym though, which was illuminating. If I remember correctly, you said they didn't speak to you, and that you were jumped from behind.'

Lorcan said nothing.

'The thing is, when me and my colleagues back at the station looked at the footage, we could see you and the yobbos having a bit of an exchange when they first approached. Now, that interests me for two reasons.' He paused, letting Lorcan feel the heat of worry build up.

'Firstly, I want to know why you lied.'

'It all happened so fast. I didn't exactly have my wits about me.'

Danny jotted his response down in his notebook as a way of giving Lorcan time to consider his reply. 'Okay, so you're saying you forgot that they spoke to you?'

'I was ambushed. It was dark and frightening. I don't remember most of what happened.'

'The second thing that concerns me is the content of the exchange. What could they possibly have had to say to you? What were they warning you about, Lorcan?'

He said nothing, wrapping his arms around his body as if he was cold.

'The way it looks to me . . . well, let's just say it doesn't look good. There's you getting a hiding not more than a week after your friend has been murdered. That makes me all kinds of concerned but I don't know if I should be concerned *for* you, or *about* you. Which is it, Lorcan?'

Danny sat forward and stared straight at him. 'You see, I believe that deep down you want to help us with our investigation. Your friend has been murdered and I think you know something about it.'

Lorcan shook his head. 'I don't know what you're talking about. How could I know anything about what happened to James?'

'If there's one thing this job has taught me, it's that there's a thin line between being on the side of what's right and falling into the descent of hell. One crooked action, one dirty lie, and before you know it, you're in the shit and rushing to cover your tracks. But I figure you're not one of the bad guys, Lorcan; you'd rather do the right thing. Except, it feels beyond your control this time.'

'I don't know what you're on about.'

'Maybe not. Time will tell. We'll leave it here for today but next time we will have to make it all official like. Bring you in to the station, see if that helps jog your memory.'

CHAPTER 35

Emer Ward was busy strapping a squirming toddler into the back seat of her Volvo estate car when Rose and Danny approached her.

'Ms Ward,' Danny stated.

She lifted her wheat-blonde head out of the car while keeping one hand on the child. 'Yes?' There was a brittleness about her, a sense that she was pulled taut, like an elastic close to snapping point.

'Me, again, and this is Dr Rose Lainey. We'd like to ask you some questions about James.'

'As you can see, it isn't a good time. I am just about to head out.' She turned back to the child and secured him in the car seat with a click.

'I appreciate that, but if you don't mind, we'd like to go inside. It shouldn't take too long.'

Emer sighed and released the child, lifting him into her arms. He smiled, delighted to have escaped the confines of the car.

Rose and Danny followed her into her modern East

Belfast house. She led them through to the kitchen where she placed the child into a highchair. He began to protest until she swiftly placed a bowl in front of him and began slicing banana into it before sprinkling some raisins on top.

'Awk, he's a handsome young fella, isn't he? You've another one, isn't that right?' Danny asked.

'Yes, another boy, but he's at school. The childminder isn't around to help today which means I'll have to collect him at three o'clock. So, if you don't mind . . .' She trailed off.

Danny smiled. 'Aye, no problem at all. I bet he keeps you on your toes, am I right?'

'Look, what's this about?' She chose to ignore Danny's friendly preamble.

Rose noticed that she busied herself with the child, offering him the raisins while he was perfectly capable of lifting them himself. He ignored his mother, his fat fists clutching at the banana and squashing it to a pulp before placing it into his mouth.

'It's about James McCallum's murder.'

'Yes, I was at the funeral. It's terrible but I really don't see how this has anything to do with me.'

'How would you describe your friendship group at school?' Rose asked.

'I'm sorry but I don't see how me, or my friends, have any bearing on James' death.' She frowned and folded her arms under her chest.

'Humour us,' Danny said.

She sighed. 'As I told you the last time we spoke, at school none of us were exactly rejects or nerds but we didn't get the invites to the best parties.'

'So after the A Levels, did you head off on a last hurrah, just the four of you?'

'Not really. A lot of the others were going to Magaluf and Ibiza but that wouldn't have been our scene. Clubbing till four in the morning and taking pills didn't sound like the type of holiday any of us would have fancied.'

'Sensible lot,' Danny said. 'So instead of Shagaluf you accompanied James, along with Lorcan Burns and Ivy Duffy, to a place in Donegal – Mistle – in the summer of 2001. Isn't that right?'

She raised a perfectly groomed eyebrow. 'So? Our parents agreed, knowing it would be safer than going to somewhere with raves and all-night beach parties.'

'Where did you stay?'

'Lorcan's family had a holiday home in the area so we stayed there. I don't know if they still own it. Look, what's this all about?' She stared intently, as if she was trying to intimidate them.

'We aren't at liberty to say yet, but we are making enquiries into the disappearance of a girl in Mistle around the same time you holidayed there.'

'And what has that got to do with me?' she asked, her voice slightly higher.

'Probably nothing, but we have to make our enquires,' Danny said coolly. 'Just making sure we tick all the boxes, you know.'

Rose could tell he was trying to put Emer at ease to keep her talking. No point rattling her too much until they had more information. The last thing they needed was for her to send them packing and demand to have her solicitor present.

'You didn't hear anything about the missing kid? Maeve Lunn was her name. Eight years old. Terrible all together. They say there's nothing worse than losing a child.' He placed his hand on the baby's head and gently ruffled his blond curls.

'No. I don't remember hearing anything about that. We were staying in Lorcan's holiday home, as I said. It was outside of the village. We only went there once or twice to get food and stuff. We didn't have a clue what was going in Mistle while we were there.'

'That's fair enough. A bunch of teenagers are usually only looking out for themselves, aren't they? You were probably all getting off with each other, downing a few beers,' Danny said with a congenial smile. Rose stayed quiet, letting Danny do his thing.

'So, James. What was he like?'

Her lips were drawn into a tight line. 'I don't know. He was just James. When you know someone for a long time, it's hard to describe them.'

'Oh, I don't know, I'd say it's the reverse. The longer you know someone the more you know about them.'

'He was a good guy. Intelligent. Conscientious about his schoolwork without being a complete swot. One of those who you knew would do well. Considerate, too.'

'Any reason to think someone would want to kill him?'

She flinched and reached for the child again, smoothing his hair with her hand. 'No, of course not. James was a sweet guy. He didn't have enemies. I'm sorry but I'm going to have to go and pick up my son now. If there isn't anything more?'

'Sure, no bother. If you think of anything else, you'll give us a call, right?' Danny sat his card down on the table. She nodded and began lifting the child out of the highchair.

'Don't worry, we'll see ourselves out,' Danny said, and they left.

Out in the car as they were driving away, Danny said, 'Do you think she was hiding something?'

'Hard to say but she was anxious. Something in the way she kept touching the child, as though reassuring herself that he was right there.'

Every interview, whether witness or suspect, provided an opportunity to gain traction in the search for truth. They had a duty to plan, prepare, engage, and clarify, but at the end of the day, you often instinctively go on gut feeling. 'I think she is protecting someone. The responses to your questions were sharp and reactive, like she'd spent a while preparing. We think we're the ones planning and in control but suspects and witnesses do the same. They think about what will be asked of them and consider how best to answer.'

'So you think we need to lean heavier on her and pay her another visit?' Danny asked.

'Yes, keep the pressure on to see if she is hiding something. Make it clear that we haven't ruled her out of the investigation. We want to create a sense of jeopardy.'

Danny looked out the window. 'I get the same feeling with Lorcan; that there's something we're missing. Something just out of reach.'

Rose put the indicator on, manoeuvred out onto Belmont Road and headed back in the direction of the station. The hills surrounding Belfast were cloaked in a grey drizzle. There was no way of knowing when the mist would lift.

CHAPTER 36

Rose read through the file detailing the Maeve Lunn case, which Danny had given to her. A thorough search had been organised, with hundreds of people volunteering to scour the fields, in the hope that the girl had simply wandered off and gotten lost. As often happened in cases of missing children, suspicion fell on the family. In this case, the family was torn apart by insinuations and accusations concerning an uncle who by all accounts was just a bit of a loner, strange but harmless. Calls for an inquest into the disappearance of the eight-year-old had gone unanswered and it appeared the investigation had eventually run out of steam after hitting a series of dead ends.

She sighed, rubbed her eyes, and leaned back in the chair. It was possible that James' interest in the case was innocent. He could have been nostalgic for a time when he was happy and carefree. Maybe, in some twisted way, he associated the lost girl with that good time in his life? She knew she was reaching, hoping that the missing child had nothing to do with their current case.

* * *

Rose was helping herself to some coffee from the vending machine a while later when she heard Danny behind her.

'That stuff will kill you, you know. It's pure shite.'

She smiled before turning to face him.

'Listen to the coffee snob. We can't all treat ourselves to a fancy state-of-the-art coffee machine.'

'The fecking thing has ruined me. I'm unable to drink anything but the best Columbian blend of beans these days. I've taken to bringing my own supply in with me and heating it in the microwave.'

'In the absence of anything better, this'll have to do me,' Rose replied, lifting her cup.

'What are you doing for the rest of the day, Rosie?'

'I've a feeling you're about to tell me. What's up?'

'I want to go have a word with Ivy Duffy. If the four of them were in Mistle together we need to establish what the set-up was. Did they all stay in the holiday home and not venture much into Mistle, as Emer Ward claimed? Or was there more to their little holiday than we realise? Are you up for coming along? I could do with you having a read of the situation, in case I miss anything.'

'You don't want to invite her to come in and do it here?' Rose asked, wary of overstepping the mark.

'Nah, I want to play this cool. If we bring her in it will suggest we know more than we do. Let's just get a feel for the dynamic between the friends first.'

'Sure, all right, but go easy. You've a tendency to make every conversation sound like an interrogation.'

He winked at her. 'It's all part of the Danny boy charm. I bring you along for the rapport-building. We're just like Steve and Kate.'

'Who?'

He shook his head. '*Line of Duty*? Jesus, Lainey. Get a life, would you, and watch a bit of television.'

'Try reading a book once in a while and I might be more likely to catch your cultural references. Let me grab my coat and bag and I'll meet you out front.'

They had discussed the encrypted files on James McCallum's computer at length the day before. Danny was becoming more certain that James McCallum's interest in the missing girl case had to be significant in some way. What that was they couldn't say yet. Rose had looked into the case notes, but the information provided by the Gardaí was sparse. It wasn't their fault. Having worked with the Historical Enquiries Unit, Rose and Danny both knew enough about unsolved cases to understand that when a lead dies, all that remains is cold hard facts. The nuances, the on-the-ground knowledge gained from those who lived alongside the victim, are what breathe life into dead leads. A trip to Mistle would be the only way to get a real sense of what was known and what was suspected about Maeve Lunn's disappearance. But first, they needed to speak to Ivy Duffy and pay Lorcan Burns another visit.

CHAPTER 37

Rose rang the doorbell and a few moments later the door opened to reveal Ivy Duffy, looking every inch the professional in a fitted charcoal shift dress with black tights. She was wearing high, black patent heels that accentuated her height, which must have been around five-nine in her shoes. Her subtle make-up enhanced her dark, cat-like eyes, and her mid-length hair glinted with hues of reddish brown that suggested expensive colouring.

'Hello, again,' she said, extending her hand and smiling. Her handshake was firm, leaving no doubt that she was in control and used to taking the lead. She was the type of woman you could tell straight off owned every room she ever entered and knew how to work her audience to get whatever she wanted. She welcomed them into her home and led them through to her study. 'Excuse the mess.' She waved her manicured hand expansively over the piles of papers.

Rose and Danny sat down on a small leather sofa while Ivy sat at her desk, swinging round in the chair to face them. 'What can I do for you?' she asked, picking up a sliver pen, as if they were patients who had come for her medical expertise.

Danny leaned back on the sofa, his arm along the back of it, looking casual and relaxed.

'You holidayed with James in the summer of 2001 in Mistle, Donegal, isn't that right?' Danny asked.

'Yes, we did. That was a great trip.' She smiled, as if remembering a particularly nice moment.

'A young girl went missing around the time you were all there, kicking back after the exams. Did you hear anything about the girl at the time?'

'No. We were too busy "kicking back", as you say, Detective. We were in our own wee bubble of post-exam celebrations. Anything could have happened, and we wouldn't have noticed. We were eighteen, enjoying the last summer together before we all went our separate ways. You know what it's like at that age; getting hammered and hooking up.'

'So, are you married, Ivy?' Danny asked.

She made a noise that sounded like 'ha', crossed her legs, and leaned back. 'No, I like my own company too much.'

'Married to the job, am I right?'

She shrugged. 'Probably. I like what I do, Detective.'

Danny raised an eyebrow. 'Plenty of people hate what they do. You're a lucky woman.'

She pursed her lips and tapped lightly on the pile of papers with the stainless-steel pen, as if to indicate that she was also a *busy* woman.

'Did you always plan on being a doctor?' Rose asked.

'Pretty much. My father is a doctor so, you know, it

was kind of expected.' She reached for a hair clip and twisted her hair into a knot at the back of her head in one fluid movement. She was on safe ground talking about her career and her father. Rose could read the subtle relaxing of her shoulders, the slight shift of her weight back into the chair.

'When you were at school, were you close to James?' Rose asked.

Something flitted across her face and she shrugged. 'We were good friends; the four of us, I mean. I went out with James for a while – first love and all that – but we both knew it wasn't going to last forever.'

'Aww that's a shame, isn't it?' Danny said.

'Like I said, we didn't expect it to last forever.'

'Nothing like teenage love though, is there?' Danny said. 'All that passion and hormones. You can't beat it with a big stick.'

Ivy turned her head towards Rose. 'It was nothing. A teenage romance, not important and nothing of particular significance.'

Rose nodded. 'And later you all went your separate ways?'

'Yes, I studied medicine at Bristol. James stayed in Belfast and went to Queen's.'

'So, the holiday in Mistle was the last big blowout before the serious work got underway,' Danny said.

She looked at him stonily. 'We took a break at Lorcan's family holiday home. Hardly the stuff of legendary spring breaks. We weren't going mad.'

'Fair enough. I'm sure the memories are hazy, all the same.'

Rose leaned in. 'When the four of you got together

184

the odd time over the years, partners weren't included. Any particular reason for that?'

She shook her head. 'No, we just liked to meet as a foursome. It was easier that way.'

'Easier in what way?' Danny asked.

She sighed. 'Easier in that we didn't have to accommodate partners. There's no law against having a friend outside of marriage is there, Detective?'

'The last time James was seen,' Danny flipped open his notebook, 'let's see . . . was the evening of October 17th. That was a Friday. He had dinner with his family, went to bed as normal around eleven, and when his wife woke up on Saturday morning, he was gone.' Danny looked up from the notebook. 'Any idea where he went to when he left the family home that night?'

'Well, I assume he went to Osbourne House as that's where he was found.'

'Aye right so. He could've gone somewhere first though. Does no harm to wonder.' Danny spoke as if he was merely musing, inviting Ivy Duffy to speculate alongside him.

'Could he have been meeting someone, do you think?' Danny said it casually.

Ivy Duffy shifted in her chair. 'I was working that night, as I have already told you, if that's what you're getting at, Detective.'

'Aye that's right, so. A workaholic like yourself would be burning the midnight oil.'

Danny allowed a brief moment while he finished making notes. 'So you were at work all night on the evening of the 17th, until midnight or thereabouts. We are checking that out. No harm giving you the opportunity to remember if you had your dates or times wrong.'

'Well, I haven't got my dates or times wrong.' A hint of exasperation crept into her voice. She narrowed her eyes and rubbed at her jawline.

'Great. Well, I think that's all we need for now, Ivy. If you can think of anything else, I'm sure you'll give me a call, won't you?'

'Of course. Let me see you out.'

'Well, what did you make of that little performance?' Danny asked Rose once they were back in the car.

'She was bristly, that's for sure. And she was prepared. Maybe it's down to her medical background. That assuredness that doctors seem to have. I had the sense that she was resisting wrong footing us.'

'Yep, I had the feeling that she was withholding something. I also think that someone in her line of work would normally have asked questions about the death, out of curiosity as much as anything.'

'Exactly. She was too disinterested,' Rose said. 'She also echoed your phrasing. It's a typical tell in someone wanting to ingratiate themselves. She is either a people pleaser who accommodates or she was deliberately setting out to win us over. And another thing: don't you think it was a bit of an overreaction to say that her relationship with James didn't mean anything? First loves are often the most impactful romantic relationships we have.'

'Yeah, and I'm still curious about that holiday and what the dynamic was between them all back then. There has to be some reason why James was so interested in the Maeve Lunn case.'

'We need to do our best to get ahead of it and we could definitely do with visiting Mistle.'

'Yeah, I think so too. I'll speak to the boss and let you know but expect to do an over-nighter. In the meantime, I'll get Malachy or Gerard to check out Ivy's alibi for the night of the 17th. Right, let's get back to base and see what the rest of team are working on.'

Ivy Duffy had been hard to read. Rose knew she was trained and equipped to work under pressure though. A GP might be seen as an easier career than other, more hospital based, medical roles, but she'd have had the same on-the-ward training. She certainly knew how to keep her cool and to deflect questions. Lorcan Burns, in contrast, came across as less able to maintain a cool façade. If there was something going on, he'd be the one for them to put the pressure on.

CHAPTER 38

Danny could remember the summer after he left school. The heady feeling of freedom. The expectation that his life was about to start in Liverpool, far away from home and the suffocation of everyone knowing his business. He longed to wake up in a strange bed and know that the day was his to do what he wanted with. No more six o'clock starts helping his da on the farm. No more routine of home and the drudgery of school.

Liverpool was going to be a blast. He knew it before he'd even arrived. He'd decided on the boat on the way over that he was going to enjoy every minute of his student life. He was going to go to every party, kiss every girl, and live his best life.

Then he met Rose. She was like a challenge, an experiment in how to live without giving a damn. She dared to be her own person without accommodating anyone's expectations. Danny was a people pleaser, always trying to fit in and make friends, whereas Rose floated around, self-contained and fearless. She needed no one. Danny

188

felt himself drawn to her immediately and with her everything changed.

What seemed like fun the week before – getting hammered on shots and chatting up random girls, with the direct intention of shagging them – no longer appealed. With Rose, everything felt heightened and sensual. Extraordinary.

Rose studied and so he did too. The library was his new go-to place, knowing that was where he'd most likely find her. Happy to have some little moment of contact. He enjoyed trying to keep up with her and the hard work had paid off. Without Rose's high expectations for herself, he was sure he would have never got a first.

There were times when he marvelled at his good fortune to have chosen the same subjects as Rose – criminology and psychology. What were the odds, he'd wonder, and then he'd smile congratulating himself on his choice as if it was cosmic gift. When he'd go for a run, he'd find he could pass the time thinking of her, imagining new conversations and going over old ones. He fantasised about bringing her home, showing her around the farm, and watching her chat away with his mum at the table.

Soon though, he realised that there was no having a hold over Rose. She didn't feel the same way about him. There was a bluntness to her, a granite certainty in everything she did, which could irritate Danny. He wanted to ask her how she could be so sure, so certain? Wasn't one of the joys of life not knowing what to expect? She'd laugh and shake her head, the dark hair falling like a curtain around her face. 'No, Danny boy, life isn't all nice surprises and picnics.'

When they discussed politics – global, never the

bipartisan farce of home – she'd come alive, debating and challenging his opinions, listening intently before annihilating him with a well-executed argument.

The girls he'd known at school would've been no competition for her. They had hung around acting like the rest of the lads, almost too familiar to be of any real interest.

The night he'd almost blown it all had come after their exams. They'd spent weeks studying, working side by side, surviving on coffee and sausage rolls, toast and KitKats. The last exam had been statistics and they had both left the exam hall intent on getting wasted. The bar was packed and the music loud but before too long the good humour and banter had fizzled to nothing of worth, so they decided to call it a night and head home. Danny had walked Rose to her halls and like any other night he followed her inside. This time, instead of sprawling out on her single bed, he gently pushed her against the wall and moved in to kiss her.

Immediately she froze, her body going stiff with rejection. 'What's wrong?'

'I just don't think it would be a good idea, that's all.' She looked down at her hands, picking at the navy nail polish.

He needed to know why she was giving him the brush off, to understand if she felt awkward with him or if it was more than that. If it was that she didn't feel anything for him.

The girls at school had never made him work this hard. Before, he'd had no trouble pulling any girl he set his sights on, but Rose was different.

'You're acting like you're shocked that I would make a move.'

She shrugged. 'I figured we were just friends. Good friends.'

'And what's the harm in good friends becoming something more?'

She laughed. 'Come on, Danny. You know it wouldn't work out. We'd end up hating each other and then who would I have to hang out with?'

He knew there was some truth in what she said. She didn't have lots of friends, preferring to hang around with him and whoever he was hanging out with.

After a moment he stood back, feeling the pain of rejection course through him. He wanted to get out of there. To go get pissed and not care so much about anything or anyone.

'Well I'll head on out then. I'll probably see you around.'

'Danny, don't be like that.'

'Like what?'

'Distant, angry.'

'Sure, no worries. I'll see you.' He left the room and headed back to his halls.

The next day he'd blushed when he saw her. Felt the heat of embarrassment rise up from his neck.

'About last night,' he began, cringing as he said the clichéd words.

'Shush,' she said. 'It never happened.'

Sometimes the memories of back then caught him unawares. When it came down to it, he had to reconfigure who he had become with how Rose was now. They were both different. Older, and wiser too, he hoped.

'You listening to one of those seventies bands you like so much? Let me guess, Pink Floyd or Led Zeppelin?'

191

he asked, having walked in to find her with her earbuds in. Despite being given her own office on the third floor, she seemed to prefer working down here in the basement.

She pulled the ear buds out. 'Wrong on both counts. It's work.'

'What is it?'

'It's a podcast called *The Lost Girl*. It covers the story of the Maeve Lunn case.'

Danny smiled. He liked to see Rose digging around, investigating like a real cop. The psychology stuff was her area of expertise, but her perception and her ability to sniff out relevant information was first rate too.

'Have you learned anything from it?'

'Nope. The host – Ryan McKeown – has been hitting dead end after dead end. It still might be worth giving him a call though. He claims that the investigation was impeded by some high-up individuals who will never let the truth be known.'

'That could just be for dramatic effect and an excuse for not getting to the bottom of the case.'

'Yeah, I'd considered that, but McKeown's based in Dundrum so it would be easy to ask if he'd come in for a chat. Sure, the claim of being kept quiet could be a ruse to excuse the lack of a real story, but what if it's not?'

'Okay, let's set it up. Bring him in and let's see what he has to say.'

CHAPTER 39

Rose checked her reflection while washing her hands. She reminded herself to check in with Kaitlin. The novelty of having her sister close by hadn't worn off but with the murder case on top of her other work, she'd very little spare time to offer at present. Pearse had fallen into the habit of sending her stupid WhatsApp memes and funny videos. Mostly she replied with a smiley emoji but sometimes she inquired as to how he was. Kaitlin, though, she wanted the whole sisterly package. After drying her hands Rose left the toilets and headed down the corridor.

Danny had scheduled a meeting with ACC Boyne for them to discuss the Mistle case. They both knew that Boyne might not buy a connection, that it would be a push to get him to sign off on their road trip to Donegal, but Danny was keen for them to check it out.

Battle had his own bosses to answer to, but Danny was keen to see the house where the four friends had stayed and to talk to the local Gardaí. It could all be a waste of time, but they wouldn't know that without investigating. Danny had kept going back to the notion that the holiday had been significant in some way as it was the last time they were all firm friends. After that they seemed to have scattered to the four winds, only meeting up occasionally. She trusted his instincts.

Danny was already in the basement office when she arrived. 'The boss says he can see us at ten so I thought we should gather the team now and see where we're all at.'

'Okay, I'll see you up there,' she replied. 'I want to finish the Mistle case notes before we go in to see him. No point going in half-arsed.'

When Danny left, Rose opened the folder on her computer. She had been trawling through the files obtained from James McCallum's home computer. Rose agreed with Danny that his searches went beyond a passing interest. James had also carried out Facebook searches on members of Maeve Lunn's family. In particular her sister, Ciara, who had run a campaign to call for more to be done to find Maeve. He hadn't gone so far as to make a fake Facebook identity to befriend Ciara but her account was public so he had been able to scroll through it any time he pleased. Why was he so interested in the Lunn family? What possible reason could there be to explain his borderline obsession?

ACC Boyne was waiting on them when they arrived at his office. 'Come on in. Get yourselves a seat. Where are we with the McCallum case?'

'Sir, we have interviewed friends and family members of James McCallum and subsequent searches on his home computer have led us to believe that he may have had something to do with the disappearance of a young girl in Donegal back in 2001.'

Battle put his hands up. 'Wait a minute, that sounds like a bit of a stretch. Can you back this haunch up?'

'We have established that James McCallum, along with three friends, was holidaying in Mistle at the time of Maeve Lunn's disappearance. Now, it could be that James had a macabre hobby of researching true crime. But we found no evidence of other such searches on his computer. All of the information he had saved and the searches he made were linked to this one case.'

'Doctor Lainey, what do you make of this? Could it simply be that he was curious about something that happened in a place he knew?' Boyne asked.

Rose cleared her throat. 'Research shows that humans like reading about survival, fear, and the sense of threat. It's satisfying for the thrill-seeking element in us all.'

'So, do you think James McCallum was a true-life crime aficionado?' Boyne asked.

'No, I agree with Danny – there's something more to it. If James McCallum was a fan of true crime, we would likely have found many other equally fascinating cases among his files. James' significant interest in the Maeve Lunn case could signify something more than a macabre curiosity. It suggests that he felt connected to it in some way. For that reason, I think it's necessary to explore the Donegal case further,' Rose said. 'Yes, it could all be nothing, but what if there's something in it?'

'Something like what? How old was James McCallum when the girl went missing?'

'He'd just turned eighteen,' Rose said.

Battle raised his eyebrows. 'So, what, you think he had a thing for young girls? That he abducted her?'

'No, not necessarily. There was nothing sexual in the information saved on his computer. No hint of anything untoward in that respect,' Danny said.

'Well, what then?'

'It's possible he saw something. Or was told something. Whatever it may be, we need to check it out,' Rose said.

Battle took a moment to consider. 'Fine, fine. So you want to head up to Donegal? Have you made contact with our counterparts in An Garda Síochána?'

Danny nodded. 'Yes, they've sent over the case file, but you know yourself, sir, nothing beats being in the area and meeting the people involved. We want to take the time to talk to Maeve's family. It shouldn't take more than twenty-four hours and Mal Magee can keep things ticking over with the team here in the meantime.'

Boyne placed his hands on the table. 'Remember that you don't have carte blanche here. You have to be sensitive. Don't be stomping in with your size elevens, telling another squad how to do their job.'

'Of course not,' Danny said.

Boyne sat considering for a moment before saying, 'Right, I'll sign off on it, but keep your heads down. Don't be going annoying the locals, or stirring up hopes that you can find that wee girl.'

'Of course. Thanks, sir,' Danny said as they both got up to leave.

'One more thing. Dr Lainey, if you need to discuss your findings or need some guidance about working with the PSNI then know that my door is always open to you.

I know that it can't be easy coming in as an outsider.'

Boyne seemed to let his eyes linger on her for a second too long. She knew the gossip in the station was that he was considered a great catch, good looking and available. Rose smiled. 'Thanks, sir, but I'm finding my way. DI Stowe here keeps me right.'

When they were out of earshot in the corridor, Danny turned to Rose. 'What was that all about? "My door is always open." The fecking chancer fancies you.'

Rose laughed. 'Behave, Danny boy, he's only being nice.'

'Nice, my arse. He was looking to get into your knickers.'

'Awk Danny, don't be jealous. You know you're my best boy.' She laughed but Danny's protective response heartened her. It was nice to know he cared.

CHAPTER 40

Danny did some of his best thinking while walking at night; if it was raining, even better. There was something about the persistence of rain driving down that ordered his thoughts and helped him think more clearly. When he was at home his mind turned treacherous, seeking out thoughts of Amy, and the old familiar guilt would creep in. Could he have done more? Should he have fought harder to save his marriage? Rationally he knew the marriage had been doomed from the beginning. Amy had her problems and they were too big for either of them.

Now, walking along Ravenhill Road, his mind turned to Rose and he found himself cheered by just the thought of her.

Earlier that day she had sat poring over academic journals and studies of killing methods.

'I don't know if you're going to find the murderer in the pages of your books,' Danny had joked.

'Very funny, Danny boy. You know as well as I do

that a profile of what the perpetrator might act and look like can help. Have you any better ideas?'

He gave her a half shrug. 'The trouble with this case is that we are looking for more than one perpetrator.'

'Yeah, but one of them will have taken the lead. I think we should focus on the instigator and see where that takes us. If we identify one, the other should fall in to place.'

'What have you got so far?'

'The fact that this crime was so precisely planned and organised suggests a degree of intelligence.'

Rose leaned back on her chair with her hands behind her head and yawned. He couldn't help noticing how her hair fell in waves down her back and that it was now as long as it had been when he first knew her in Liverpool. She lifted her head up and for a second he felt that familiar tug. The one that made him fearful that he'd one day risk their friendship by making the wrong move again. Even though there were times when he felt a tension between them as electric as the air in the moments before a thunderstorm, he had the sense that it still wasn't something she wanted.

Rose looked straight at him and sighed. 'Most of the current literature focuses on identifying a killer's static traits, like ethnicity or IQ, or biomarkers, like physical illnesses or disorders. I'm more interested in behavioural and psychological development. What kind of person were they before they murdered?'

'How do we uncover one without the other?'

'All the advances in technologies and algorithms aim to provide information to help narrow down a list of suspects, without ever directly referencing the killers' specific psychoses. I think if we had a sense of what made them tick, we'd be closer to finding out who they are. But, of course, we also need to explore the Maeve Lunn angle. I really think there could be something in it.'

Danny thought of all the questions that arise when it comes to cold cases. Can old blood samples found at the scene be retested? Can modern forensics build a DNA profile? Is there any circumstantial evidence that can be seen in a new light? What more could be found within the apparently unimportant details, with the benefit of hindsight? Part of him wanted to say 'This isn't our investigation or jurisdiction and we should focus on the hanging tree case.' But what if James and the three friends did know something about Maeve's disappearance? A trip to Mistle may be a complete waste of time, but they'd only know for sure if they went.

Later in the day, he caught up with his team.

'Mal, did you look into James McCallum's text message to Lorcan Burns?' Danny asked.

Mal nodded. 'We can pretty much determine the exact location of a call when it connects with another. James' phone sent the text from the school grounds.'

'Okay, so that doesn't give us anything further to go on.'

'What about his phone records from the house?' Tania asked Mal.

'Now that was interesting. On the day before he was found dead there were two calls – one for twenty minutes and the other for fifteen minutes – to a mobile in Holywood. Both calls were from James' phone to the Holywood number.'

'That's where Ivy Duffy lives. She didn't mention the calls to us. Get her number checked out and see if the calls were definitely to her. We may need to pay her another visit,' Danny said.

CHAPTER 41

Rose parked the car and sat taking a minute to herself before facing the relentless rain. The sky was a purple bruise and the leaden clouds looked swollen, promising more rain to come. The deposits of the previous night's storm had been strewn across the road – a thin, knobbly branch and a broken blue slate lying among the last of the autumn leaves. It all looked so threatening, as if the environmental catastrophes long warned about were finally here. The day was mapped out for her. First, they would speak with the podcaster, Ryan McKeown, and then she had a meeting with human resources to look at mental health strategies for the department. Her job was certainly varied. The trip to Mistle was planned for next Tuesday.

DI Robert Conlon greeted her as she entered the station.

'Robert, how's it going?'

'Better. Definitely getting there, thanks.'

'Well you know where I am if you need me.'

She made her way to the conference room to find Danny.

'The podcaster is coming in this morning for a chat, if you want to join me?' she asked. There were rules and regulations around what she could and couldn't do alone. Interviewing, in particular, had to be treated with caution to ensure anything unearthed could be used in court.

'Sure, give me ten minutes here and I'll meet you in room seven,' he said.

Ryan McKeown looked every part of the hipster podcaster – his hair was curly and shaved at the sides so that it looked like he was wearing a woolly cap, and he sported a thick, dark wiry beard and round horn-rimmed glasses. He completed the look with a red and white striped T-shirt and tight black jeans with a pair of oxblood DM boots.

'Hey, Ryan, thanks for coming in.' Rose led Ryan and Danny into the interview room and offered their guest tea or coffee. He declined, taking a purple water bottle out of his backpack.

'No trouble at all. You said on the phone you were interested in *Little Lost Girl*?'

'Yeah, we are following up some leads on the Maeve Lunn case and came across your podcast. I suppose we were interested to know if your investigation led anywhere after the end of the podcast or if it was a total dead end.'

Ryan shook his head. 'As I said on the phone, we didn't really get anywhere. I don't know what I can say that would be of any use to you.'

'Worth having a chat all the same. Did you find the research difficult?' Rose asked.

He shrugged. 'There comes a point in every investigative story where you have the breakthrough moment – the point where the work starts to pay off – but we never got that far with the *Lost Girl* story. The podcast became more about the dead ends than the mystery itself and we eventually ran out of steam.'

'How come? Why didn't you stay on it?' Danny asked.

Rose knew he had listened to the podcast and had been surprised to find the storytelling aspect of the case compelling. The low, melodic voice in his earbuds, taking him on a journey of intrigue. It was easy to see why the podcast was so popular.

Ryan leaned forward. 'We were told to stop digging.'

'By whom?' Danny asked.

'Your lot, that's who.'

'What do you mean, "our lot"?'

'The police, or at least your Irish cousins, the Gardaí.'

Danny jerked his head. 'Really?'

'Yep, told me that the investigation was closed and that if I persisted in harassing the people of Mistle they would have to arrest me.'

'On what charge?'

'We didn't get that far. I got the message and stopped asking questions. The truth is I'd hit so many dead ends that I was almost relieved to have a reason to stop.'

Rose sat in the empty conference room later, staring at the white board of photographs and maps, a visual chronicling of the investigation. It helped to have this type of graphic illustration of the evidence, a visual depiction of every possible angle. She absorbed the images. The hanging tree, Emma McCallum and Martin Kilburn, the four friends – James, Ivy, Lorcan, and Emer – and the more recent addition of the Mistle images – little Maeve Lunn and her red bike.

Could they be wasting time travelling to Donegal? Nothing in the Gardaí notes linked James or the friends to the case. What drew the different elements of their findings together? What could James possibly have known about Maeve Lunn?

CHAPTER 42

Still with no major breakthroughs in the case, Danny's team were stagnating. He hated this sense of feeling like he wasn't doing enough. The Mistle trip was scheduled for the next day and he vacillated between thinking they'd find something there and knowing the odds were stacked against him. He had been in two minds as to whether or not to call the whole thing off.

In the meantime, the update from the animal forensics specialist was due in.

Doctor Harriet Cardwell, 'the dog woman' as Malachy referred to her, arrived with Fiona Madden. The veterinary expert was in her late forties with shoulder-length curly brown hair. She arrived with a laptop and asked to be hooked up to the white board. 'It's easier if I show you what I'm talking about rather than expecting you to follow.' She began explaining how reference databases for animal hair identification are rare.

'Pet hair is frequently found at crime scenes but is not the best source of nuclear DNA. However, because animals groom themselves, we can sometimes extract nuclear DNA profiles from shed hairs. The transfer of pet hairs to the victim or crime scene may also occur when the suspect is a pet owner and has animal hairs on his or her clothing when the contact occurs. This is referred to as a secondary transfer of trace material.'

Danny watched his team as they all studied the expert's findings.

'Fiona has indicated that there were a few hairs caught in the knot on the rope as well as a couple on the victim's clothes. Though there was not sufficient DNA in the roots for standard DNA profiling, we did find very small amounts of DNA in the hair shaft and used mitochondrial DNA testing. From this, we were able to create a partial dog DNA profile,' Harriet said.

Fiona put her elbows on the table. 'The small quantity of hairs found on the deceased could suggest two things: firstly, that the murderer did a fantastic job of cleaning up, or secondly, that it is a random sample of hair picked up through transmission, such as via a brief moment of contact with a friend or neighbour's dog.'

'So, the dog hair is of little use to us?' Danny asked.

'Not entirely,' Harriet said. 'It tells us that you're not necessarily looking for a dog owner. It also tells us that based on the hair cuticle scale pattern, type and diameter of the medulla, and the differential features, you are looking for a tan-coloured boxer.'

Something was better than nothing.

DS Gerard Kinley approached Danny's desk after the team meeting with Harriet had wrapped. 'Hey, boss.'

'What's up?'

'Ivy Duffy's alibi checked out. She was on-call on the night of the 17th in the Knockbreda Health Centre. I was going to leave it at that but then I thought it would be useful to have a list of the surgery calls she had that night.'

'Go on.'

'Well, the thing is . . . she had calls between six p.m. and ten, but there's no record of her being in the duty surgery beyond that. I took the liberty of looking at their CCTV, and I'm fairly certain it's her leaving the building at 10.05. I've sent you the file of the clip.'

Danny let out a whistle. 'Good work, Ger.'

'Unfortunately, I don't know where she was going but she definitely lied. I checked some of the surrounding CCTV at Forestside Shopping Centre and the Saintfield Road but there's no sighting of her car.'

Danny opened his email to retrieve the CCTV clip. It was grainy and dark but there was no doubt that it was Ivy Duffy pictured leaving the health centre building at 10.05 p.m. Where was she going and why had she lied?

CHAPTER 43

The sounds of revelry and music met Rose at the door of Bert's Jazz club. For once she had agreed to Friday night drinks with some of the work crowd and she'd actually taken time to blow dry her hair and apply make-up. She was also wearing a red coat she'd bought from Zara with a pair of high-heeled black boots that made her feel good.

It was busy but she spotted Tania straight away and made her way through the heaving throng of Friday night revellers to take her place at the bar next to Mal, who was waiting to order.

'Dr Lainey, what will it be? The boss is buying,' Mal shouted over the music and the conversations happening around them.

'A vodka tonic, thanks.'

'Grab a seat and I'll be right over.'

Rose turned to the table where she'd first seen Tania and caught sight of Alastair Boyne. He looked different out of the office, more relaxed and less pompous. He was regaling the team with some story from his glory days and she couldn't help smirking at the faces all drinking him in.

'There she is!' Battle greeted her with a hug as she joined their crowd. She wasn't used to his 'one of the gang' management style, but she figured it was better than having a boss who treated his team with disdain.

'Glad you made it. Hey, move round lads and give the woman a seat,' Boyne said, smiling at her. She couldn't help noticing the dimple in his right cheek, visible through the rough stubble. He gestured for her to sit next to him, even though there was very little space. She felt her arm push up against him, feeling the heat of his body through his shirt.

'What are ye drinking Dr Lainey?' he asked over the noise of crowd.

'Malachy is getting me a vodka tonic.'

She smiled at the others and joined in the conversation, scanning the crowd for Danny. It looked like he hadn't arrived yet. She chatted to DS Collette Quigley across the table about Christmas plans, which seemed far off to Rose. Those with kids were saying that you had to start shopping early and that every year it gets a harder to know what to buy. That the expense of phones and iPads was ridiculous. They'd be needing overtime to keep up with the bills.

Mal came back with her drink then and they clinked glasses.

As the night wore on, the conversation moved to work and then back to home life and they all chatted with ease. Still no sign of Danny. Soon the others were heading off to meet partners or friends, or to head home, and before she realised it Battle had managed to move her from the main group so that they were standing apart from the others in a nook, where a table with two stools had just become free.

'Shall we?' He jutted his head towards the stools and Rose felt his hand on her back as he guided her towards them.

'You're looking good, Dr Lainey,' he said, smiling at her as he sat down.

Rose could feel her cheeks flush. Battle was attractive in a smooth, older man sort of way. It was strange seeing him out of his suit. Tonight, he was wearing jeans and a Gant shirt, opened at the neck to reveal some dark chest hair.

'How do you like being back in Belfast?' he asked. He was close to her, almost shouting into her ear to be heard over the music. It felt uncomfortably close.

She hadn't told him that she had been living in London for years, but she supposed he had read her file. What else did he know about her, she wondered. She noticed Tania and Collette looking towards them and talking conspiratorially with their heads close together. No doubt they were gossiping about her and Battle. So let them, she thought, taking a sip of her vodka tonic. She wasn't doing anything wrong. Having a drink with her boss wasn't a disciplinary offence. She sat her glass down and saw Danny across the bar, talking to Tania. He looked over at her, his face stony, then turned abruptly and left.

What was his problem? Then she realised that Battle had his arm around the back of her chair, looking proprietorial.

CHAPTER 44

Danny knew he'd no right to feel put out seeing Rose and Battle together. When he left the bar, he headed up towards Dublin Road, not sure where he intended to end up. The wind battered him, and he wished he'd never bothered going out. He could have stayed in and watched a film on Netflix while downing the best part of a bottle of whiskey. Some clichés exist for a reason.

Seeing Rose snuggling up to Battle had infuriated him. She was better than that. Or at least he'd thought she was. Boyne was out of order going anywhere near her. She was his subordinate after all. He checked the time on his phone and found that it was only a quarter to nine. Just as he went to put his phone back in his pocket it rang. Rose.

'Hey, why did you leave? I was hoping to buy you a drink.' Her voice was light and intimate with a background cacophony of clinks, cheers, and music.

'Didn't fancy watching you crawling all over Boyne.' He heard the bitterness in his voice and instantly regretted it. 'Sorry. I'm being a dick. I've no right to judge you.'

'Danny boy.' She sighed. 'Wise up. Battle might have had his arm draped over the back of my chair but there's no way I'm getting involved with him. Where are you?'

'Dublin Road. Thinking of getting a taxi and heading home.'

'Well, if you can get a taxi, circle back and pick me up. We can do our usual "let's pretend we have social life" and then talk work all night.'

He smiled.

'Rose, don't cut your night short because of me.'

'Get a taxi, Stowe. I'll be waiting outside Bert's.'

By ten they were at Danny's house pouring drinks. 'This is much better. I think my days of enjoying crowded bars are in the past,' Rose said, clinking her glass against Danny's.

'Thanks for doing this,' Danny said, trying not to sound too grateful. If she hadn't called him, he'd have most likely spent the night getting shitfaced and feeling sorry for himself.

Rose shrugged. 'Always happy to leave a party early. In case you don't remember, I'm not the most sociable person.'

He laughed. There had been many occasions when she had turned down invitations, claiming she had deadlines to meet. He'd occasionally been able to persuade her to go out but more often than not they left early and spent the evening together quietly.

'This is just like old times,' he said.

'I'll drink to that.' They clinked glasses again and sat quietly, contemplating the years that had passed and how fate had brought them back into each other's company.

213

They moved from the kitchen into the living room and inevitably the conversation turned to the case.

Danny placed his glass on the arm of the chair. 'Lorcan Burns bothers me. What does he know that warranted getting a hiding?'

'You still think his attack was related to the case, then?'

'No reason for it not to. Burns was the one with the text from James McCallum. When we checked his phone records, we found he'd made calls to each of the other three over the weeks preceding the murder. They all play it cool, as if they aren't living in each other's pockets – friends but not super close – and yet . . .'

'Yeah, I know what you mean. And then there's the whole Mistle case angle. What's that all about?' Rose said, half lying back on the sofa with her glass in her hand.

'Hopefully we'll know soon enough, now that Battle has agreed that we can take a day to speak to the Gardaí in Donegal. Sure it's a long shot but it's worth checking out the locals and seeing if any of the Lunn family will talk to us.'

'From what I've read they haven't a notion what happened to the girl.'

'There has to be some reason why James McCallum was keeping up with the investigation and news on the case.'

Rose swirled the remainder of her drink in her glass, the ice clinking. 'I don't care what Mal says about his sister and true crime stories. Anyone taking such an intense interest in one particular case has to be emotionally invested. People can have morbid fascination with murder. Carl Jung even says that we need that darkness – to be complete we have to acknowledge our darkest, most demonic inclinations. We need to know what James' motivation was born out of. Everything I have learned about him from his family and friends suggests he wasn't the type of fella to get a cheap thrill out of reading about a lost child.'

Danny felt the warm glow of alcohol mixed with anticipation. 'Sounds like you think we might be getting somewhere. Hopefully the Mistle trip will be worth the trek.'

CHAPTER 45

Milltown Cemetery was a large tapestry of graves. Some had fallen into ruin, sunken-in plots with victorious weeds and remnants of long-rotted potted plants sitting at the headstones. Others were immaculate, adorned with freshly cut flowers and proclamations of love: *Our daddy, so very missed. Gone but not forgotten.*

Rose nodded in greeting as she passed an older woman tending to a grave. Someone further down the path was walking a collie, and the sound of traffic droned from the busy Falls Road. She walked past the Republican plot, which was enclosed with a low sandstone wall, complete with tricolour flags, before reaching the row where her mother was buried. She stood at the rectangle plot and wondered why she had come. It wasn't as if she believed Evelyn would know. The husk of who her mother had been was slowly rotting in the ground beneath, yet there was this compulsion to somehow honour her mother by paying her respects in this traditional way.

How Evelyn had lived knowing that at any time she could be killed for being a tout, Rose would never know. She likely never felt safe; never felt free of danger. How close had her mother come to being found out? Rose knew how their community worked. One wrong word, a sighting of Evelyn getting into a strange car, or a leak from within the security forces themselves could have seen her being taken, tortured, and ultimately murdered, left lying naked in the ditch to warn others. Rose felt a shiver of fear at the nape of her neck.

Then there was the whole other side of living with what she had done. Had she been directly involved in killing people? Rose tried to picture her mother directing covert operations; playing her part in setting up attacks. It seemed ridiculous, almost fanciful, but she knew it wasn't beyond the realm of possibility.

The recent resurgence in violence with teenagers rioting on the streets had unsettled Rose. Two Catholic families had been burned in North Belfast, their homes petrol bombed in the night. For the first time, the media had called it 'ethnic cleansing'. When Rose had been growing up that kind of thing was so common that it was almost accepted and expected. Most people kept to their own areas.

This place, with its complicated history and point scoring politicians who weren't fit for purpose, could never take peace for granted. It felt like they were always playing for time.

She'd tried to get on with her life, to put this new information about her mother in the 'family history' compartment of her brain, but gradually it had eaten away at her. Now she found her thoughts were dragged back to her childhood and the conversations she thought she'd heard, the late-night knocks at the door that took her mother away for business she couldn't imagine. It all took on a new, freshly sinister slant.

The grave still looked relatively fresh even though it had been six months. Rose's brother Pearse had organised the granite headstone inscribed with the words: *In memory of Evelyn Lavery, devoted mother and grandmother. Forever missed.*

Rose had grown up believing that her mother's assignations were in support of the IRA. There was no doubt that women like Evelyn performed an important role in the Republican movement. They certainly weren't passive in the struggle, both within the factions and on the movement's political front. Rose had resented Evelyn's clandestine activities, had hated Sean Torrent for his hold over her mother. But now, in death, Evelyn had become something else entirely. Now, Evelyn was more deadly than Rose had thought possible. Evelyn was a secret agent, working her community on behalf of the British government. That was a whole other head melt for Rose.

Rose bent down, placed the bunch of white roses she'd brought, and stood back. 'I never really knew you, Mum,' she said quietly before walking back to her car.

Back in her apartment, Rose pulled the curtains against the bleak autumn sky. The rain had been relentless recently, and a bitter cold that felt intrusive and brittle had crept in. She had a notion for the comfort of an open fire and a real sense of home. The rented apartment no longer seemed sufficient. This place was temporary and too clinical. She promised herself that when she and her siblings had sorted through the last of Evelyn's stuff and sold the Bond Street house, she would consider buying a place of her own. At least property in Belfast was more affordable than London. It was a nice thought – to be putting down roots and staking a claim in her new life.

She opened a bottle of Copeland gin and poured herself a generous measure before topping it up with tonic water. The first sip of the night was always the nicest. She lay back on the sofa and closed her eyes.

Pearse has been their mother's favourite. As a child he had been wickedly funny, quick to fight, but even quicker to say sorry and give a hug. Rose supposed her mother saw herself in him. He had so far resisted her attempts to reconnect in any meaningful way, but if she was sticking around, she wanted to try to develop some sort of relationship with him and Colm.

The annoying thing about being a psychologist was that she understood her own personality pathology too well. Her early experiences of her father's murder, the sense of her mother withdrawing from the family, coupled with a working-class upbringing in an area of Belfast marked by violence, had formed her into someone who didn't trust easily. She never wanted to rely on anyone but herself. She initially dismissed any parallels between her upbringing and her chosen career, but the older she became the more she could see a direct correlation. Rose had set out to systematically become everything she believed her mother would hate. Evelyn had never been introspective, never sought reasons as to why someone might act a certain way. Her outlook was black and white. Them and us. Or so Rose had believed. And for

Rose to now be working for the PSNI . . . well, she didn't know if it was ironic or hilarious.

She opened the freezer and lifted out some ice cubes. Poured herself another gin and tonic. A past-its-best lime sat forlornly on the counter so she sliced into it and squeezed its juice into her drink. When Rose thought back to her family home it was with a certain fear. The unspoken rules to be careful, to watch what they said, where they went. All of it now took on a new hue and Rose knew that in order to process that which had happened she needed to unearth all the facts, no matter how difficult it might prove. For some reason it made her think of James McCallum. His middle-class upbringing would have been so different to Rose's, but she knew money and the privileges it brought didn't necessarily make for happiness. When she returned to the sofa she reached for her laptop and opened her document detailing the personal life of James McCallum and typed: *what was James' relationship with his father like?*

CHAPTER 46

The thing about investigations, Danny thought, was that time was the crucial factor for a successful outcome. That was why cold cases were so hard to crack. When the heat goes out of an investigation it is near impossible to find what you need. Unfortunately, cases peter out for all sorts of reasons, such as lack of evidence or lack of due care and attention to the details. Time passes and suddenly the desire to catch the perpetrator isn't so strong. When years go by, people can take the opinion that nothing will be achieved by incarcerating an old man. That nothing will bring a dead child back to life, so what's the point in turning a person in? Danny had heard it all. Like any cold case, the Maeve Lunn investigation needed new life blown into it. Danny's enquiries with An Garda Síochána in Mistle had amounted to little but a call with Guard Cillian Leahy ahead of his and Rose's planned visit had given him some useful background information.

'The case has lain dormant for a number of years now,'

Leahy said. 'The Gardaí Review Team tried to advance the investigation a couple of years ago, but all avenues had dried up and they found nothing new of significance.'

Danny ended the call with a promise from Leahy to forward case notes.

While he wanted to re-question Lorcan Burns, Emer Ward, and Ivy Duffy and see what they had to say about their time in Mistle, they had decided to leave the questioning until after their trip to Donegal. It would be better to have all information available to them gathered in advance. Danny stood looking at the display on the conference room wall at the station. Photographs of Ivy Duffy, Emer Ward, Lorcan Burns, and James McCallum stared out at him. What had happened to make them separate? Or was it only normal to move on from some friendships as you got older? People change and grow. Danny hadn't exactly stayed in touch with his school mates. Most of them were married with kids now. A couple had emigrated to other countries. Rose was as close as he got to having a proper friend, not just a work colleague to share a pint with after a hard week.

His train of thought was halted when Rose arrived at the door.

'Hey, I've been looking for you,' she said.

'What's up?'

'You know the file you found on my mother? Do you think I could get a look at it?'

He shook his head. 'Rose, that isn't a good idea. We could both get fired. Besides, it isn't easily accessed. I don't have that kind of clearance.'

He wanted to tell her there was nothing good to come out of going down that particular dark rabbit

222

hole. If Evelyn Lavery was the informer he believed she was, then Rose wouldn't find any comfort in researching her activities.

Informers were a breed unto themselves. He knew that anyone who went down that path had to develop heightened senses. Had to accept that every encounter could be their last. Why or how Rose's mother had put herself in that position might never be answered. He knew the dead often take their secrets with them.

'Hey, put it behind you. Some things are not meant to be uncovered.' He was close enough to her to smell her scent – lemon, and a slight muskiness that reminded him of forest walks through the rain. Earthly and sensual.

'It's not that easy, Danny. We don't all have the normative family unit like you.'

He'd spoken of his family to Rose often enough over their uni years. How he felt stifled by his parent's desire to keep him at home and have him take over the farm. He knew that his parental woes where nothing compared to hers though.

'Neither of us can get hold of that file without a good reason,' he said. 'Let it go, Rose.'

She said nothing but he could tell she wasn't going to take his advice.

'Every family has secrets and troubles. Whatever your mother was involved in has died with her and that's probably for the best. Sure we've bigger fish to fry. How are you finding working on the case?' he asked.

'I'm getting there. Haven't resorted to surviving on a diet of reheated sausage rolls and doughnuts just yet, but give it time.' She checked her watch. 'Seven thirty and we're still working.'

'Murder squad waits for no one. A case like this demands long hours. Besides, I've nothing and no one to rush home to.'

'Well how about we get a takeaway tonight and be two loners together?' She smiled at him.

'Yeah, I'd like that,' he said.

CHAPTER 47

Rose showered and changed into leggings and an old, washed-out, comfy Neil Young T-shirt that she had acquired long ago from an ex-boyfriend. Danny had phoned to ask what food she wanted ordered and he was due to arrive any minute with her honey chilli beef and rice.

She would've tidied up, but in truth she spent so little time in the rented apartment overlooking Belfast Harbour that she rarely created any mess. She was, by nature, neat, preferring to go about her day making the barest impression on her surroundings. Life was messy enough without any help from her.

The doorbell chimed and she spoke into the speaker. 'Come on up.' When she opened her door, she was surprised to find Pearse standing there instead of Danny.

'Pearse, what are you doing here?' She tried to keep the surprise out of her voice.

'Thought I'd drop by. No harm in that, is there?'

'No, none at all. Come on in.'

'By the way, for a peeler your security is pretty lax. "Come on up"? Not even checking who it was?'

'Yeah, I was expecting someone else. A friend. That'll be him now,' she said as the doorbell went again.

Danny arrived with the bags of food and Rose made the introductions.

'Listen, I'm in the way. I'll head on and let youse get your dinner,' Pearse said.

'No, sit where you are. There's plenty of food and I'm not going to let the opportunity pass to find out more about Rose from an actual relative,' Danny joked. Rose frowned. Her two worlds were colliding, and she didn't know if she could handle it. She'd spent years keeping her professional and private lives separate, so Danny meeting Pearse left her unbalanced. It was a strange new terrain.

She fetched plates and cutlery and poured a glass of wine for each of them. They sat around the glass dining table.

Danny and Pearse talked football for a while and by the time Rose had had her second beer she'd relaxed a little. Maybe it wasn't so bad for Danny to meet her brother. Pearse was good company when he wanted to be. He regaled them with stories of his teenage misdemeanours – nothing too bad, but enough to make Rose regret not being around to guide him.

'Was your sister always the goody two shoes I know?' Danny asked, setting his bottle of beer on the table.

'Oh now, our Roisin, she was something else.' He looked at Rose and smiled. 'She was destined for big things; we all knew that. Just didn't expect it to be with the peelers.' They laughed but Rose knew there was some animosity behind his words.

'Nothing wrong with working for the police. Your way of thinking is a bit outdated, Pearse. The PSNI are not the RUC,' Rose argued.

He shook his head. 'Roisin, come off it. You can't tell me that institutional sectarianism doesn't exist.'

Pearse was never going to see Rose's side of things. 'Maybe you should learn to think for yourself, not rely on the old nationalist propaganda machine to tell you what to believe.'

'I'm my own man. No one tells me what to think. You're the one spouting the corporate line.'

'I don't want to argue with you Pearse. It feels too much like when we were kids.'

'No one survives childhood without a few psychological scars. Sure, isn't that what makes us who we are?'

Rose nodded. 'True. In our line of work, you see patterns. No one – or at least, very few people – is intrinsically bad. The rot usually stems from childhood. How they've been treated or mistreated.'

'And is that how you see our childhood? A wasteland of mistreatment?'

'No, that's not what I'm saying at all, Pearse. Why don't you listen instead of making your proclamations from your high horse?'

She could sense Danny's unease. He'd stopped eating and was silently watching their exchange.

Pearse leaned back on his chair. 'You know, I saw a counsellor for a while. Tried to make sure that I didn't let the past trip up my future.'

'Sounds like a sensible thing to do.' There was a hint of a sneer in Rose's voice, but she couldn't help it. Pearse had pissed her off.

'You should try it, Rosh. A bit of self-awareness would do you good—'

'So, Pearse,' Danny interjected. 'Do you fancy another beer?'

He moved the conversation on to safer territory and Rose was grateful. She didn't want to argue with Pearse, and she certainly didn't want to do it in front of Danny.

At half ten, Pearse called it a night and left Rose and Danny to it. Settled on the sofa, Rose directed the conversation back to her mother and the file.

'Why do you want to know? What good can it do?' he asked before tipping the bottle of Peroni to his mouth.

'In all the years you have known me, have I ever talked about my family?'

'Nope, definitely not. I learned back in Liverpool that that topic was out of bounds.'

'Growing up wasn't easy with my mother. She was hard on all of us but particularly me. If you had asked me a year ago what she was like, I would have said without hesitation that she was a bitch. But now . . . I don't know. Everything seems different. I had one idea of who she was and now everything has gone from black and white to colour with the flick of switch.' She hesitated. 'She was respected where we lived, yet I always sensed that people were wary of her. She seemed to command an authority that I had assumed was born out of her paramilitary involvement. It blew my mind when you told me that she had worked for the security forces. It changed everything. I feel like I owe it to her to discover who she really was, what she did, and to use that knowledge to realign how I feel about her. Does that make sense?'

'Fuck no. You're talking about digging in the past and we both know the past here wasn't a nice place to be. Rose, please, just let it go.'

CHAPTER 48

There was so much of the past that still haunted Rose. Leaving her family behind had seemed easy at the time. Now she realised that in trying to create a new life in Liverpool, she had buried any longing for Kaitlin, Pearse, and Colm as deep down as possible. She had refused to acknowledge how she truly felt. It was easier to walk away from her childhood if she didn't think about those she had left behind.

Now, parked outside Colm's house off the Andersonstown Road, she turned off the engine and considered what she would say to him. He had phoned her the night before, asking if she would stop by. He'd said he wanted to talk about the past, their childhood, the old days.

The house was a semi-detached in a cul-de-sac, the inky dark outline of Black Mountain hovering in the distance like a sleeping giant. In the orange glow of the streetlights the houses looked like something out of a film; something noir and full of secrets. She could imagine the lives lived out behind the windows as being full of the mundane with moments of high drama and tragedy laced through.

The white PVC door opened as she made her way up the driveway and Colm greeted her with a smile.

'So, you found it okay then?' he asked.

'Yeah, no trouble at all.'

His home was tidy, and she wondered if he had cleaned it especially for her arrival or if he was particular like that. She sat down on a grey leather couch and accepted the cup of coffee he offered. The smoky, peat smell of it was comforting. She wrapped her hands around the pink mug and welcomed its warmth. He lived alone, as far as Rose knew, though she didn't feel like she could enquire as to his living arrangements, sensing that he liked to keep his relationships to himself.

'It's a lovely house.' She looked around the living room, with its navy feature wall and copper light fittings. 'All very swanky.'

'I like doing up houses. This is my third.'

'Wow, look at you, you little property developer.' She laughed and he grinned at her, his eyes lighting up in the way she recalled from childhood. They made small talk for a while until Rose finished her coffee. 'So, what did you really want to see me about?'

He looked down at his hands and shrugged. 'Just feeling nostalgic like. Thinking about the old days, what it was like at home.'

'Ah,' she said. 'So you don't remember?'

'I remember . . . most of it. I just want to hear your take on it all.' He looked down at his coffee again, suddenly shy.

'There's a lot I could say. I just don't know how much of it you want to know.'

'All of it. I want to know.' He stared at her, his

expression earnest. She could see so much of the child in him up close like this, his barriers lowered, and he suddenly became her wee brother again.

They talked. Went over old ground. Their father's murder. The late-night errands that their mother would go on. The sense that their family was treated differently by those around them; that Evelyn was either feared or respected by their neighbours. Neither of them could agree on which it was. Rose filled him in on what she had learned about their mother's work for the security forces. That she had most likely been an informant.

'If what you say is true, I want to know why. What drove her to it?' Colm said.

'Yeah, no one does that without good reason. Either the security forces had something on her, something bad that could be used against her and she felt like she'd no choice, or she'd had enough of the war and wanted to play a part in ending it.'

'Which theory are you more inclined to believe?' he asked.

'That she was coerced. It's unlikely the state would intervene to save her; much more feasible that they used her. We need answers. She was known and respected within the Markets, but the hard men she worked along-side wouldn't have hesitated to put a bullet in her if they felt that she had shared information about them with the British.'

Colm smirked.

'What's so funny?' she said.

'You are, with your talk about the Brits.'

She rolled her eyes and playfully thumped him.

It was gone midnight when they were finishing up.

Rose stood and shrugged her coat on. 'You look after yourself,' she said.

'You, too. Don't be doing anything too heroic for the job.'

She kissed him on the cheek and when she was back in her car, pulling out onto the Andersonstown Road, she began to cry. She needed to know more in order to move on.

CHAPTER 49

The journey to Mistle was pleasant. They'd listened to Danny's Spotify playlist – a mixture of nineties Britpop and seventies rock bands – while talking about work, global politics, and everything in between. Rose enjoyed how they never ran out of conversation and when a lull did occur, it felt natural and comfortable.

As they approached Mistle, their talk turned to the job in hand. 'We need to suss out any backstory here that could possibly expose a link between the four students and Maeve Lunn. We've already acknowledged that there's a chance this is a wild goose chase, that James could have been affected by Maeve's disappearance only because he had been in Mistle at the time it happened, but we should still keep an open mind,' Rose said.

'Noted,' Danny replied. 'Let's see if Cillian Leahy can fill us in. The case notes didn't make any mention of the students so we can assume they weren't questioned at the time.'

Mistle was a small place used to harbouring secrets

and protecting its own, but the disappearance of a child? Now that was something else. To understand what had happened, they'd need to gain trust and to understand the people of the town. Unfortunately, Danny didn't have the time to do that. Instead, he'd told Rose he was relying on her and her intuitive way of working.

'No pressure then,' she'd joked. 'I've googled everything I can about the case, from the original reports to the more recent stuff. While there's plenty of salacious rumours and stories in the notes, none of it has ever been corroborated,' she said.

'Let's see how far we get with the Guards first.'

Their first appointment was at the Gardaí station, which was situated on the road into Mistle and looked less parochial than Rose assumed it would. She'd some notion that it would be a station house, like something out of *Ballykissangel*, that show from years ago.

When they arrived, Cillian Leahy greeted them and offered tea and coffee.

'I hope you had a good drive. The weather's behaving itself, at least. I don't want you thinking Mistle is a drab wee backwater. We like to show ourselves off in our best light, now.' His congenial face broke into a wide grin as he spoke. 'So, settle yourselves down and we can get started.'

'As I said on the phone last week, we are investigating a murder case in Belfast and our investigation has thrown up a link to the Maeve Lunn disappearance. It appears that the deceased had a particular interest in the case.'

'An interest in what way?'

'Well, files relating to the case were found encrypted on his computer. We wouldn't have necessarily thought too much of it except for the fact that the victim and his three friends were holidaying in Mistle at the time of the disappearance. They were all eighteen, had just finished their A Levels.'

Leahy whistled. 'Is that so?'

'The case notes you emailed to me didn't make any mention of the students,' Danny said.

Leahy shook his head. 'First I've heard of them, but then, I wasn't on the case at the time. I was still at the old training school down in Cork. Mick Hickens would be your man. He was the case lead at the time. Retired now, but I can put you in touch with him if you like?'

'That would be helpful. Why was the case never reopened? Did it never come up for review?' he asked Leahy.

'Listen, cold cases aren't exactly top priority round here. The usual factors – lack of evidence, limited resources, an ineffective investigation in the first place – all make opening an old cold case pretty futile. No one's going to start digging around on a case that isn't likely to throw up a good conclusion. People move on.'

'I'm sure the family hasn't moved on,' Rose interjected. She couldn't help thinking of the Mulligan case and how the family had suffered for decades, living without their mother and never having the answers they needed.

Leahy nodded. 'Aye, that's the truth.'

'Was the case ever officially closed?' Danny asked.

The Garda looked at his file. 'Yeah, in September 2009.'

CHAPTER 50

Within twenty minutes they were in the car driving out of Mistle to Dungloc, where Mick Hickens was living out his retirement. Leahy had called on ahead and Hickens had agreed to see them. His house was a pretty retirement bungalow, complete with a well-kept garden and a painted yellow rowboat sitting in the front drive.

Hickens greeted them from the doorway as they were getting out of the car. 'Come on in and I'll stick the kettle on.'

Rose got the immediate impression that he was glad of the company.

A large brown dog was sitting on the sofa as they entered the living room. 'Aye now, never mind her. Tara, down with you and let the visitors take a seat.' The dog raised her head and reluctantly ambled down.

'So I hear you're up from Belfast to check out the Lunn case?' Hickens said, handing them hot cups of dark tea.

'Yes, we are interested in knowing if four Belfast students were ever part of your investigation?' Danny said.

Hickens shook his head. 'Not that I recall.' He thought about it for a minute. 'Though there was a car with a Northern Irish registration that was mentioned. It was seen around Mistle at the time. Not that it was unusual for Northern Irish registrations to be here. We get plenty of visitors, especially in the summer months.'

'Was the car checked out?' Rose asked.

'I assume so. If I remember rightly, we went in another direction.'

'Why?'

'We'd had a tip off.'

'What kind of tip off?' Rose asked.

'It was an anonymous call to say that if we wanted to find wee Maeve, then we should take a look at Jack Mahoney since he had an interest in little girls.'

Rose remembered seeing a reference to Mahoney in the case file she had reviewed.

'On one hand, you hear something like that and your skin crawls, but when you know the individual, it's hard not to dismiss it as an employee with a grudge or a jealous neighbour, especially as Mahoney was well thought of round here. He was a bigwig from just outside Mistle town. Owned a few pubs, as well as the undertakers, and had plans to buy a plot of land and open a caravan park up at Malin Head.'

Rose nodded. 'But you took a look at him?'

'His alibi checked out. He was working in his pub at the time young Maeve disappeared. He'd forty drinkers, including my boss, Garth, standing around watching the big game.'

'So, what happened?' asked Danny.

'The strange thing was, I'd the bit between my teeth

about Mahoney at the time. I thought if he was that way inclined – a deviant, as we called them back then – then he could have had someone else snatch the girl for him. So I wasn't happy to take the word of forty drinkers, never mind if one of them was my paymaster.' He paused and made a dismissive sound, as if to say he wasn't going to bow down to authority for the sake of it.

'We asked him to come in for an informal chat. Even sent the sniffer dogs from Dublin around his farmhouse to check if they could pick up the scent from the wee girl's clothes. The boss wasn't happy about that at all. He gave me a hard time about wasting resources and harassing an innocent man, but he agreed I could question Mahoney, just to make sure that we'd covered all angles.'

He paused and leaned back into his armchair.

'The interview was straightforward. "Where were you on the day of" and that sort of thing. I'd Bridie Craig sitting in with me. She was only starting out, but I knew that she had the makings of a good Garda. Mahoney was an arrogant bastard. He sat there looking like he owned the place. It wasn't until Bridie asked him if the rumours were true that it got really interesting. "What rumours?" he said, his voice full of disdain. "The rumours that you have a penchant for children. Little girls, like Maeve," Bridie fired back.

'Now here's the thing, the colour drained out of him, but he smirked. Like he felt untouchable. It's an accusation that no sane person would want put to them and if you were to accuse an innocent man of such things, he'd soon lose his cool. But Mahoney was so sure of himself you could almost feel the smugness radiate off him. Then, just as Mahoney leaned forward in his chair, as if to say something, Fallon came in the door and terminated the interview. I can remember thinking that in all my years of interviewing suspects, Fallon had never once pulled a stunt like that. It struck me as odd.'

'Was Fallon protecting him?' Rose asked.

'It seemed like that or, I don't know, he owed Mahoney a favour or something. Either way, it didn't matter. At the end of the day, Mahoney had an airtight alibi and the dogs threw up nothing of concern so we eliminated him as a suspect.'

'What happened after that?' Rose asked.

'Mahoney went on his way and Fallon gave me a bollocking about needing to treat innocent people with respect. "You can't go around throwing false accusations at respectable businessmen," he said. I can remember thinking since when did money make you respectable round here? We're all from the same wee bog town, trying to make our way.

'Half the town wouldn't say a word to me afterwards. Some of them wouldn't even look me in the eye. It was as though they thought that if Mahoney could be pulled in for questioning, then anyone could. The same ones would have plenty to complain about if I wasn't doing my job right.'

'Where's Mahoney these days?'

'Dead. Suffered a massive heart attack a few years back. It still niggles me, you know? If you don't get a good crack at the suspect in an interview how do you ever know for sure? Alibi or no alibi.'

'And the known sex offenders in the area, were they all checked out?' Danny asked.

240

'Aye, we questioned a man called Nick Cooney. He was living in a hostel several miles away in Burton and had several witnesses to say he was watching the match, too.'

'Who made the decision to close the case?'

'That would have been my boss, Garth Fallon.'

CHAPTER 51

Ciara Lunn was recognisable from the photographs in the press. She had long hair the colour of whiskey, and the same freckled complexion as her sister. Now twenty-eight years of age, she was the driving force behind the campaign to keep the memory of Maeve alive and seek answers.

'Ciara?' Rose said as she approached the solitary young woman sitting at the table near the window of Castle Mistle Hotel. The view across the purple heather cliff gave way to the dramatic, slate-coloured Atlantic.

She turned to Rose. 'Yes. You must be Dr Lainey.' Ciara half stood to greet them and then abruptly sat again.

'And I'm Detective Inspector Danny Stowe from the PSNI,' Danny said, reaching out to shake hands with her.

'Thanks for meeting with us, Ciara,' Rose said, taking a seat. A waitress arrived and asked if she could get them anything. They ordered teas and a coffee for Danny and settled down to discuss the case.

'People think that after a while you have to move on

and just get on with your life. But you can't. My family hasn't been the same since the day Maeve went to the shop and never returned. My father died a few years after Maeve disappeared and my mummy isn't able to deal with the press intrusion or talk about it – it's too painful for her – so it falls on me to make sure Maeve is never forgotten.'

'We've been reading up on the case and it seems that there was little to go on for the Gardaí.'

'So they say. From day one we had our suspicions that the case wasn't being given the necessary resources. It was as though they didn't want to find Maeve. Local people turned out in droves to search for her, but more often than not, the searches were badly organised, and nothing came of them. Looking back, we can see that evidence was possibly even destroyed or damaged by those trying to help.'

Rose could hear the bitterness in the tone of her voice and see the pain in the hunched set of her shoulders. Talking about Maeve clearly wasn't easy for her, but it was necessary.

'We need to know what happened. An inquest would give us some sense of closure. It would help us to have a new view of the events leading up to her disappearance. Someone, somewhere, knows something. Mistle is a small town and secrets can't stay hidden forever. My family have endured years of wondering what happened to our Maeve, the bright, sunny girl who everyone loved.' She smiled at the memory of her sister, her eyes brightening slightly for a moment.

'Can you tell us about the day she disappeared?' Danny asked.

She sat back into the chair, took a deep breath, and began. 'The day she went missing she was wearing her favourite outfit – dungarees and her Clark's sandals. I can still see her, rushing out the door, delighted to be going to get sweeties. The Gaelic football match was a big deal and the whole town was jubilant watching one of our own do well. It felt like a special day.' She shook her head sadly and her eyes filled with tears.

'I'm so sorry,' Rose said.

'Maeve was a great wee girl. The apple of my daddy's eye and Mummy's pet. We all doted on her. Over the years we have all asked: why Maeve? Why was she taken? What if we hadn't sent her to the shop? Our father went to his grave never knowing what had happened to her. The pain of it killed him. Anyone who knows our family, knows we have never given up hope of finding her and that we will all continue fighting for answers. We owe it to Maeve.'

Rose wondered how it would feel to have your child taken from you. To have no sense of what had become of her. Motherhood was something Rose had deliberately avoided, refused to even consider. It was firmly in the realm of things not for her. Yet now, with this cataclysmic shift in who she knew her mother to be, her relationship with her own mother no longer defined or limited Rose. And for the first time, she thought that her future did not necessarily have to be childless.

Ciara reached into her handbag and found a tissue. She wiped her eyes and blew her nose.

'I've written to politicians, the minister for justice, the chief of the Gardaí, and all in vain. You'd think the disappearance of a little girl would be top of everyone's agenda but apparently not. We're meant to live with no answers. To accept that she won't come back.' She shifted in her seat, lengthening her back, as if eager to take on the system that had failed to find them answers.

'Maeve doesn't matter to any of them. They say she's gone and that's the end of it. How would they feel if it was their sister or daughter?'

'Early on in the investigation the Gardaí questioned a man called Nick Cooney,' Rose said.

'Yes, they did. They even arrested him. Apparently he was known to the Guards as a sex offender who had moved from another part of the country. There had been talk that he had been seen about the town, but it later turned out that he was living in a hostel several miles away, in Burton, and had several witnesses to say he was watching the match, same as every other man in the town that day.

'There've been organised searches of the farmlands around the area, but some of it's bogland and it's nearly impossible to do it properly without specialist equipment. We keep thinking if only we could find her, we could at least bury her with our daddy. That would ease some of the pain.'

Rose could understand the need for a proper burial. A Catholic upbringing ingrained certain things and the pressing desire to have the dignity and respect of a sacred burial was one of them. The family would gain a semblance of peace in finding the child and burying her, though Rose knew it would just leave them with a different sort of pain.

When Ciara was talking about her sister, she seemed older than her years. From Rose's research, she knew

Ciara had been vocal about her sister's disappearance, calling out politicians and the Gardaí commissioner for their lack of compassion and inability to do more, ensuring that the case wasn't forgotten. The tireless campaign had obviously taken its toll on her.

'We refuse to allow the passing of time to diminish her memory. Somebody out there knows what happened to Maeve.'

Rose thought about Maeve. She had been only eight years old. The age when many children made their first holy communion, a rite of passage. Rose could remember the day she had made hers. The dress with stiff net lace that itched and prickled her skin, the plastic comb of the veil biting in at her scalp. Unusually, Evelyn had made a fuss of her, making sure that her hair was styled and that the dress sat perfectly. At the time she had batted her mother's fussing hands away, wanting the spectacle of the day to be over, but looking back now, she was glad to have the memory. Not every interaction with her mother was about being locked in dispute. Arguing and posturing. Funny how she had manipulated their shared history to paint Evelyn as a consistently contrary, difficult woman. Memory of traumatic events could so easily be distorted, tinting everything, she mused. It was clear now that her bias against Evelyn had amplified certain events and feelings from her past.

'Ciara, there was a car with Northern Irish number plates seen in Mistle around the time Maeve went missing. Did the Guards ever mention that to you?' Danny asked.

'Yes, we heard about the car, but I think it was ruled out as holiday makers staying up near the cliff walk. Northern number plates aren't unusual around here, especially in the summer months.' Strands of her red hair fell across her face and she tucked them behind her ear.

Rose leaned forward and set her teacup on the table. 'Maeve, do you know a man called James McCallum?'

She shook her head. 'No, I've never heard of him. Why?'

'It's part of another investigation so we aren't at liberty to say at this point,' Danny interjected.

'We just wanted to check if the name was familiar.'

Ciara nodded. 'If there's some sort of connection to Maeve you'd tell me, right?'

Rose nodded. 'Of course. We need to do some digging but if anything concrete comes out of it, we will keep you informed.'

CHAPTER 52

The coast road provided them with breathtaking scenery. The Atlantic was grey and stormy, with gigantic waves crashing against rocks, creating a spray of foam that reached out to the pale gold sand. The stretch of coastline they were driving along took in Bundoran and Mullaghmore Head, renowned for drawing surfers. Danny could see the attraction of buying an isolated bolthole in this part of the world, and hunkering down for the winter months with only the call of the seagulls overhead for company. Jesus, he was getting wildly romantic in his old age. Next he'd be smoking a pipe and wearing an Aran cardigan. Acquiring a dog.

They planned on going to see the Burns' holiday home. They didn't necessarily expect to find anything of interest, but since they were in the vicinity, it seemed worth having a look. They followed the SatNav directions until they came to a narrow road and there before them was the Burns house. It would have looked modern back in the nineties. The property boom had seen second homes being built by northerners, tempted by the relatively cheap land. The original cottage had been modified to an architect's vision of avantgarde. Now though, it looked tired and dated. It was a Swiss chalet-style design, all wood apart from a triangular expanse of glass looking out onto the sea, and had the cold, weary look of a house not lived in and locked up for the winter months.

Danny walked around the outside of the house, peering through the windows, while Rose checked the outbuildings. They consisted of little more than a run-down croft and a stable that had most likely been the original house on the site. Planning had ruled that new homes could only be built on land with pre-existing abodes.

Through greasy, rain-smeared windows, Danny could see the house was furnished simply – a three-seater sofa and a dining table with an assortment of chairs around it. A pile of board games sat in the corner of the living room, and a telescope stood on a tripod stand in the bay window, pointing towards the coastline. It was a quiet spot with no other houses close by. A perfect retreat.

Danny could feel the springy and dry heather underfoot, covering the moist clay beneath, as he walked across the field towards Rose. The wind whipped around him and he pulled up the collar of his jacket against the cold. The original croft house was reduced to rubble on one side with the partial south-facing wall standing around six foot. A small slit where the window would have been remained. The footprint of the small house was still clear among the undergrowth, but the remains of the interior layout had been eradicated by nature and time.

Danny put his hand to the carving on the plinth above the doorway. 'Where have I seen that before?'

'That's an old Celtic symbol. Probably wards off evil or something,' Rose said.

He peered at the carving in the stone, tracing the outline with his fingertip.

Rose called out as he went to step inside. 'Watch your step there. I think that might be an old potato pit.'

Danny cautiously pressed his foot against the remains of a rotting wooden door in the floor. Dandelions had sprouted up through the cracks, their long stems waving in the wind.

'How do you know about potato pits?'

'We learned about them in school when we studied the famine. It's an underground chamber – usually about seven-feet deep and covered with straw and clay – used to store potatoes during winter to preserve them. Every house probably had one back in the old days.'

Danny pulled at the remaining rotted wood and peered into the deep, black darkness of the cavity below.

He turned to Rose. 'You don't suppose . . .?'

'What, that Maeve's remains are down there?'

He shrugged. 'You never know.'

'Nah, that would be too easy. But if you need to be sure, away you go. I'll hold the torch.'

Danny lowered himself into the hole. It had a mouldy, starchy smell that he assumed came from the storage of the potatoes long ago. It was darker than dark. His phone's torch light seemed to be sucked into the blackness. The sudden, unwelcome thought of being trapped down there made him shudder. He felt something crawl on his neck and slapped it away. Rose was right, it was stupid to think that Maeve would be found here after all this time. He reversed his course and the stark coldness hit him like an assault as he climbed back out of the pit.

'Claustrophobic down there. It's not pleasant,' he said, dusting a trail of cobwebs and dirt from his clothes. They continued trampling around the croft remains until they were satisfied that there was nothing more to see, and then headed back to the car.

Danny thought about the four friends, fresh out of school, still thinking the world owed them everything. The arrogance and privilege of youth. Nowadays, they'd be heading off to Ibiza or Magaluf for a fortnight of debauchery and sun. He'd never had the luxury of a holiday like that. His father had too much for him to do on the farm. Summer holidays meant hard graft.

James, Emer, Ivy, and Lorcan were from a different background – one of self-entitlement and money. What had they really got up to that summer? Was it as innocent as it appeared?

CHAPTER 53

They climbed around the boulders set into the landscape and jumped over soggy parts of emerald moss-covered ground. Suddenly, Danny stopped dead in his tracks.

'Shit. Rose, look.'

She turned to see where Danny was pointing.

'What is it? You look like you've seen a ghost.'

Her gaze followed the direction of Danny's pointing finger towards a boulder, where she saw the same old Celtic symbol as the one on the croft house.

'James McCallum. That's where I've seen that symbol before! He had that symbol tattooed on his body.' He took out his phone and found the photograph he'd taken of McCallum's tattoo in the mortuary.

'From what we've learned about James McCallum, he didn't strike me as the sort to get a tattoo on a whim. It would have to have some significance.'

'What do you think this place is?'

'I'd say it's an old crypt. A burial place from years ago.'

The crypt, if that's what it was, was overgrown with

ivy and thistles and part of it had sunk into the bog land. They moved carefully into the gaping mouth of what appeared to be a shallow cave, and Danny illuminated the interior using the torch on his phone. Nature had reclaimed it. It was damp and full of flora fighting against the dank darkness to thrive. Some sort of mulch smell of putrid bracken rose up as their feet tried to gain purchase on the damp floor.

'We can't go any further in. It's too dangerous. This whole structure could collapse. We'll go back up to the town and ask around. See what the locals know about this place,' Danny said. Rose could sense he was frustrated not to be able to get stuck in and order his own search. But this wasn't their case, nor their jurisdiction.

'We can also grab some lunch.'

'Sure, I'm starving,' he answered, reluctantly stepping out of the crypt.

Within half an hour they settled into seats near an open turf fire and looked at a menu that appeared to be designed for tourists. It had enough braised cabbage, ham hock, and potatoes to suggest the 'authentic Irish culinary experience', a dish more suited to the American idea of what Irish people ate.

The friendly waitress looked like she had barely left school and was practising her best flirty smile on Danny.

'What can I get you?' she asked.

'Still deciding,' Danny said. 'Out of curiosity, do you happen to know anything about an old crypt up by Cionn Road?'

'No, but Henry Beck will know. He's the local historian. You'll find him up at the crossroads. The big white house. You can't miss it. He's been campaigning to save the old crypts. Bit of an old relic himself, but don't tell him I said that, mind.' She smiled again.

After they had eaten, they made their way up to the historian's house. As promised, it wasn't hard to find.

The house sat built into the cliff wall and they caught sight of the view behind the house, of the Atlantic sparkling in the weak, late autumn sunlight, as they were walking up the driveway.

'Wow, that's some view,' Danny said as he pressed the doorbell.

The door was opened by a distinguished man in his seventies. 'Hello, can I help you?'

Danny did the introductions. 'We were wondering if you could tell us about an old crypt we found up by Cionn Road? The waitress in the pub said you were the one to ask.'

'Oh, that'll be the Bonar family crypt. Must be over three hundred years old.'

Henry welcomed them into his home. The back of the house overlooked the ocean and they could see for miles.

'There are a few old crypts around these parts. Back in the old days the bodies were mummified – some of the old boy nationalists would have been preserved in that way too – and many of the tombs had secrets concealed within the walls. Hidden messages left for others to decipher.'

Danny opened his phone and found the photograph of the tattoo on James McCallum's hip. 'We found this symbol carved into one of the boulders near the crypt. Any idea what it means?'

The man looked at the image and nodded.

'The symbol itself is the Triskele. It reflects the Celtic belief that everything comes in threes. The physical realm, the spiritual one of ancestors, and the celestial world of the sun, the moon, and the stars.'

'And the words?'

Henry peered at the photograph. '*Taw bro-in orr-um* – I'm not much of a Gaelic scholar but I know that it means "brother in Christ", or "brother-in-arms". Some sort of declaration of companionship in this world and the next, I would say.'

Danny jotted it down in his notebook.

'I've been fighting to save that burial site. There are many small, furtive burial grounds scattered across the landscape so to have an actual crypt dating back hundreds of years is worth preserving. Of course, the developer who hopes to build a hotel on the Cionn Road doesn't see the damage to our collective history.'

'The site is going to be built upon?'

'Yes, but first they were going to dig up the crypt. Remove it all together.'

Danny looked at Rose. 'That's interesting. Thanks, Henry, you've been a great help.'

CHAPTER 54

Rhea McCallum was entering her house when Danny and Rose pulled up outside. She turned as soon as she heard the engine and Danny could see the annoyance in her features as she recognised them. Broomhill was a wealthy area in South Belfast. The houses were all large, older houses, some built in the Arts and Craft style with good-sized gardens. It was a ten-minute walk from her son's architecture practice and twenty minutes to Osbourne House Grammar.

She placed her canvas shopping bag down in the hallway and turned to them as they walked up the path to her front door.

'Detective, has there been a discovery? Some news on my son's murder?'

Danny glanced at Rose. 'Mrs McCallum, we apologise for the intrusion. We don't have anything new to tell you but we do need to speak to you again.'

The woman sighed and made to lift her bag of shopping, but Danny swooped in and carried it for her. 'Here, let me.'

Her hair was glossy and coiffured, as if she had recently had it styled, and she was wearing a smart trench coat. Despite her outward appearance, there was a sense of despondency in the way she carried herself. It was visible in the slope of her shoulders and the slow gait.

Her heels clicked along the wooden floor of the hallway as she followed Danny into the kitchen. 'I've been running low and thought it was time I left the house,' she said as she began unpacking the provisions of bread, milk, cold meats, and a bag of lettuce. 'My daughter, Jenna, is calling round and if the cupboards are empty, she'll start on me. I'm expected to carry on as normal. Cook meals and keep the house tidy. None of it seems right.' She looked visibly frailer than the last time they had visited her, as if the recent events had aged her overnight.

Rose shook her head. 'This can't be easy for you and we apologise for the intrusion, but it would be helpful if you could answer some further questions.'

Rhea sighed again and led them through to the living room. The curtains were open this time and the room had been tidied. A pile of books, with a Boden catalogue placed on top, sat in a neat stack on the coffee table, which gleamed as if it had recently been polished. The scent of lavender and beeswax still hung in the air and someone had set the fire ready to be lit.

'What is it this time? I don't think there is anything more I can tell you,' she said as she sat on the wing-backed armchair in the bay with her hands clasped on her lap.

Danny sat and leaned forward. 'Mrs McCallum, what was James like as a teenager? Did he ever get into any trouble? Hang around with the wrong crowd?'

'God, no. James never gave us a day's trouble in his life. He didn't go through a rebellious stage of staying out late or drinking and smoking. He definitely never did drugs.'

'Ah, good. Good lad. When he did his exams, did he head off interrailing or on any mad holidays to Greece or the like?'

She shook her head. 'No. He was always studious, and he worked hard for his A Levels. Jenna, now, she was a different story. She was more likely to get into trouble than James.'

'You confirmed previously that James went on holiday with some school friends to Mistle in Donegal after his A Level exams. Is that right?' Danny asked, for the sake of the recording device.

She hesitated. It was just a beat, but it was evident. 'Yes, he did. One of his friends – Lorcan, I think it was – his family had a holiday home in Donegal. In fact, when he said he was going away for the week to Donegal with his friends we were pleased. He was a serious boy and we thought it would do him good to have some fun.'

'When he came back from Mistle did you notice anything different about James? Was he quiet, or withdrawn, or acting up?' Rose asked.

Rhea McCallum reeled slightly, looking from one to the other. 'James' grandfather had a heart attack while James was away in Donegal. I thought it was best to not tell James until he was home. What good could it do to upset him? My father was in hospital waiting on surgery, and the day James was due to come home, he had another heart attack and died. When James came back, we were in the throes of grief and he took the loss hard. It was a difficult time for us.' She pursed her lips in a tight line and sniffed.

'I'm sorry to hear that,' Danny said.

'His office isn't far from here. He used to pop in for lunch and check up on his old mum. That's the kind of good son he was.' Her eyes filled with tears and Danny noticed her hands were trembling.

'After the A Level results, James went to Queen's University, isn't that right?' Danny asked.

'Yes, James did very well in his exams. All A grades and he went on to do his degree.' She lifted her head as she spoke, clearly proud of her son's achievements.

'Your daughter-in-law mentioned that your husband died last year, and that James had been deeply affected by his loss,' Rose said.

Something flickered in the woman's eyes. 'Yes, James was very close to his father.' Again, that defiant jut of the chin. 'It's only to be expected that James was upset. James loved his father very much.'

She swallowed, as if willing herself not to cry again. 'Now, if there isn't anything else, I'd like to get on with my day. Jenna will be here soon and I was planning on making her some lunch. I don't see what all these questions about James have to do with finding out who killed him.'

CHAPTER 55

Rose got out of her car and zipped her Barbour jacket, all the way up to her chin, against the biting chill. She'd forgotten how cold Belfast could get. How the wind could cut right through you and make you long for a warm bath and a hot whiskey for company. But a bath would have to wait. Right now, she wanted to speak to Emma McCallum. Danny had suggested the meeting take place without him in the hope that she would open up more if it was just Rose asking the questions. The time would come for formal interviews when they had more to go on.

The McCallum house looked stark where it sat amongst the autumnal landscape. The bank of silver birch trees had lost most of their leaves, and in the fading early evening light their branches looked eerily like bones. Rose rang the doorbell and waited. A moment later, Emma McCallum opened the door dressed in leggings and a sweatshirt. Her hair was pulled back into a pony-tail and she looked like she had just finished a workout. A light sheen of perspiration coated her skin.

'What do you want?' There was no animosity in her voice, just a weariness.

'Can I come in?' Rose asked. She made sure her tone was conciliatory, since the aim was to build a rapport with Emma. Danny was brilliant in intense interview situations but Rose recognised that not every suspect or person they questioned needed to be handled in that way. This was a place where Rose could be of real value.

Emma didn't move from the doorway and took a long drink from her water bottle. 'You can't have more questions. I've told you everything.'

'I think there's more that you want to say.' Rose had the impression that Emma had held back when they first met. There was something in the way she'd held herself – contained and rigid, even in her grief – that suggested she was withholding information.

Rose waited a second before saying, 'Emma, I think you lied when you said you didn't know what troubled James and I think you need to talk about it.'

Emma stared at Rose before sighing and standing back. 'You better come in then.'

They walked into the kitchen and Rose was struck by how isolated the house seemed in the dusk. The wall of glass reflected her image back at her and beyond it she could see the outline of the skeletal trees and the swing-set. There was no sign of Grace or Emma's mother.

'All alone this evening?' Rose said.

'Grace is at a friend's house for tea. I'm picking her up at seven.'

Rose sat on the chair beside the island. 'Emma, James knew about your relationship with Martin, didn't he?'

'I've told you. Martin and I are friends – good friends – but nothing more.'

'Then why did you open a separate bank account in June?'

'Excuse me? It's none of your business what I do with my money.' Her eyes had a flicker of anger in them. Good. Rose wanted to rattle her, to push her. Emma McCallum was too controlled, too calm for Rose's liking. She appeared to be resigned to the loss of her husband, but her acceptance felt too soon, as if his death had been a shock but not devastating.

'If you had been straight with us from the beginning, we wouldn't have had to go digging through your business, as you put it. Your husband has been murdered and someone has gone to great trouble to make it look like a suicide. Until we find out who did it and why, your business is my business.'

Emma sighed.

'I wanted to manage my own income, okay? It's not a crime, is it?'

'That's perfectly reasonable, but you have to admit it seems suspicious when you consider the timing. Why, after having had a joint account for years, did you feel the need to make separate arrangements now?'

'I knew that James wasn't well, that his head wasn't in the right place, and I worried that his business would suffer. To protect myself and Grace I wanted to have complete control over my own money.'

'So, James had been struggling? You suggested that he was emotionally absent from the marriage at times, that he appeared distracted. If it was something more than that why not tell us?'

'I didn't know for sure. James could be a closed book at times. There didn't seem to be any point in making him out to be some kind of head case.' Her eyes skated away from Rose. 'I didn't lie, I just didn't tell you the whole truth. As for the bank account, well, I was future-proofing my finances, that's all.'

'Did he know you intended to leave him?'

Emma looked straight at Rose. 'What does it matter now?'

'In order to understand the circumstances around James' death we need to have insight into of all aspects of his life.'

'Look, it isn't easy to break up a marriage. It isn't something I would have done lightly. I would have waited for the right time.'

'You were going to lend Martin Kilburn money for his property venture, weren't you?'

Her eyes flitted to the floor. A brief second of uncertainty breaking through the in-control façade.

'Listen, I don't know why any of this has to be raked over now. Yes, Martin and I were talking about building a life together. I don't care if you believe me, but I've never been unfaithful to James, not physically, anyway. Martin and I . . . well . . .' She broke off, as if needing a moment to find the right words. 'Martin and I, we were together years ago. Long before I ever met James.'

'Did James know?'

'Yeah. We even laughed about it when I realised that Martin was his business partner. It was a bit awkward the first few times we all got together but gradually it was just one of those things. A past love that meant nothing in the present.'

'So what changed?'

She dragged her hair out of the ponytail and sighed. 'Life changed. Things with James were boring, and safe, and predictable. Martin made me feel young and attractive again.'

Rose couldn't imagine a time when Emma McCallum didn't feel attractive.

'When you have a child, you lose your identity. A bit of undivided attention is nice once in a while. Martin did that for me. Then, without even realising it had been happening, I was in love with him all over again.'

She stood up and walked over to the oversized American fridge to get some more water. 'I made it clear that I didn't want an affair. If Martin felt the same way about me then we would do it properly. I was going to tell James after Christmas.'

Rose watched as Emma stared out at the garden, now blanketed in darkness.

'James was a good father. So, while things weren't exactly perfect, I knew that, for Grace at least, we were better as a family unit. But after a while that wasn't enough for me.'

Rose considered that for a moment. She understood how Danny had struggled with the break-up of his marriage. She was annoyed with herself for not being as supportive as she could have been. It was always difficult with him – never knowing how far to push the friendship, when to offer a shoulder to cry on.

'Did James ever talk to you about Mistle, a town in Donegal he visited after his A Levels?'

'No, can't say he did.'

'Do you remember where you went after your A Levels?'

'Yeah, I went interrailing round Europe. Six weeks of hostels and trains. It seemed fun at the time.'

'Did you talk to James about it?'

'Yeah, of course I did.'

'And you don't think it strange that he never mentioned his own end-of-school holiday? The big celebration you spend your days dreaming about, thinking the end of the school term will never come.'

She raised her eyebrow. 'I don't understand. What are you getting at?'

'James' computer had files relating to the disappearance of an eight-year-old girl in Mistle during the same summer that he was there. Her name was Maeve Lunn. Have you ever heard James talk about her?'

'No, why would he? We don't know her.' She looked puzzled and then exasperated. 'I really don't get this.'

Rose could see the concern in the creases of Emma's forehead. The strain of the last few weeks was starting to show.

'Do you know why he would have encrypted files about the case on his computer?' Rose asked.

Emma shook her head. 'I don't know. That's not something James would have an interest in.'

'James researched the case extensively. He had saved files of newspaper reports and Facebook posts by Maeve's family.'

'No, you've got it wrong. James wouldn't have anything to do with that.' She looked down at her hands. The nail polish was chipped on one finger and she worried at it. For the first time, she seemed truly spooked.

 Rose paused for a moment. 'Emma, we have been looking at the possibility that James had something to do with Maeve's disappearance.'

Emma's eyes widened. She shook her head.

'No, that makes no sense at all.'

CHAPTER 56

The light was bleeding out of the day and no further progress had been made. The case room, located on the first floor with large windows looking out over the car park, was quiet for a change. The mood was subdued. Danny knew that he needed something to shake up his team, to take the investigation to the next level. He felt the old familiar sense of something being just beyond his grasp. Some entity, unknown as of yet, that would connect what had happened at Mistle to the current case. Maybe bouncing a few ideas around with the team would help clarify his thinking and spark that breakthrough moment they were chasing.

'Listen up, troops,' he called. 'We are on day nine of this murder investigation. I want everyone gathered here tomorrow morning, first thing, to appraise our findings to date and to plan what we do next. You have tonight to dream up some new initiatives and to look for angles not previously covered.'

A general murmur of 'Right, sir' rippled round the

room. Danny wasn't one to pull rank and give out to his team, but they needed leadership and it was down to him to make sure everyone stayed motivated.

Danny was about to call it a day when Malachy Magee sauntered over and pulled up a chair.

'Hey, boss. Can I have a word?'

'Sure. What is it?'

'I've something for you that's going to perk your pecker right up.'

'Magee, the day you perk up my pecker I'm out of here. What have you got? Hit me with it.'

'The car you got me to look into. The one seen in Mistle around the time of the Lunn disappearance?'

'Yeah, what have you found?'

'Well, according to log notes from the Gardaí back in 2001, the witness, Ellen McKay, said she saw a dark blue car with a Northern Ireland registration. She said she thought it was BFZ something but she couldn't be sure.'

'Go on.'

'Well I ran it through the system and found a navy Vauxhall Astra registered to an Arnold Burns. So, I wondered, could he be related to Lorcan Burns, and lo and behold, he's Lorcan's father. The logbook says it was sold on the 28th of August, 2001. Bit suspicious, isn't it?'

'Fuck. Why did they sell it so soon after staying in Mistle?'

'Don't know but it's definitely worth looking into.'

'See what you can find on Arnold Burns and hopefully we'll have something to take to Battle. In the meantime, I'll have another dig through the Lunn case files and see if there's any further mention of the car.'

Danny did what he used to do when they were given an assignment at university that he'd no clue how to make sense of – he went to find Rose.

'Fancy working late?' he asked as he walked into her new office.

'Do I have a choice?'

'There's always a choice, Lainey.'

Rose shook her head and laughed. 'As if. I know that look when I see it. You've a lead or an idea that you want fleshed out and I'm your sounding board.'

'How well you know me! Come on, I'll buy you dinner. Pizza with all the trimmings. I might even throw in some dough balls.'

'How can I say no?'

Danny filled her in on the information about the sale of the car registered to Arnold Burns. They spent some time considering the angles, trying to find a supposition that could hold.

'Talk me through your theory again,' Danny said. 'If we're to get Boyne on board we need to have the proposition watertight.'

The remaining light outside had dwindled as they worked and now all that could be seen out of the high rectangle slot of a window was the dark, inky sky.

'James, Ivy, Lorcan, and Emer were staying in the holiday home in Mistle in August 2001, at the time of Maeve Lunn's disappearance. So, we are hypothesising that the friends were in some way involved in the child's disappearance.'

'All circumstantial and pretty thin on the ground there, Rosie. We need something more substantial than proximity. There's no physical evidence, no witnesses. Nothing of true worth to bring to Battle of the Boyne. Not yet, anyway. We need to keep digging, Rose.' He looked at the boxes of files sent from the An Garda Síochána. All the reports from the Mistle case were contained within and they needed to go through them, line by line, to find something that would give them a solid connection to James McCallum and his friends.

'Let's keep going until we crack this thing. There has to be something in these boxes that points us in the right direction.'

An hour later, they had eaten pizza and washed it down with Diet Cokes from the vending machine. Danny was reading a witness statement provided by a Mistle publican when he felt the first kick of something stirring. 'Rose, listen to this: "A racing green Jag type car was reported to have been seen in Mistle around the time of Maeve's disappearance." Ivan O'Reilly, the publican from the Kildowney Street, was the one who gave a statement citing the car. He said he had taken note of the registration plates, thinking if anything went missing, he could point the Guards in the direction of the traveller site situated outside the town. The green Jag had a Northern Irish number plate of MRZ 3882. This would mean the car was relatively new at that point. He said he recognised it as a Northern Ireland registration because their number plates have black characters on a white background at the front of the car, and a yellow background on the rear plates.'

'Hang on a minute,' Rose said with urgency. 'The car belonging to Lorcan Burns was dark blue. Your witness statement says the car he saw was green. Did anyone consider that there may have been two cars with Northern Ireland number plates seen on the Kildowney Road right around the time Maeve disappeared?'

'Yeah, it's possible all right.'

'Look, the other witness Ellen McKay, she said she saw a blue car with Northern Irish number plates and the R sticker indicating the driver had recently passed their driving test, parked outside the Burns holiday home. This is the car we assumed the friends had driven to Donegal in, but the pub owner, Ivan O'Reilly, claimed he saw a dark green car with the northern plates.'

'What if the Garda had assumed that there was only one car with Northern Irish reg plates? They never investigated the second car reported by O'Reilly. Who owned the green car seen near the holiday home, after Maeve went missing?'

CHAPTER 57

The buzz in the office had reached fever pitch. Pressure from above ACC Boyne had forced them into holding a press conference even though they were reluctant to release any new information. Rose and Danny had watched from the side-lines as Battle delivered the prepared statement, ending with, 'James McCallum was a much loved husband, father, and son. We will not rest until we find who has killed him.'

'Do you get the impression that Battle loves the cameras?' Danny whispered out of the side of his mouth to Rose. She nodded as the journalists clamoured to ask questions.

'Looks like he has styled his hair for the occasion too.' She smirked.

Boyne had agreed that it was vital to keep the link to Mistle out of the media as there was no point stirring up false hopes of finding the girl after all this time.

When the press conference had wrapped, Rose returned

to the main office. She saw she had a missed call from one of her HR colleagues, Pedar, who was looking to book a meeting with her. They had been working on rolling out a training programme designed to help officers understand the importance of language and different communication styles. Rose enjoyed using her psychology skills and knowledge to enact this kind of change for the better.

Not for the first time, she thought of how policing had to be one of the hardest jobs to do. They saw the worst of humanity up close and were expected to deal with horrific scenes on a regular basis. The complex history and community distrust the PSNI faced on a daily basis certainly made it even more difficult. Her mind flitted to Danny. While she knew he'd never appreciate talking to her in a professional capacity, she also knew him well enough to sense that something other than the case was bothering him. The wise cracks and the smile had been absent lately.

Later, with a cup of coffee in both hands, Rose sought him out. 'Hey, you know if anything's bothering you, you can talk to me, right?' She sat the cup on his desk, sitting on the spare chair next to him.

Danny looked away. An unconscious reaction to avoid her reading his face. She could tell he was stilling himself, trying not to give in to the wave of emotion that appeared to have crashed against him.

Eventually, he shook his head and gave her a weak smile. 'There's nothing to talk about.'

'We both know that's not true. You can't expect to let go of the past if you don't deal with it.'

'Dr Lainey, is it now? And here's me thinking you were just my friend bringing me a cup of coffee. Am I expected to lie down on a couch and pour my heart out? In case you hadn't noticed, we're in the murky depths of this here case.'

'The problem is, Danny, there's always going to be a case on the go. Always a pressing job that has to be done. Sometimes we have to put the work aside and take a minute to think of ourselves. Consider what we need to do to work better, be more effective, and to stay sane in this crazy profession we've found ourselves in.'

'Oh spare me the psychology shite, Rose.'

'Don't be a dick, Danny. I am your friend but if you want me to give you my professional opinion, then I will. You can't shore up anger and hurt without it causing you damage in the long run.'

'Well thanks for that, Dr Lainey. I'll be sure to take your professional opinion into consideration.'

'Suit yourself. I'm here if you need me but I won't be your punch bag.'

She felt like heading to her office in the basement. At least there she could have some peace and quiet.

Danny could be bloody pig-headed at times. She didn't deserve to be spoken to like that. She was only trying to help him.

If he wanted to wallow in his misery, then she would let him. She'd watched from the side-lines as he had beat himself up about his failed marriage. Seen how he had been full of recriminations and regret. If he drank a bit too much or felt remorse about something to do with work the conversation always came back to Amy. If he wasn't over her, then Rose didn't want to know.

Sometimes you have to go back, to try to work out that which was wrong in the beginning to understand why it was no more.

It was near the end of the day when Danny turned up at her office door.

'Sorry about earlier, Rose. I don't like feeling as though you're treating me like one of your head cases.'

He came in and sat on the small sofa.

'I was only trying to help but I get it; we've too much history for me to be analysing you in a professional capacity. I can recommend someone else if you think it would help to talk to someone.' She spoke gently, unsure if he would throw her suggestion in her face and storm off.

'Nah. It's not for me, all that talking about your feelings. I'd rather move on and not look back.'

'Ah, but that's your problem isn't it? You can't move on from Amy, can you?'

He sighed and put his head back against the wall. 'Okay, so tell me what I need to do.'

'Forgive her. Forgiveness allows you to correct the distortions in your relationship and to work through the pain and hurt to find a new meaning. It might make you see that there is something worth fighting for underneath all of the resentment.' She spoke softly, careful of his bruised heart.

'But how in hell's name do I do that?'

'It requires you letting go of past resentments so that you can reframe them in the present. Even if you do not feel like forgiving Amy, you can enact the process of forgiving to release you from the hold of the past and allow you to experience your relationship in a new way. Fake it until you make it. Forgiveness enables you to step outside of the hurt, where concepts from the past dominate, by eliminating fear and anxiety, weakness and vulnerability.'

'Fuck. You're sounding like a shrink again. Not my mate.' He rubbed at the back of his neck.

'Can I not be both?'

They both fell silent.

Eventually Danny said, 'I can't see how to move on. I don't even know what I want, let alone what I need.'

Rose clasped her hands. 'First, you decide on the kind of life you would like to lead in ten or fifteen years. This will give you a benchmark for making decisions in the present and will reduce the inclination to keep looking back. Ask yourself: how would I handle this situation if I was the person I hope to become? And then make decisions and take action in line with that vision. Let the past relationship you had with Amy, when it was good, be the goal to work towards.'

He looked weakened by her words. How easy it would be to walk across the room and put her arms around him, drawing him close.

'I'm sure you can find a way back from this. That you and Amy can make it work.'

Danny hesitated, as if he was struggling to find the right words. 'What if I don't want to go back? What if the future I want for myself is right here in front of me?'

CHAPTER 58

Danny was on his phone when Rose entered her basement office the next morning. Thankfully she didn't make reference to his near confession yesterday.

'Are you hiding from your team?' she asked, smiling.

'Not exactly. I've been trying to get my head around some of the stuff Lyons has sent over. Apparently there's a problem with his initial findings. He wants to see us.' Danny felt on edge. All this work only for Lyons to raise doubts about the original post-mortem findings. It could only be bad news.

'Sounds ominous.'

'Yep. If we're lucky it could mean we have something new to work with. If not, it could be that he got it totally wrong in the first place and we've been investigating a suicide as a murder.'

'I don't think he'd have got it that wrong. The universe has a way of throwing up new leads when you need them most so let's remain optimistic for now. Did Lyons say anything else?'

'He sent some images of the markings on James McCallum's neck and lots of medical terminology. You know what he's like, full of his own self-importance. Are you able to go over with me this afternoon?'

'Yeah, definitely.'

Lyons kept them waiting in the foyer for over ten minutes. When he showed up, he greeted them, apologised for the wait and directed them into his office.

'Sorry about this. I thought it was better to discuss the new information in person. I've just been on a call to a colleague in Edinburgh, Caroline McGill. I had emailed the initial report to her along with some images and wanted to discuss the case with her before I saw you.'

'And?' Danny asked.

'Well, I am glad to say we were not mistaken in our initial findings.' He passed an enlarged photograph across the table to them.

'Now, most hangings result in brain asphyxia due to compression of the carotid arteries and or the trachea. We see this happen with strangulation as well.'

'So what are you saying? We already believed that whoever had killed James McCallum had done so before moving the body to the hanging tree,' Rose said.

'Manual strangulations will leave a fairly horizontal ligature mark at the neck – absolutely straight across – however, with a hanging, you would expect the ligature mark to show a diagonal line from the ear down to the neck.' He indicated with his finger along his neck to demonstrate. 'There is also frequently a mark where the knot of the ligature is present in a hanging – often at the back or side of the neck. But, as you know, we found markings to suggest a belt or lead beneath the rope markings.' He paused and looked at them.

Here it comes, thought Danny. *The big reveal.*

'I now believe that the killer was behind the victim, tightening the belt or lead around the neck. If you look at this image . . .' He placed another enlarged photograph of the back of James McCallum's head in front of them and traced his finger along the markings. 'The marking left behind was angled and the pattern injury of the belt buckle has been mistaken for the mark usually left by a ligature knot.'

They stayed quiet, waiting for Lyons to explain further.

'It didn't help that when the deceased was removed from the tree, the rope was cut away. I'd have preferred to have the rope remain attached to the neck or, if removed, cut with a sharp object, leaving the knot intact for examination and comparison to the pattern injury on the body.'

Danny sighed. 'Come on, Raymond. What are you telling us?'

Lyons clasped his hands together. 'I think we are dealing with autoerotic asphyxiation.'

'He did this to himself?' Rose asked, her eyes widening.

Lyons shook his head. 'No, there was another party and the pattern injury of the belt or lead suggests a buckle was used to secure the strangulation. Whoever did it was behind and on top of the victim. Either it was a sex game gone terribly wrong, or he was set up to be murdered in this way.'

CHAPTER 59

'Just when we thought this case couldn't get any more complicated, along comes Lyons to throw an absolute spanner in the works,' Danny said as he placed his hand on the bundle of files sitting on his desk in the basement office. The smell of mould and dampness was heightened with the heating going full blast, but he found it strangely comforting in its familiarity. You could grow mushrooms down here, he thought.

Rose looked thoughtful. He could tell she was processing this new information, reconsidering everything that had gone before and the assumptions they had made.

She stood and walked across the room. 'I don't know what to make of this. The thing about sex games gone wrong as a defence is that it is normally women who are killed, not men. In most cases it ends with them getting off with a light sentence for what the courts call "rough sex".'

Danny reached for the white board marker and began writing. 'Let me get this straight in my head.

James McCallum was into autoerotic asphyxiation, strangling or suffocating himself to heighten sexual arousal. That would suggest that whoever killed him was in some sort of relationship with him. After he was killed in this manner – whether intentionally or not – his body was then moved to the school and hanged from the tree in an attempt to make it look like suicide.'

'Wow, this case is so fucked up.'

'Just another day at the office, Rosie.' Danny grinned at her.

'So, do we go back to Emma?'

'Yes, but we can't assume it was her. We were so busy looking at Emma McCallum's relationship with Martin Kilburn that we didn't think to consider whether James might have also been playing around.'

'Whoever did it had help to the move the body. Could it have been Emma, and Martin Kilburn helped her?'

Danny raised his eyebrows. 'Possibly.'

'What's the motive?'

'Maybe she wanted to be with Martin and wanted James out of the way?'

'A bit contrived, don't you think? It would be a hell of a lot easier just to divorce him.'

Danny crossed his arms and leaned back in his chair. 'Or it could have been a crime of passion. Maybe the whole strangling thing is what the McCallums were into but it went too far and Emma got caught up in the moment. Instead of owning up to it, she panicked and asked Martin Kilburn to help her stage James' death as a suicide.'

Rose shook her head. 'I can't see it. If it happened accidentally why would Emma have tried to cover it up?

281

'We need a search warrant for the house. Let's see if that throws up anything and we can bring Emma McCallum in for a little chat.'

CHAPTER 60

Rose thought about how much of policing involved managing people and paperwork. She'd watched Danny navigate both and seen how he resented them for keeping him from the part he liked – strategy. The interesting part was found in the thinking time; the time away from the scene and the suspects when you could process it all and let it ferment in your brain until it produced a whole scenario you didn't even know you should be looking for. At that stage, it came down to a game of chess with heightened drama thrown in for good measure.

The new break in the case gave rise to a buzz in the conference room. The new information had been circulating among the team and everyone was fired up and ready to make the next move.

Rose stood at the front alongside Danny as he addressed the room.

'Right, listen up. As you've all probably heard by now, we've been talking to the State Pathologist again as he has come back with some interesting findings that were not apparent during the initial autopsy report.' There was a rumble of comments.

'We know James didn't die of natural causes, nor was his death the result of suicide. The placement of the ligature marks around his neck led us to wonder about the third option – murder. Lyons now believes that his death was caused by a game of autoerotic asphyxia gone wrong.'

'What, like a sex game?' Magee asked from across the room.

'Yes, autoerotic asphyxia is the initiation of oxygen deficiency to enhance sexual excitement and orgasm. It's a practice that has been around for centuries and has led to many fatalities,' Rose said.

'So, where does this leave our investigation?' Danny walked forward with his hands on his hips. 'Was it a sex game gone wrong or was it something more sinister and pre-planned?'

'We also have to consider the roles of dominance and submission in the dynamic between James and his killer,' Rose said.

Danny wrote 'dominance' and 'submission' on the white board.

Danny took over. 'We still don't have information on the primary murder scene. Since the victim had a history of depression, and the investigation of the death context and environment suggested suicide, we had to work within the perimeters of asking who knew that James had mental health issues? Who had he talked to about his problems?'

Rose sat on the edge of the desk. 'Dr Lyons believes that the pattern of the injury markings on James

McCallum's neck suggests that a belt or lead was attached and pulled from behind.'

She clicked on the remote for the computer screen and the image of the neck markings came up on the screen. 'If someone is doing this practice with a partner there is usually a safety override, a safe word. In some cases, however, it goes too far or something goes wrong, leading to injury or fatality. But how often does it happen, and the partner just leaves? If a thorough investigation is not carried out, a second party's involvement in the death can be easily missed.'

Rose stood again. 'In this instance, James McCallum's body was moved and his death presented as suicide by hanging. This leads to several questions: Who was he engaged in the auto-erotic practice with? Who was he with on the night in question? Was it accidental death or pre-determined murder and who was involved in moving his body to the hanging tree in the school grounds?'

CHAPTER 61

Danny was sat at his desk typing up notes when Mal walked into the basement office.

'Working late, boss?'

'Aye, sure, might as well. Nothing to rush home to. This case seems to be giving us all the run around. Just when I think I'm getting a handle on it, something turns up to make me question what we thought we had. You doing okay, Mal?' Danny could see the tension in the man's shoulders, and now that he looked at him properly, he could see he'd lost a bit of weight, too. Maybe he'd started to eat better and spend some time in the gym?

'Awk just a few things going on at home. I'll be fine. You need anything done or am I okay to head off now?'

'Nah, away you go. I'll see you tomorrow.'

Danny imagined Malachy going home to his wife and kids. He probably had a nice dinner waiting for him too. He thought of what that must be like, to be checking in on a sleeping infant, the pride he would have felt swelling in his chest along with the fear that he would have to protect this precious life for ever more. Amy had stolen it all from him, yet he still felt that gnawing guilt that he should have done more to look after her. He had spent the last year trying to block it all out; trying to move on. Seeing her again had threatened to unleash everything he had worked so hard to hide from himself. Things weren't right and he didn't know if he'd ever reach a point of feeling that he and Amy were truly over, done and dusted. The emotion was draining. It was as though he had a constant inner dialogue trying to keep him on an even keel. Sooner or later Rose would see through him and call him out on it.

He needed some coffee to shake this weariness. At least he knew where he was with work, knew what was required of him and what he could give. He was still thinking about this when his phone rang. Battle wanted an update on the new findings.

CHAPTER 62

Rose woke and immediately felt that something was wrong. The remnants of a dream lingered, something about her father and the shooting. Faces pressed too close together lining a hallway, making her feel claustrophobic and dizzy.

She got up and had a shower and then drank some coffee before reaching for her phone to text Colm. They had been in more regular communication of late, each checking in with the other, asking how they were and both making an effort to build on the ruins of their relationship. Rose appreciated the effort he was making and felt it was only fair that she played her part too. But for all their renewed closeness, she hadn't told him that she had reached out to an intelligence agent with knowledge of their mother's past. She told herself it was to protect him, but she knew deep down that it was also to protect their mother's memory. God knows what she was going to uncover, and she wanted to deal with it before she involved her siblings.

She had researched Special Branch and their tactics. Their function had been to collect information on subversive groups and those with any paramilitary links. They were a force within a force, operating with a freedom that rendered them dangerous and extreme in their methods. Rose had read how they preyed on women like her mother to do the dirty work of informing. It was the women not directly linked to paramilitary organisations being made to grass on their families and neighbours that had made her quake with an indignation she didn't know she had. One case she'd read about had involved a young girl, only seventeen, who'd become pregnant and told her parents she'd been offered a job in Dundalk, where she went to have the baby, in quiet, before having it adopted. Months later, she was home and doing a nursing course when she was approached by two men. They had photographs of the child with its new family and implied that the child might come to harm if she didn't help them with their 'enquiries'. The girl had ended up saying a whole lot of things she knew – and some she didn't – just to protect the child. When the pressure, fear, and dread became too much she'd walked over the Albert Bridge and jumped into the Lagan with chunks of masonry in her pockets, leaving behind a letter detailing what she'd done.

Rose's mind went to her siblings. They had suffered just as she had and just thinking of them made her stiffen with resolve. The past was a place of shadows and fear. She hoped that by finding out more she would illuminate the corners of her mind that scared her.

In the end it hadn't been too difficult to find someone undercover who would talk to her about Special Branch.

The meeting with David Bridal, if that was even his real name, was scheduled for six o'clock. She had been told to park her car on University Road and walk to College Green where a black SUV with tinted windows would be parked. She was to get into the back seat.

As she walked down the street, she felt anxiety in the pit of her stomach. She'd dressed that morning as if going to an important work meeting, choosing to wear a structured, dark green blazer over slim-fitted trousers and high-heeled black boots. Now the click of her heels on the footpath only served to remind her that she would fool no one; she was a bundle of nerves.

It was a Sunday, so the street was less busy than usual. The rain had ceased but a dampness hung in the air.

As she turned the corner, she saw the black car. For a second she thought about turning back, forgetting the whole thing and spending the day curled up on the sofa watching shite TV and drinking wine. Anything to numb the memories and the conjecture that her mind inevitably turned to. Instead, she took a deep breath to steady herself and continued walking until she reached the car. As she approached, she heard the clunk of the automatic locks. She opened the back door and slid inside.

'Why did you request this meeting?' The man in the driver's seat spoke with a mild English accent. She couldn't tell if he was English but had lived in Belfast long enough for it to mellow or if he was Irish and had lived in London.

'My mother – Evelyn Lavery. I want to know what she did. What role she played.'

He looked straight ahead. All she could see was his

greying hair. It was cut army-style short. His suit jacket was navy and from what she could see, expensive looking.

'Some things are best left alone.'

'For who? Not for me. I need to know what my mother did. How she was involved.'

'Loyalty. It means something in these parts but people never know where true loyalty lies.'

'She passed on information that was used against people she grew up with, lived beside, and saw every day. That's not loyalty.'

'Aww, now it depends on your perspective, doesn't it? Look down the viewfinder and see where the red dot lands. Them or us.'

Rose felt cold to her bones, as if the damp air had seeped into her clothes, and she longed to be home. To shut out the world and the feeling of revulsion that David Bridal gave her. He had that professional glint she'd seen in some police and army types. Like they had no sense of compassion or empathy. It was all about getting the job done.

'Was she in an active unit?'

'She was. That was why she was so well placed for us to use her.'

Rose paused, unsure of how to proceed.

'How did it start?'

'You mean, how did she begin working for us?'

She nodded. 'Yeah.'

'I wasn't her handler, but I would assume she was lifted for something. Probably something that would have seen her go away for a long time. I know she was held at Castlereagh for two days. A mother on her own with four kids to look after . . . well, I'm sure she was happy to take the alternative route.'

Two days in Castlereagh. Rose couldn't think of when that might have been. Acknowledgement that Evelyn had been put in an impossible position was what she had come here for, even if she didn't have the details. Her imagination could do that for her. Evelyn had been questioned, perhaps tortured, and eventually offered a way out. Except it was anything but a way out. It was a way in, right up to her neck in boiling water.

'She would likely have been told that she had been set up, sacrificed for the greater good. That she had to talk, or she'd never see her children again. It was the way it was done back then.' His voice was silken-smooth, as if he was describing an innocent jaunt to the countryside, something pleasant and innocuous.

He lowered his voice. 'If you want to know more – the details of it all – it can be arranged. After all, you're one of us now. You are well placed to help us out in return when needed.'

'Fuck off,' Rose said, reaching for the car door, her heart racing with anger and a bitterness as corrosive as acid burning in her throat.

'Wait! There's one more thing,' he said, reaching over to the passenger seat and lifting a brown envelope. 'Your mother asked for this to be passed on to you, should you ever come asking about her.' He thrust the envelope towards Rose.

'What? My mother left it this for me?'

He shrugged. 'She obviously knew you'd come looking for information. Don't worry, there's nothing incriminating in it. We wouldn't have passed it on if there was. Just a reckoning of sorts, from a mother to a daughter from the grave.'

CHAPTER 63

'Hey, Danny, I've managed to track down a teacher who taught the four friends – a Ciaran Bradley. He taught them maths A Level,' Malachy said as he passed Danny a slip of paper with the teacher's details scrawled on it.

Danny looked at the Ormeau Road address. 'Ta, good work. I'll take a run out to speak to him.'

Ciaran Bradley was busy with a leaf blower when Danny pulled up outside his red-brick semi in Haypark Avenue in the south of the city.

'Mr Bradley? DI Stowe.' Danny presented him with his ID card. 'I wonder if I could ask you a few questions about some past pupils of yours?'

The man looked intrigued. He wore a trilby hat on his balding head and the silk cravat at his neck gave him an air of someone who liked to think of himself as debonair. 'Certainly, anything to be of help to the PSNI.'

When they were settled in his living room, Danny asked if he recalled the four friends.

'Yes, I remember them well. Always together in the senior school. In fact, if I'm not mistaken, I'd say James and the girl, Ivy, were inseparable. We didn't condone any physical contact at Osbourne House – heavens above, it's not like some of those American high schools you see on the television – but one can always tell if there's a little frisson between pupils.' He smiled. 'Do you know, I think I might have some photographs of them at the annual formal.' He hurried away to fetch the pictures.

'Yes, here we are. That's Ivy and there is James. I was in charge of the school newsletter, so I have a lot of old bits and pieces squirrelled away. Haven't the heart to throw them out.'

Danny looked the photograph. Ivy was wearing a purple satin dress and James was dressed in a tuxedo. He had his arm around Ivy's shoulders, and she was smiling up at him. They certainly looked like a couple. Young and infatuated. Danny thought of his own school formal. He'd attended with Michelle Kirk. A good-looking girl with dark blonde hair. She'd gone on to do French and the last he heard she'd had a squad of kids.

'Thanks for this,' Danny said. 'Do you mind if I keep it?'

'Not at all. Help yourself.'

'Well, thanks for all your assistance. I'll leave you to get on with your day.'

CHAPTER 64

Before going back to the station, Danny thought he might as well drop in on Ivy Duff's GP practice in Ballyhackamore. Most people felt thrown when cops turned up at their place of work so he hoped that it would unnerve her and make her less sure of herself. He pulled in to the crowded car park just as she was exiting the building.

'Dr Duffy, a word, if you don't mind?' He gave her a smile as he approached, one that he hoped said 'I come in peace'.

'What is it this time? I'm afraid I'm busy,' Ivy said.

'Oh, I don't doubt that. Sure we're all busy people. I just need a word. It won't take long.'

An elderly woman walked by and nodded in greeting. Ivy watched Danny, waiting, her eyes narrowed into suspicious slits. She tutted and turned to go inside. Danny followed her. The reception area was busy, filled with mainly mothers and children. Danny could feel the germs brewing in the atmosphere. He wasn't one for visiting his

GP; come to think of it, he couldn't remember the last time he had. His annual health check-up through work was as much medical attention as he needed or sought.

In Ivy Duffy's office, he sat down while she hung up her coat on the back of the door.

'What do you want now?' she asked, sitting at her desk. She gathered herself, putting on her professional mask now that she was in her usual habitat, but there was a look of something on her face – fear? Annoyance? He wasn't sure.

'I would like to talk about your friendship group again.' He took the photograph the teacher had given him and placed it on the table in front of her.

She gave an exaggerated sigh. 'We've gone over this before.'

'Humour me. You and James were an item for a while. Why did you break up?'

'Christ, we were teenagers. It ran its course.'

He said nothing, waiting for her to keep talking.

'Some people aren't meant to be together forever. That was us. It was a teenage romance and once school ended so did our relationship. There was no big fall out and certainly no great mystery, Detective.'

Danny stared at her. There was something in the way she said 'mystery', as if she was taunting him. He knew that anyone holding on to secrets can go through life contained and satisfied that they are safe. Then one day they wake up and suddenly the fear of being found out becomes too much. They lose their nerve and find that the certainty that had been their armour is no longer as secure. If that secret is shared with others the risk and fear is greater.

What secret did Ivy and her friends harbour?

'Aww, now I always say where there's history there's a mystery.' He smiled at her. He wanted desperately to get something out of her and hoped that in keeping up a measure of pressure that she'd be spooked. Rose had shared that she didn't think the other two, Emer and Lorcan, would be as tough to crack.

'If you are trying to pressurise me into saying something that may have some sort of bearing on James' murder you are in for a big disappointment, Detective. As I have already told you, I was working on the night James died.'

Danny gave her a little shrug and raised an eyebrow.

'Oh, now, Dr Duffy, I'm glad you brought that up. You see, there's a few questions concerning your alibi that we need to clear up. Namely, where did you go when you left Knockbreda Health Centre at 10.05 p.m.?' His voice was steady and steely. He wanted her to know that he was just as clever and astute as she was.

'I had a house call. You can see the address logged into the system.'

'Then why tell us you were there until midnight?'

'I must have forgot.'

'Someone knows what happened to James and why and it's my job to find that out.'

She glared at him, her chin jutting out in defiance. 'That's what we all want. I suggest you go and do your job, Detective, and stop harassing me.'

CHAPTER 65

Danny pulled up outside Lorcan Burns' house at five forty-five. There was no one at home but he decided to wait, hoping that Burns and his partner, Brody Sullivan, wouldn't be much longer. If they had left work at five, they should be about to arrive any minute.

Brody turned up first and Danny watched as he parked his blue Clio and then removed a laptop bag from the back seat. As Brody was putting the key in the door of his house, Danny approached him.

'Lorcan's not home,' Brody said without even turning to look at Danny.

'So you saw me sitting there, then,' Danny said.

'If you're trying to be discreet, you'll need to try harder.'

'Nah, sure I've nothing to hide. I'm the good guy, remember? Just partaking in a bit of neighbourhood watch and checking in on our boy. See how the wounds are healing.'

'As I said, Lorcan is still at work. He's not due home till after six.'

'Aye sure, I don't mind waiting. Give me a chance to chat to you.'

Brody didn't bother to hide his annoyance. 'I don't know what more you could possibly need to speak to Lorcan about. He's told you everything he knows.'

'It's the nature of the job. A bit like picking at a scab. Sooner or later you get to the good stuff.'

Brody opened the door and Danny followed him in without waiting to be asked.

'Well, I'm about to start to cooking dinner, so you can sit and watch me.'

He hung up his coat and set the laptop bag down in the hallway before walking through to the open plan living and kitchen area.

Danny stood looking around and noticed a framed set of photographs hanging on the wall above the dining table. It was one of those collective frames holding eight pictures of varying sizes. All of the photographs appeared to be taken on holidays. There was one of Brody and Lorcan sitting in a yacht, surrounded by a deep cyan-blue sea, which must surely have been the Mediterranean. Another showed them in what was unmistakably a New York street in winter.

It was the next picture that caught Danny's full attention though. In it, Lorcan Burns and Brody were sat on a mountain top – possibly somewhere in the Mournes – complete with hard hats, harnesses and ropes. A flicker of excitement coursed through Danny. Lorcan Burns knew about ropes, knots, and pulley systems.

'That's a great picture,' he said casually to Brody. 'Do you two go hiking a lot?'

'From time to time. That was taken last summer up Slieve Binnian.'

'You both look well equipped. Do you know a lot about mountain climbing and all that?'

'We did a rock-climbing skills course at Tollymore Outdoor Centre. We both like learning new skills and pushing ourselves.'

'Fair play to ye. I wouldn't have a head for heights. Must have been hard going if you needed all those harnesses and ropes and stuff.'

Just then they heard a key in the door. Lorcan was home.

'Detective Stowe, hello. Has there been a development?' he asked Danny, throwing his keys on the kitchen counter.

'Just checking in on you. See how you're doing.'

'I'm doing fine. Still hard to take it all in. James was a good fella. He didn't deserve for this to happen to him.'

'Well, you were friends. It's bound to hit you hard. Then there's your wee altercation in the car park. That can't have been easy to deal with.'

'Of course I'm upset, but that doesn't mean to say I can't go to work and go about my life as normal.'

Danny held up his hands in a peace offering. 'Sure, I'll get out of your hair. Let you boys enjoy your night.'

He walked towards the door before turning. 'One more thing, Lorcan. If you don't mind popping down to the station tomorrow, there's a wee issue I need to straighten out in my head and I think you're just the man to sort it for me.'

'What issue?'

'Awk, sure we'll worry about it tomorrow. Don't want to ruin your dinner, now do I? See you at ten. Don't be late.'

Danny got into his car and called Rose's number.

'Guess who knows a thing or two about ropes and pulley systems?'

'Hello to you, too.'

'Lorcan Burns. This is the break we've been waiting on.'

Rose gasped. 'Frigging hell. How did you find that out?'

'First-class policing work, Rosie. The stupid fecker has a picture of himself and his boyfriend in their mountaineering gear on his kitchen wall. The pair of them were sat on top of Slieve Binnian. I didn't notice it the first time we called to his house.'

'So, what's the plan?'

'We do a bit of mountaineering research overnight. Find out all we can about the type of equipment he would be familiar with. I've told him to be at the station tomorrow morning at ten for a little chat.'

CHAPTER 66

The following morning, Rose and Danny waited for Lorcan to arrive.

By eleven, they were fed up.

'The wee shit thinks he can stand us up. He'll soon learn that we can stop playing nice *very* quickly,' Danny said.

'We could get a search warrant for the house?' It was one of the new things Rose had learned while studying police procedures. She was determined not to be a hindrance to Danny or the team.

'Nah, too soon. Besides, I doubt he has anything incriminating lying around. Maybe we should drive to his place of work?'

'Give it another fifteen minutes. I have a feeling that he has resisted turning up on time to wrong foot us. He's asserting his power. He might even hope that if he turns up late we'll have gone out on another job. That way he can say he tried to see you, but you weren't available.'

Before the fifteen minutes was up, the front office

called to tell Danny he had a visitor; Lorcan Burns was waiting for them in reception.

Rose couldn't help smirking.

Danny did a hand gesture to mimic that his mind was blown. 'You're a freaking weirdo to be able to read people like that!'

'I might have just got lucky this time.'

'Lorcan, thank you for joining us, even if you did keep us waiting,' Danny said.

He stared straight at them, providing no excuse or apology, watching as Danny sorted out the recording device.

'Take a seat,' Rose offered. He sat down with a deliberate reluctance, like a pupil going before the school's principal.

Danny placed his elbows on the table, stated the date and time for the benefit of the record, then began. 'So, Lorcan, we would like to ask you about your mountaineering. Been a hobby for long?'

Lorcan looked surprised. 'Mountaineering? Don't know what you're on about.'

'That nice fella of yours told me that you and he went on a course to learn all about mountain climbing.'

'It was hiking, actually. Yeah, it was something we did for a short while.'

'And what kind of things did you learn?'

'How to be safe when hiking up mountains. It's not something you should do without the proper preparation.'

'So, it's a hobby you shared with Brody. Did you ever go with any of your other friends, say . . . Emer, Ivy, or James?' Danny asked.

'No, just Brody. We like to take on new challenges. The hiking was something we did for a while. End of.'

Rose leaned forward. 'We need your help with something, Lorcan. James' body was found hanging from a tree. Now, we know he didn't put himself up there, which means somebody else did, and to do so required either a lot of brute strength or some knowhow when it comes to ropes and pulley systems.'

'You can see where we're going with this,' Danny interjected.

Lorcan flushed. 'I don't like your insinuation. You're treating me like a suspect.'

'The penny drops,' Danny said. 'You were the person who received the text message from James, and you're knowledgeable about ropes and moving a dead weight. Excuse us if we are more than a little suspicious.'

The colour drained from his face. 'My mate is dead. I've tried to be helpful at every turn. I'm not prepared to sit here being treated like a criminal. I won't answer any further questions. Not without my solicitor.'

'You are within your right to have representation, of course, but before this all gets too complicated you have the opportunity to talk to us. Tell us what you know, Lorcan. What you did.'

Lorcan sat up straight in the chair. 'I didn't do anything.'

CHAPTER 67

The letter had lay unread for long enough. Rose knocked back the remains of a glass of Pinot and reached for the envelope. The gummed flap was easily opened. She'd no doubt that David Bridal and his colleagues had approved its contents before placing it in her hands. Whatever Evelyn had chosen to share with Rose had been approved and possibly sanitised.

The pages were thin, blue, and lined, like old-fashioned writing paper. There in her trembling hands was her mother's distinctive handwriting. The swirling tilt of the letters suggesting she was writing in a hurry, laying down the words as quickly as her hand would allow.

Roisin,

This letter has been entrusted into the hands of my protectors, my handlers and my one-time enemies.

What I am asking of you is a massive leap of faith. To take what you knew of me, or what you thought you knew of me, and see it reconfigured into something else. Each of us has own experiences, our own set of preconceived notions of right and wrong. The trouble with you, dear Roisin, is that yours are set in stone. You are so like me when I was young. Life changes a person, if you let it. That's where the growth comes from. Don't stay locked into the person you think you are, be prepared to grow, to see the world differently.

After your father was killed, the Republican movement was there for me. The comradeship was seductive and besides grief is easier to deal with if you wrap it up in anger. Find a purpose within it.

For a long time, I thought that freedom would bring peace. Gradually I realised that I had it the wrong way round. Peace would bring freedom.

You don't need to know of the circumstances that led me to my awakening. Just know that I had the best of intentions for you, Kaitlin, Pearse, and Colm.

Love from beyond the grave,
Your mother.

The letter said everything and said nothing. It was Evelyn's way of having the last word.

When Rose returned to Belfast, she knew there would be ghosts to contend with. Memories that would catch her out, making her face the old realities she had run from. She didn't expect to find them in her nieces and nephews. Watching them, heads close together looking at some TikTok video on an iPhone, reminded her of the closeness she used to share with her siblings. Her mind felt stretched from the present to the past, dropping her right back into the nineties when she was listening to Britpop and dreaming of a life beyond the streets of Belfast.

'Hey, you okay?' Kaitlin sat down on the sofa beside her.

'Sure, just thinking, you know.'

'What, about the old days?'

'Yeah, us as kids. All the stuff that we used to get up to.'

'Do you remember the time our Pearse's friend, Tommy Reynolds, sent you a Valentine? Pearse was furious.'

'Oh god, I'd completely forgot about Tommy! What happened to him?'

'Emigrated to a sheep farm in New Zealand, the last I heard.'

'Good for him.'

'I suppose I should be grateful you never made it that far. You might never have come back.'

Rose sipped her tea. 'This is nice.'

'What, the tea?'

'No, being back, sitting here with you, watching the kids. A whole new generation. I suppose I didn't realise what I was missing out on.'

'I'm glad you're back.' Kaitlin rested her head on Rose's shoulder. 'I like having my big sister around.'

Rose liked the mess scattered around Kaitlin's home. Muddy football boots and a gym bag lay in the hallway, and a coat had been draped over the bannister post along with a Hype school bag. The faint lavender scent of fresh laundry hung in the air along with the lived-in smell of cooking. It spoke of family life and love. Rose's apartment, in contrast, was a clinical shell of orderliness and dullness. She came to Kaitlin's to grasp moments of family life like a drinker seeking out the last dregs at the bottom of the bottle. The funny thing was, she didn't even know she'd craved this until she'd experienced it. In London, family life had been something she thought of as part of childhood. Now she realised how short-sighted she had been to think that she didn't deserve or need this kind of connection.

They chatted away about their days over a glass of wine and prepared the evening meal together. Kids came in and out of the kitchen looking for homework books or grabbing snacks before being told off for ruining their appetite before dinner. They appeared to accept Rose as part of the furniture now and she liked it that way. She was one of them.

'Right, it's ready!' Kaitlin shouted and everyone made their way into the kitchen, jostling for attention in that way kids do, competing with one another for airtime. The chatter over dinner drifted over Rose. It had felt so alien to her to think of herself as being part of a functioning family unit, yet here she was passing the jug of diluted orange juice and listening to her niece and nephew complain about school and too much homework.

'So, how's work going?' Tony, Kaitlin's husband, asked.

'Good. I actually like it a lot more than I expected. No two days are the same.'

'Who'd have thought a Lavery would end up working for the PSNI?' He said it lightly, with no hint of malice, a smile playing at his mouth.

Rose shrugged. 'I'm not your typical Lavery.'

* * *

308

Later on, Rose helped Kaitlin scrape the plates and stack the dishwasher. This felt right. Like she had never been away all of those years. That they were just two normal sisters enjoying each other's company.

'What?' Rose asked as she caught Kaitlin staring at her with a soppy grin on her face.

'You're good at this being part of the family thing. Being the doting aunty. The kids love you, you know.'

Rose smiled. Kaitlin's words were a balm for all of the papercuts of her childhood.

The brown envelope still lay like a threat on the table in her apartment. She'd stared at it, placed her fingers on it – had even smelled it – but couldn't bring herself to share it with her sister or brothers. Whatever lay inside could only open old wounds, wounds that had never healed, but were at least not infected. This calling from the grave could do all sorts of stuff to her head.

She'd told none of her family about the meeting with David Bridal or the letter. This part of her investigation into their mother's past was for her alone. She didn't want to drag them emotionally or physically into something she may not be able to handle herself. Evelyn's letter had left only a sense of unfinished business. There was more to it, Rose was sure.

CHAPTER 68

The rain had eased off to a faint drizzle, but the weather forecasters had warned more was on the way. Winter had taken hold, and everyone looked glum at the prospect. The heatwave so many had complained about a few months previous was taking revenge for all their moaning. Belfast people could never be happy, thought Danny. They always wanted what they couldn't have.

Lorcan Burns was sitting at his desk in the accountancy offices when Danny approached him. He looked up and annoyance immediately darkened his face as he recognised Danny.

'Lorcan, can I have a word?'

'What's it this time, Detective? And does this really have to happen at my place of work? I've been more than good about cooperating.' There was annoyance in his voice, but also an undercurrent of fear. Danny could sense the panic creeping in. Good. He wanted him rattled.

'And there's me thinking I was doing you a favour by coming to you rather than asking you to come down the station again. Is there somewhere to get a cup of coffee round here? Something decent, mind. I don't want no Nescafé house piss.'

Lorcan looked at Danny with something that could be contempt or annoyance. 'There's a café across the road. Meet me there. I need a minute to finish up and let my manager know I'm heading out for a few minutes.'

'Good man. I'll get the order in. Coffee's on me.'

Danny was sitting near the window when Lorcan arrived. 'I took the liberty of ordering you an Americano. Sugar's on the side if you take it.'

Lorcan sat down and stared straight at Danny. He was playing it cool, but Danny could play that game too. 'Awful bloody weather we're having. Keep thinking I'll take up running and then I look out the window and the storm clouds convince me I'm better off on the sofa, do you know what I mean?'

'I doubt you came here to discuss the weather with me. What do you want, Detective?'

'Aww, now what we want and what we get, they're two different beasts, aren't I right?'

Lorcan looked like he had had enough of Danny's messing around.

'I can't stay long, so whatever you need to say, say it.'

Danny leaned back and took a long, slow drink of his coffee, and set the cup back down.

'The thing is, Lorcan, I've been feeling a bit uneasy. You know when you think you have the measure of something and then it turns out to be not as it seemed?'

Lorcan stared at him.

'Well, I've been feeling – how would you put it –

311

discombobulated. Yeah, that's the word. Discombobulated. I can't say I like feeling this way. Me, I'm a man of simple desires. I like to do my day's work and go home with a clear head, you know? No hangover work worries niggling at me. But, here's the thing – since your good mate James died, I haven't been able to do that. What with autopsy reports, rope fragment forensics, day trips to Mistle, and pondering what it all adds up to, I haven't had a night's peace. Not one night.'

'I don't know what you want me to do about that,' Lorcan said, angling his head in a show of insolence.

'Ah, but you might be able to help me out. There's one thing I'm sure you could clear up for me.' Danny took out a piece of paper from his jacket pocket and set it on the table in front of Lorcan's untouched coffee.

'It's a copy of the logbook transaction for a car, registered to your father, Arnold. A car that I believe was seen scooting about the town of Mistle in August 2001.'

'And, so what?'

'Well, I don't know if you've heard, but that same summer, on the 17th of August to be exact, a young girl – little Maeve Lunn – went missing. Never seen again. Dreadful all together, wouldn't you say?'

'So? What has that got to do with me?'

'Oh, nothing, I hope.' Danny laughed. 'Unless you want to tell me otherwise?'

Lorcan looked at him with either fear or hate. It was hard to say which. Danny had seen that look before. The guilty always distrust and hate their accuser while innocent people tend to look hurt and scared. But which was Lorcan? Scared and innocent or distrustful and guilty?

'The thing is, the car – the same navy blue car seen

scooting about Mistle – was sold by the end of August.' Danny leaned forward and put his hand to his head. 'I can't seem to work out why that wee car had to be sold. I bet your parents bought you the car as a gift for finishing the old exams, or maybe it was for your eighteenth birthday? In my day you got sod all. Pat on the back if you were lucky.'

Lorcan looked pale.

'Like I said, it's one of those things that have been niggling at me when I come home from work at night. There's me trying to get my Netflix and chill going and my thoughts are dragged back to that navy blue car. It just seems so strange to me that your father bought the car in June and sold it in August. Who does that?'

'I didn't like the car. I was heading off for uni so it didn't make sense to keep it.'

'Aww so, that's the reason. Glad you cleared that up for me. Still . . . it makes me wonder. I don't like wondering, you know. Wondering takes me down all sorts of paths. And me? All I want is an easy life.'

'Well, if that's everything you came here for, I need to be heading back to work now.'

'Sure, sure, away you go. I'll be in touch if I think of anything else – you know me and my wondering – but in the meantime, if you feel like having another wee chat, here's my number.'

'You've already given me your card.'

'Sure, does no harm to have another one.' Danny grinned at him, certain that he'd intimidated him. 'Next time we do this though, we'll do it down the station. Make it all formal, like.'

CHAPTER 69

There are points in every case, hinge moments, when the investigation moves from being one thing to another on the spin of a bottle, and this was it for the McCallum case. Danny could feel the heightened tension in every sinew of his body. He was primed and ready for the final showdown, he just didn't know in what form it would be. So much was still unknown. They were closing in, but one wrong move and they would lose their advantage. The next twenty-four hours were crucial.

When tiredness overwhelmed him, seeping into his very bones, he called it a day and headed out of the station. He couldn't shake this feeling of being depleted. The case had worn him down and he needed to find the reserves to see it over the final hurdle. He knew a good night's sleep would help but didn't hold out much hope.

Just as he exited the front doors, Rose came up behind him. The office lights spilled out onto the tarmac, casting shadows as they made their way to their cars.

'What's the plan for tomorrow?' Rose asked.

Danny sighed. 'More of the same until we get what we need. I've instructed Mal to get the three of them in and keep them in separate rooms. Spook them a bit. It's time to do the interviews in a formal setting. If they each think the other is talking, they might start to slip up. We need to know what secret they were all keeping and was it all too much for James? Did he threaten to come clean?'

'You think one of them will crack?'

'I'm hopeful. I'll need your input and expertise.'

She nodded.

The misting rain fell on them like a veil, making everything feel gauzy and out of focus.

'You want some company? We could get dinner,' she said.

'Nah. I'm wrecked. Need an early night to be ready for whatever tomorrow brings. Rain check?'

'Sure,' she said and walked off towards her car, leaving him standing there.

CHAPTER 70

'Interview room 0809. DI Danny Stowe and Dr Rose Lainey interviewing Lorcan Burns,' Danny said into the recording device. He turned back to Lorcan and stared at him across the table.

'Thanks for coming in,' Danny said. 'We appreciate your cooperation. Your friends are here helping us with the investigation as well.'

He sat stony-faced, giving nothing away, and reached for the paper cup of water. He was dressed in a baggy grey cable-knit jumper and looked like he hadn't shaved.

'In your own time, can you tell us about your trip to Mistle in 2001?' Danny could feel his heart racing. If he was wrong about the friends, then everything would be shot down by a good solicitor in minutes. He needed to keep his cool and get Lorcan Burns on the tape saying exactly what had happened, before he demanded his counsel join them.

'I've told you before. We went for a few days' break after the exams.'

'So, humour me, what did you do there?'

Lorcan rolled his eyes. 'We drank vodka, we might have smoked some weed, we swam in the sea, we went on walks.'

'And what was the set-up? Did the boys sleep in one room and the girls in another?'

He glared at Danny. 'We didn't care where we slept. We were all mates.'

'So you and James never had anything going on?'

He sat up straighter. 'No, we didn't. I find that insulting. As if a straight man and a gay man can't be friends,' he said with evident annoyance.

'So, then, who was James sleeping with: Ivy or Emer?'

Lorcan sat with his hands in his lap. 'I don't think I have to tell you anything, Detective.'

'No, you're right there, lad. You don't have to say a thing. But if you'd rather we find answers another way, I can get my boss to sign off on a search warrant for your house and start flashing the cuffs around. Me, though, I like to do things the easy way. You see Lorcan, I'm reasonable. My colleague here though, not so much. If Dr Lainey had her way you'd be arrested by now.'

Lorcan looked concerned, his complexion flushing. 'On what charge?'

'Withholding information pertaining to a crime. That would do to begin with,' Rose said calmly.

'I don't have to prove anything to you. You can't make me say anything. My solicitor has told me my rights.'

'Lorcan, we think you know something about James' death and we think that in some way his death is connected to the disappearance of Maeve Lunn. If we are right, then what you are doing is obstructing us in the pursuit of the truth. That's a crime and you will do jail time, I promise you that. We think you were attacked as a warning. Someone wanted to make sure you kept your mouth shut. So, tell me, who are you protecting?'

Lorcan jutted out his bristly chin. 'I'm not protecting anyone.'

Danny slammed his hands down on the table, making both Rose and Lorcan jump. 'I will not have you wasting my time, do you hear me? At the heart of this case is the disappearance of a little girl and I will not spend another night tossing and turning and wondering what happened to her.'

Lorcan flinched.

Danny paused for a moment before saying quietly, 'Now, in your own time, please tell us exactly what happened in Mistle.'

Lorcan began to cry. 'I wish none of it had ever happened.' His left eyebrow was twitching as if in time with some unheard rhythm, and he was clenching his fists as if readying for a fight.

'None of what, Lorcan?' Danny said softly, his voice barely above a whisper.

'No, I want my solicitor. I'm not saying another word.'

CHAPTER 71

'Do you think we're getting close?' Rose asked. They were back in the office, waiting to make the next move.

Danny nodded. 'Yes, I could feel the tension radiating from him in there. He wants to talk.'

'Boss, Diane Quirk, Burns' solicitor, is ready for you,' Tania shouted over. 'The front desk has rang through.'

'Here we go,' said Danny to Rose.

Diane Quirk was wearing a dark green trench coat over a fine knit cream polo neck jumper with black trousers. 'DI Stowe, I believe you've been harassing my client.'

'Is that what you're calling conversation these days, Diane? How are you, haven't seen you in a while?'

'I'm good. And you?'

'Grand. Working hard. You know what it's like – the bad guys don't seem to give us a break. This is my colleague, Dr Rose Lainey.'

Rose and Diane shook hands.

'Are we ready to go in there?' Danny asked, nodding towards the room where Lorcan was waiting.

'Yes, I've spoken to him. We're ready.'

'So, Lorcan,' Danny began once the recording device was on. 'We need you to tell us about Mistle. What happened on the 17th of August, 2001?'

'We were low on supplies. Milk, cheese, bread, and sausages. I can still remember the bloody shopping list. James offered to go into the town and pick them up. It should have been me, but I was hungover from the night before. "No worries," he said, "sure I can take the car. I won't be long."'

The rough, bristly curve of Lorcan's cheek was pale as marble, and shadows had settled beneath his eyes, giving him a look of a gargoyle, something contorted and hideous. It was as if the telling of what happened was physically altering him.

'You have to understand that we didn't set out for any of this to happen.' Desperation was making his voice rise. Danny could see the cords of veins in his neck pulsate.

'What happened, Lorcan?' Rose said. 'What happened when James took the car to go into Mistle?'

He looked at Diane. She gave him a gentle nod.

CHAPTER 72

Rose and Danny took a break from the interview room and headed to the basement office.

'Let's release Lorcan Burns at the same time we bring Emer into the interview room so that they see each other,' Danny said. 'Keep them on their toes. You lead on this one.'

Rose nodded and gathered her folder of notes. Her phone pinged with a text – a reminder from Kaitlin that they had plans to meet at the weekend. It was comforting to know that she had a life outside of work, perhaps for the first time in a long time. The case had been all consuming, but her family were rather good at making sure she didn't forget about them.

Ten minutes later, Rose sat looking at Emer as she fiddled with a paper cup of water. Her hair was tied back in a messy ponytail and tiredness was etched onto her face. Her black bra was obvious under her pale grey shirt, suggesting she had dressed in a hurry. There was something vulnerable about her under the interview room lights.

'Emer, I want to talk to you about your days at school,' Rose said.

'What has school got to do with anything? Is all of this really necessary? I should be at home with my sons.'

'Bear with us. We don't know yet, but it could be relevant. We would like you to tell us about your friendship group.'

She sighed. 'School wasn't fun for me. Not at the beginning anyway. I came from a single-parent family. We'd not much money and those things matter when you're at a grammar school full of Malone Road kids. They'd the nicest clothes, summer holidays spent in their villas in Portugal, even Longchamp school bags for god's sake. I stuck out for all the wrong reasons. I was tall, freckly, and geeky. The perfect combination to attract the wrong sort of attention.'

'Were you bright academically?'

'Yeah. Sure, I had to pass the transfer exam to get a place at Osborne House, but that didn't set me apart or help me as everyone was smart. I did all right. Held my own. For the first three years I had no friends. Not a single one. My life was one long, fretful existence. In first year, it was lonely, but no one messed with me. That came later.'

Emer looked straight at Rose with her eyes wide and unblinking. 'Do you know what it's like to feel different? To know that every person you are forced to spend your days with detests you and takes every opportunity to make that clear to you?'

Rose nodded encouragingly.

'There was no let up. My weight, my skin, my clothes – they were all fair game for them to attack me. They

322

wrote things like "muesli face" on my locker. It was torment. Even outside of school there was no peace. Then, in fourth year, the year groups were changed. I was sitting in English Lit when Ivy walked in. Gorgeous, dark-haired Ivy with her shiny life of privilege. She started talking to me as if we'd always been friends and everything changed overnight for me. I never understood why Ivy suddenly decided to befriend me. She'd never been one to say mean things to me, but she had been there, part of the pack. The change was like feeling the sun on my face for the first time. With Ivy walking down the corridor with me they treated me differently. When she chose to sit beside me in the cafeteria no one spilt drinks down my back.

'Then Lorcan and James joined us, making up the rest of our little unit. Lorcan had endured his own hell for the crime of being gay. The lads treated him like he was contaminated. As bad as I had it, he experienced worse. And James, well, he was just quiet, not one to draw attention to himself, but when the four of us were together he was funny and cool, and we all loved him. I felt like my life only truly began when the four of us became friends.' She reached over and took the paper cup of water, drinking it fast before setting it down.

'Ivy made my last years at school fun. She had a way of making everything feel like an adventure. That the four of us could do anything. That life was ours for the taking.'

'After the A Level exams in August 2001, the four of you went to Donegal, to stay in Lorcan's family house, isn't that right?' Danny asked.

Emer nodded, looking down into the empty cup. 'Could I have more water, please?'

Danny stood, walked over to the water cooler, and poured a fresh cup. He gave Emer a moment to drink the water before taking it again and refiling it a second time.

Rose leaned forward. 'So Emer, what happened at Mistle?'

Emer looked away. 'It was a holiday. We had fun.'

'We know there was more to it than that. Emer, you have a lot to lose. Your family, your career . . .'

'Why are you saying that to me? Threatening me?' She started to cry softly.

'Emer, James is dead. Your friend has been murdered. I'm certain you want to do the right thing by him. Your silence is helping no one. This is your opportunity to tell us what you know.'

She sat looking at them, her hands clasped, her skin mottled and flushed from crying.

Rose sat back in her chair. 'Emer, I understand that you feel you have to protect your friends – you all have a strong sense of loyalty to each other – but sometimes loyalty is misguided. Misplaced. You need to think really hard about your husband – John, isn't it? – and your two little boys. We don't take well to being messed around or lied to. This is a murder investigation. If you are withholding information, no matter how small, we will be forced to charge you with perverting the course of justice.'

'Now,' Danny said, his voice low and soothing. 'Tell us about your holiday in Mistle.'

Emer closed her eyes for a moment. 'God, it started out so good. Freedom from exams, celebrating the end of school, and all of us bursting with plans for the future. The four of us had a blissful week. Long walks on the beach, meals cooked over a makeshift barbecue with the sea air on our skin and the taste of salt on our lips, swimming in the Atlantic sea until our toes were numb . . . It was to be a new start for us. We could strike out on our own, yet know we had each other in our lives forever.

'Ivy was the smartest of all of us and she was going to Bristol to study medicine. Lorcan wanted to do accountancy and James was doing architecture at Queen's. I'd a place to do English at Trinity. We imagined ourselves in these new places, still keeping in touch but with new friends who knew nothing of our years of feeling uncomfortable and at odds with the world. Everything about our futures seemed to sparkle. It was as if our time had finally come.

'The rest of the sixth year had booked interrailing trips or party weeks in Ibiza but staying in Lorcan's family holiday house in Donegal was perfect for us.' She sniffed and took a tissue out of her sleeve. 'I don't think I've ever felt as happy as I did that week. We drank, smoked some weed that Lorcan had managed to buy before we headed to Mistle . . .' She looked up sheepishly, as if suddenly realising she was telling two cops about taking drugs.

'None of us were used to partying. It didn't take much to make us feel the effects.' She gave a hollow laugh. 'We thought we were invincible. On the first night we stayed up all night, just drinking and talking. Lorcan told us an old ghost story about the cottage. The nearest beach is called Murder Hole Beach, so it seemed fitting that there was a ghost story to go with it. Apparently, when his family were renovating the cottage, they found an old newspaper hidden in the rafters. The front page of the paper had a photograph of the original cottage with the owners and their family standing outside of it. The story told of how the father and the two sons had gone fishing and had perished in a storm. When they didn't return, the wife, mad with grief, took her two remaining children, a three-year-old and a baby, and walked into the sea. Lorcan told us that the cottage was haunted and that when you fall asleep you can feel hands tugging at you. "It's the fisherman trying to save himself and his children," he said. It was a tragic story and it spooked us.

'The next day we went exploring and Lorcan took us to the old crypt. The names inscribed on the stone were hard to read but we had convinced ourselves that it was the drowned family.'

Her breathing faltered and she closed her eyes for a moment. 'There was something so eerie about it.'

CHAPTER 73

Danny bided his time, letting them settle and stay with their own thoughts for as long as possible. Experience had taught him that there is nothing worse than your own imagination when it comes to second-guessing tactics. The friends would be fretting about what the others had said.

'It's frustrating, isn't it?' Rose asked.

'What? The job?'

She nodded. 'Yeah, it's hard not to rush it. To try to force the process,' Rose said.

'Yeah, I know, but when you've been doing it a while you learn to trust the process. It's not our job to judge. I afford them all the same respect, guilty or innocent. The courts get to decide the rest. I just bring them in and provide the evidence. Set it all up for the lawyers and say "here you go, finish it." Then I do it all over again with the next case.'

He knew they were getting closer. The friends were starting to crumble. Each folding under pressure. When it comes down to it most cases end up like this: people telling their side of the story, hoping it exonerates them or at least paints them in a slightly better light.

When they re-joined Emer Ward in the interview room her skin had an ashen look, as if she was ill, and her eyes were sunken marbles, darting around the room in uncertainty.

Danny looked at Rose and indicated with a sharp nod of the head for her to lead again.

'Emer, in your own time, tell us what happened after James went to town,' Rose said, her voice measured and low.

'I don't know what you're talking about,' Emer said.

Danny leaned forward. 'Emer, we know that James went into Mistle town. We also know that you were not directly involved with what unfolded, but to make sure you don't go down with your friends, you need to explain to us what happened.'

She hiccupped and clapped her hand over her mouth. 'I think I'm going to be sick.'

'Take a moment. Breathe deeply,' Rose said. 'There, is that helping?'

Emer nodded.

'We know this is hard, but we need you to tell us what happened.'

She started to cry. 'When James came back from the town, he looked stricken. I had never seen anyone so deathly pale. Lorcan was the one to ask what had happened but James just stared straight ahead, unable to find the words. He sat down on the sofa and put his head in his hands. Ivy took him by the shoulders and shouted at him, "James, what happened?" I think it was the silence that frightened me the most. He just sat there. No one made a sound for a good few moments, and then James started talking.

'"I didn't see her. She came out of nowhere." He was panicking, totally freaking out. "Who came out of nowhere? What happened? Did you have an accident?" I asked. He looked up at me and I will never forget his face in that moment. He was sort of blue with shock. His teeth chattering. Then he said: "She's in the boot."

'On the day we had arrived in Mistle we'd had a near miss with a ram on the road. He was a huge, ugly thing, and as we rounded a corner, Lorcan had to break hard to avoid hitting it. So when we ran out to the car to see what was in the boot I expected to see a ram, or maybe even a dog. I never imagined it would be a child. Her bicycle was in the boot too. The bent, tangled remains seemed to emphasise the gravity of the situation. The girl looked like she was sleeping. A red welt of an injury was blooming on her forehead and it was obvious that she had been terribly injured. As we were standing there astonished, James said: "She's dead, I've checked."'

'James had hit a child with the car?' Danny asked.

'Yes, but it was an accident. He hadn't seen her. You have to believe me.'

Rose looked at Danny. 'Then what happened?' she asked softly.

Emer shook her head. 'I can't do this. I can't talk anymore. Please, you have to let me go home! I want to see my husband, my children. Please, you have to let me go.'

Rose reached across the table and took Emer's hand. 'Emer, listen to me. You have done so well. We need to ask you more questions and then we can get your husband to come and see you, but we can't let you leave. Not yet. Not until we know the full story.'

She nodded. Her face was streaked with tears and brown eyeliner. She wiped her nose with the back of her hand.

'Here,' said Rose, passing her a tissue. She wiped her eyes and blew her nose.

'God it all sounds so terrible. So horrific. We've lived with this for years. I wanted to tell someone, lots of times. To do the right thing. To phone the police. But it was too late. Much too late. If I phoned the police, I would be destroying the life of one of my best friends, one of the only true friends I ever had. I would be signing his life away. The girl was dead. We couldn't do anything for her. Why did James have to suffer, too? In my head back then that made sense. I couldn't help the girl, couldn't bring her back to life, but I could save my friend. I could protect him. Now though, I can see it was all wrong. *I* was wrong.' She sobbed.

'What happened next, Emer? What did you do when you saw the girl in the car?'

She scrunched the tissue up in her fist. 'For Ivy every crisis is something to be solved. She grew up in a dysfunctional family. Her father was unfaithful to her mother and there were all sorts of chaotic episodes while we were at school. Ivy learned early on to fix things and that she had no one to rely on but herself. When the accident happened, the rest of us were too shocked to do anything but Ivy, well, straight away she was making mental lists of what we had to do, instructing us on how we should react, even how we should feel. "No records," she kept saying. "Never write anything down that can implicate us."

'At school she was always making planning sheets for revision. Organisation is part of her nature. She finds control in knowing what is going to happen and planning for it within an inch of her life. Ivy was the smartest of all of us and I can remember thinking it was weird that she wanted to become a GP rather than something like a surgeon. I asked her once and she looked straight at me and said, "A surgeon can't control everything." She didn't like risks.

'I realised that night that Ivy's need for control was all consuming. I, on the other hand, have built my PR career on the assumption that most people will fuck up at some time. That their actions are doomed to fail and cause problems.

'For Ivy, the plan was all about eliminating the risk of being found out. She calculated the risks and found that the best way to proceed was to carry on as if nothing had ever happened. When we went back into the cottage, she made James drink some black coffee while she paced up and down, considering the story from every angle. James kept crying. Big, heaving sobs. He was shattered. Totally broken. He kept saying "I didn't see her, I didn't see her." It was unnerving watching Ivy in action. It was as if she had been practising for something of this magnitude her whole life. She said if we went to the police, they'd never believe it was an accident. We were given no choice. Or at least that's how it felt.

'I suggested calling an ambulance and Ivy turned on me, saying, "She's dead, Emer. Dead. An ambulance won't change that. If we call the police, then we are all implicated. We can all forget university and our futures. What we do now won't bring the girl back to life. It's too late for her but it's not too late for us." James was gasping as though he was struggling to breathe, his head on Lorcan's lap.

'Ivy stood there staring, then she said, "There is no way out of this, unless you all do exactly as I say."'

CHAPTER 74

Emer's face was bone white. 'We were reeling, struggling to comprehend what had happened. We were kids celebrating the end of school, looking forward to the future, and here we were having to grapple with the most unthinkable problem we could ever imagine. We wanted someone to tell us how to make the problem go away and Ivy knew that she could direct us to her way of thinking.

'Part of me wanted to run out of that house and phone my mother. To claim I had nothing to do with the death and save my own skin, but I knew I couldn't. Ivy, Lorcan, and James were my friends. They had been there for me when I had no one. They had each taught me what a true friend was. I couldn't let any of them down. I had to stick by James. We all had to.'

She paused, looked down at her hands, bowed her head as if in prayer.

'Emer, you are doing really well. Take your time and tell us what happened next,' Rose said.

She lifted her head and breathed in deeply. 'We waited

333

until it was dark. Ivy wore her trainers and pulled on an old waxed coat belonging to Lorcan's mother. It made her look older, more authoritative and in charge. Lorcan wanted to stay with James but Ivy said no, the three of us had to do it together, and James was in no fit state to go anywhere. I can remember thinking: why the three of us? Surely someone could stay with James? His complexion was waxen and every so often he'd break down and start to cry again. James was traumatised, but Ivy meant business. I was simply reacting and doing as I was told. We wanted someone to make it all go away and that's what Ivy was doing. So we obeyed.'

Danny realised he had been holding his breath. He was frightened of breaking the spell; of jolting Emer out of her reverie of memory.

'The house was around a hundred metres from the sea and that's the direction we headed in most days. Swimming, messing around, lighting fires and cooking sausages while drinking beers. It felt like freedom and pure joy. I don't think I've ever felt that carefree again.

'The day before the accident we had gone for a walk. Lorcan said there was a creepy old crypt a couple of miles away so that's where we headed. The crypt was partially falling into the boggy ground but we messed around there for a while. Ivy told us when we got into the car that we were going back up to the old crypt. "If we can get in through the gates, we can bury her there," she said. There was a purposefulness to her; a real sense of strident determination. It was all too easy to get caught up in her rationale. To trust her.

'The journey to the old crypt felt as if it took forever. Ivy drove and made a couple of wrong turns before we found the place. Every bump in the road made me think of the child in the boot. I was terrified of seeing her. The rusted gates were padlocked but Ivy had brought a screwdriver and some pliers. Lorcan worked at the chain but it wouldn't budge so he lifted the gate itself. There must have been some land slippage as the whole gate could easily be lifted out and then put back as if it had never been touched.'

She stared ahead, as if she was seeing the scene unfold before her. 'The sky was the deepest, darkest blue I can ever remember seeing. The pinprick stars looked benevolent and I took it as a sign that we were doing what we had to. We had no choice. This was the only way out for all of us. "Right, let's do this," Ivy said. She opened the boot of the car and we peered in. I can remember seeing the flame-red hair and the pale skin of the girl and thinking she didn't look real. She was waxy like a doll and somehow that made it easier. Ivy used the black plastic bags that we'd brought with us and wrapped them around her before we lifted her out . . . and that's when it happened.'

CHAPTER 75

'That's when what happened?' Danny asked.

Emer looked away, put her hands to her face and started crying again.

Rose gave a barely perceptible shake of her head, stilling Danny. He knew to trust her, that Rose was in control. She had yet to let him down and it was all in the balance now.

A moment passed and Rose placed her hands on the table. Emer looked up and began again. 'She moaned. A low sound that we could have dismissed if it wasn't for all of us having heard it.

'"What the fuck!" Lorcan said and sat back in shock.

'We looked at the girl closely. Her eyes were shut tight and there was an obvious injury on the forehead. The righthand side of her body seemed almost mangled but there was no blood. She was still alive! I couldn't believe it. It felt miraculous that she had survived. We would call the police and get her help and the whole sorry mess could be put behind us.'

She paused, closed her eyes, and shook her head. Sorrow and regret were imprinted on her features.

'That isn't what happened though, is it?' Rose said quietly. 'You didn't call the police. You didn't get the child the help she needed.'

'No, the look on Ivy's face told me that she had jumped ahead of my thinking. "There's no going back. At best, we'll still be charged with trying to cover up the initial crime," she said. "But she's still breathing," I can remember saying. "We have to get her help. We need to take her to a hospital," Lorcan cut across me. Then he said, "No, Emer. Ivy's right. We're still fucked." Lorcan rarely cursed so it told me he thought the situation was desperate, beyond redemption. I could feel the muscles in my jaw clench. The possibility of being able to fix everything, of having the entire problem resolved, had vanished before my eyes. I had never felt so tired in all my life. It was as if a weight was pressing down on me. Ivy said: "No one is going to look at what has happened and say it was an unfortunate accident. She could still die from her injuries in a day or so and even if she's alive, she could have an untreatable brain injury. We can't turn back time."

'"Well, what do you suggest we do? Just leave her out here?" I asked. Ivy shook her head. "No, we have to take care of it and James can never know. As far as he is concerned, she was already dead, and we dealt with the body."'

'What happened next?' Rose asked.

'Ivy took the shovel out of the back seat of the car. Lorcan helped her lift the child out of the boot and they placed her inside the crypt. "You can't be serious?" I said. Ivy looked at me with contempt. "Deadly serious.

We don't have time for your histrionics, Emer." As if my hesitation was weakness. I expected Lorcan to speak up and tell her this was ridiculous, that we couldn't possibly do what she had suggested, but to my shock he said, "It has to be this way."

'Then Ivy said, "When we place her in there, we each need to use the shovel to inflict injuries to her head. She needs to die, and we all need to be implicated, that way no one will be tempted to grass on the other. We will all be guilty together."

'I can remember gasping at this plan. I felt it was abhorrent. James had hit her accidentally. Sure, he had been drinking and smoking weed the previous night, but he had not intentionally killed the girl, and now Ivy was expecting us to murder her in cold blood. "You don't get it, do you Emer? We will all go to prison for this if we go to the police now. There's no other way out." Ivy's tone was softer now. She placed her hand on my arm. "I know this is bloody awful, but we have been left with no choice. It's the only way to be able to put this behind us."

'I thought of how hard I had worked for the exams, how I was so close to getting away from home, to creating a new life for myself where I didn't have to feel lesser, different. I wanted this whole nightmare to be over, so I nodded and followed them into the crypt.'

Danny watched as she methodically rubbed her hand, as though trying to erase some invisible stain.

'I was committing to a plan that I knew was wrong, that could ruin everything, but I was convinced that if I didn't do it everything would be destroyed anyway. There was a hope that we could come out of that crypt with our lives still on track.'

'What happened afterwards?' Rose asked.

'The next day, Ivy made breakfast for everyone – scrambled eggs, thick, salty rashers of bacon, slices of sourdough bread toasted and slathered with salted butter, and mugs of strong tea. We sat around the table eating, and it felt as if the events of the night before had all been a terrible dream. When we'd finished, I'd half expected Ivy to announce we needed to phone the police and to confess to what we had done, but she didn't, she acted like it was just any other normal day. "Shall we go for a swim?" she asked. I was incredulous watching her go about the kitchen tidying away the breakfast plates, but then James smiled and said, "Yeah, that would be lovely." Before I knew it, we'd gathered our swimming stuff and were walking down to Murder Hole Beach.

'We ran down the deserted beach, into the water, screaming and kicking through the icy cold waves until we were far enough in to plunge ourselves fully into the sea. The sky was overcast, and it began to rain heavily, the raindrops bouncing off the waves. It was a baptism of sorts. We huddled together and Ivy instructed us to hold hands. "From this day forth we will never speak of Mistle again. We owe it to ourselves and to that little girl to live our best lives possible," she said. She made it feel like we were doing the right thing by moving on, keeping our secret and taking the best of what life had to offer us. God, she was so compelling. She should have been a politician. I think we were all crying but it was hard to say where the tears began, and the sea and the rain ended.'

CHAPTER 76

Rose sat nursing a cooled cup of coffee, discussing tactics with Danny. They had Lorcan Burns still waiting in the interview room and they needed to get his version of what happened at Mistle before launching into questioning about James' death.

Danny stood up, stretched out his arms and yawned. 'Okay, let's go do this. But you should know, I'm going in hard to begin with,' he said as they made their way up the corridor towards the interview room.

Danny threw the door open and strode in with a ferocity that Rose hoped he could control.

He sat down, activated the recording device and read out the date and the names of those in the room.

'Lorcan, I'm sick of listening to you and your two friends playing your silly games. Do you have any idea of the magnitude of what you have all done?' Danny was leaning across the table, so close to Lorcan's face that flecks of saliva hit him.

'None of it is down to me!' Lorcan was crying now,

gulping for air like he was drowning under the realisation that his life was about to be upended.

'We want to know what happened at Mistle. We have Emer's version, now it's time for you to speak up,' Rose said.

'I wish I could say we were drunk or high on something, but we were sober. Stone cold sober. Christ, living with it hasn't been easy. James suffered so much. We never spoke of it but it was there hanging over us. We were bound together because of it. Every good thing in life, every achievement, was tainted by guilt. Ivy said we owed it to the girl to make the most of our lives but I could never do that. It was only when Brody came along that I decided to give myself a break, to let myself feel love and be loved. I guess it's payback time. None of us deserved to have good things happen. I wish . . .' He looked down at the table, reached for the cup of water in front of him, and drank it quickly.

'What do you wish?' asked Rose.

'That none of it ever happened. That we had never gone to Mistle. That we could rewind time and that that day and night had never existed. That we'd gone interrailing or travelling around the Greek islands instead. Somewhere far away from Donegal and that bloody town.'

Rose stood with her back against the wall. She felt as if every nerve ending was tingling, on high alert. She knew ACC Boyne was watching through the one-way glass and felt compelled to show him she was worth the risk he had taken in allowing her to be part of the interviews.

'I know it's painful, Lorcan, but we need to go back to Mistle. Maeve Lunn was killed on the Saturday night, isn't that right?'

Lorcan's left eye was twitching again and his jaw was clenched. He nodded.

'Can you please respond aloud for the benefit of the recording?' Rose said.

'Yes, that's right.'

'And what time was she killed?'

'I don't know for certain. Sometime around midnight.'

Rose walked back over to the table and took her seat beside Danny. She referred to her notebook, turning the pages and letting Lorcan sit with his memories for a moment.

'James had gone to the village at 2 p.m. that afternoon and we have been told that he hit Maeve at around 2.15 p.m. Is that correct?'

'Yes. Possibly. I don't know for sure.'

Danny leaned back in his chair. 'So what did you do for the ten odd hours between James returning with the child in the boot and the murder?'

'We did nothing.'

Danny snorted. 'Nothing. You all sat about like lemmings doing absolutely nothing?'

'We talked, wondering what we were going to do.'

'And you decided you were going to hide the child's body,' Danny said.

'I know how it seems, but it wasn't like that.'

Rose leaned over and said softly, 'So, tell me Lorcan. What was it like?'

'We were scared shitless. You know that expression "your blood runs cold"? Well that was exactly how it felt, as if my blood had turned to mercury. We discussed taking her to one of the clifftops and dropping her over, but we reckoned she'd be washed up and with forensics and stuff, they'd know she had been hit by a car. Then Ivy remembered the crypt up by the old church ruins. She figured it was the perfect place to hide a dead body. No one would think of searching an old tomb. Tourists might come across it from time to time, but local people never went near it as the bogland was too dangerous. As far as I was concerned, we were taking Maeve to bury her. Nothing more.'

Rose studied him for a moment. She tried to look beyond the man in front of her, to see the scared teenager he had been in Mistle. Rose could see the dejection and wretchedness in the slump of his shoulders, the clench of his jaw, and the tight set of his mouth.

'Lorcan, we need to hear every detail of what happened. We need to hear your side of the story,' Rose said.

'I didn't kill her. I swear I didn't. And James wouldn't have hurt anyone on purpose, let alone a child. It was a stupid accident. A terrible mistake. If he could have saved her, he would have. It was bad judgement to place her body in the boot of the car in the first place. He should never have done that.' Lorcan put his hands to his head and started rocking back and forth in his chair. 'Ivy was like a machine. She's so exacting in how she operates, what she expects of us. We had to fall into line.' He sniffed and rubbed at his eyes.

'She said the only way out of this was for all of us to commit to her plan. If we were all guilty, then we were all invested in protecting the secret. I can remember thinking she was crazy, but it made sense. There was a simplicity to what she was saying – all of us would be guilty, but we could all be innocent as well as no one would know which of us caused the fateful blow. There was no way I was doing it though. I told her straight, "Do what you want but I'm not striking her." She looked at me with disgust, said I was weak and pathetic.'

Danny took a deep breath. 'Lorcan, we need to know – did you hit Maeve?'

Lorcan shook his head. 'No, I swear I didn't. I couldn't.' He massaged the back of his neck with his hand.

'I couldn't believe how stupid James had been assuming the girl was dead. If he had just called for help and owned up, none of us would have been in this situation. Ivy said that when the car hit the bike and the girl fell, a blow to the head could have rendered her unconscious, slowing down her breathing and pulse so that she appeared dead. When she was lying in the boot of the car, all we saw was what we dreaded the most.'

He paused, staring ahead before saying, 'Afterwards, when we had done it, Ivy had this eerie calmness that was unsettling. The rest of us were jittery. Emer kept crying, James looked like he'd fallen into the fires of hell, but Ivy kept going as if it was just another night of the holiday. She poured drinks, set out bowls of crisps, and even prepped a cheese board. It seemed ridiculous and wrong, but we were all ravenous. By two in the morning, we were making bacon sandwiches and drinking mugs of tea. The edginess had dissipated but there was a sinister hum left behind. It felt as though we were all tripping on some sort of mind-altering drug. Part of me wished that was the case, that we'd all taken something. That we'd come down and discover in the morning that it was all just a high gone wrong. That there had been no girl and none of the events of the night before were real. That it had been nothing more than a nightmare of the worst kind.'

The air in the room felt electrified with tension. Rose could hear Lorcan's heavy breaths, and she felt the pounding of her own heart.

'What happened afterwards?' Danny asked.

'Even though we were all exhausted, when we eventually went to bed none of us could sleep. The cottage seemed to creak and groan in ways I'd never noticed before. Every time I closed my eyes, I saw the girl, her red hair fanning out around her little head, the pale, almost blue skin with freckles. We had covered the girl with fistfuls of bog muck until she was buried within the crypt. I kept thinking of the earth clogging in her mouth, going up her nostrils, and it made me wretch.'

Rose thought about how the friends had managed to shift the blame between them. They had adopted a group consciousness rather than acknowledging their own individual responsibility.

CHAPTER 77

They took a break from the interview to discuss what they had uncovered and to plan their next move. Danny was wound up. So much of their job was in the detail, uncovering small, seemingly inconsequential pieces of evidence to build towards a more complex picture. But this case felt different, as if the truth they were uncovering was something pure and dark at the same time. Sin felt like an old-fashioned word but the phrase 'guilty as sin' had been running round Danny's head on a loop. They were all guilty as sin but who was the worst of them?

'I can't get my head around what they did to Maeve,' Danny said in frustration.

'They were kids. Stupid fucking kids.' Rose didn't swear often but she felt like the occasion called for it. She understood Danny's fury and frustration. 'We do stupid things when we are in a state of terror. Fear begins in the amygdala area of the brain and spreads through the body, fuelling the fight or flight reaction. They had been emotionally tricked by their own minds into seeing that which they feared the most. James told them she was dead so that is what they believed. The chances are none of them checked her pulse properly.'

'Fucking reckless, privileged bastards . . .' He trailed off and smashed his fist against the wall.

'Take a moment to decompress,' Rose said as Danny began pacing the room. He saw his reflection looking back at him in the window looking into the interview room. There were shadows beneath his eyes, and the curve of his cheek was rough with stubble.

Rose put her hands on his shoulders and drew him close to her. 'We can't go in there guns blazing. You know that we have to take it slowly. We're nearly there.'

The last of the day's light was fading outside and the office lights cast everything in an artificial ochre glow.

'A child, Rose. They killed a child. Jesus, when we were eighteen the worst thing we did was get rat-arsed and throw up somewhere we shouldn't. They've gone about their lives for all these years not giving a damn about Maeve's family. And there was me saying only hours ago that my job isn't to judge those who we bring in for questioning. Ha! I'm a fucking liar. How can I not judge them?'

Rose put her head against Danny's shoulder. 'You'll make sure that we see justice done, and it will help the family to know what happened.'

'Lainey, you make my job a hell of a lot more tolerable just by being at my side.' He gave her a weak smile, breaking the tension.

She shook her head, smiling. 'Are you ready to go back in there?'

'Yeah, come on.'

CHAPTER 78

Danny placed his hands on the table and stared into the dark pools of Lorcan's eyes.

His skin was a clammy grey and his hair looked like it could do with a wash.

'Lorcan, we want to talk to you about James. After Maeve was killed, how did James react?'

Lorcan took a deep breath and began. 'It was as if the events of that day were burned into James' mind. There was nothing that could ease his guilt or erase the memories. He once told me he would have given anything to forget. He would go off on benders. His mother would ring me asking me to go track him down. He'd wail and cry, talking about ending it all. He rarely mentioned Mistle but it was there all the same. Not once did he threaten to go to the police though. He didn't want to implicate us, and he knew there was no way he would get away with keeping us out of the story. He seemed better after he met Emma. More settled. Happy even.

'He married Emma thinking she couldn't have children.

He didn't feel like he deserved to be a father so when Emma told him she was pregnant, he flipped.'

'Did you ever bring Maeve up in conversation with him? Rose asked.

'God, no. The last thing I wanted to do was talk about it. I knew it was hard for James. Can you imagine what those years were like for him? The unbearable strain of holding it together. Living with the weight of that burden. Ivy, Emer, and I were made of stronger stuff. It wasn't that it didn't affect us, it was more that we could be pragmatic about it and try to move on. That sounds callous and hard, but we accepted there was no bringing the girl back.'

The girl had a name, Danny thought. *And a family who have lived all of these years not knowing what happened her.* As far as Danny was concerned, the friends seemed to have thought only of themselves and saving their own skins.

Lorcan waited a few moments, gathering his thoughts. 'Recently though, James got worse again, and Ivy began to realise that we couldn't trust James to hold it together. There was no way Emer was caving; she had her family and career to protect. And I couldn't bear for my partner or my parents to see me go to prison. I reasoned that we couldn't change the past, so we had to keep moving forward and be the best version of ourselves possible.' He gave a brittle laugh. 'I actually had hopes to adopt a child with Brody. I thought that by giving a child in need a home I would somehow be helping to make up for what we did.'

He bowed his head.

'You said James seemed worse recently. In what way?' Danny asked.

Lorcan took a deep breath. 'Like he needed supervision. He was so soft, so caring. That's why he couldn't hack what had happened.'

'Most people couldn't hack it,' Rose said. 'The death of a child isn't something most people can push to the back of their mind.'

'God, you make us sound like psychopaths! We were teenagers; kids ourselves. We made a mistake.'

Danny looked at him with disdain. It was getting increasingly harder to not lose his cool.

'What do you mean when you say "supervision"?' he asked.

'He was unravelling. We barely ever talked about Mistle. In all the years since I think we've mentioned it twice. It was easier to just never go there in conversation, but lately, James had been fixating on it. Ivy knew he was a risk.'

The light fell across his face, creating shadows. His eyelashes were damp with tears. 'James had always loved Ivy. They . . . well, they've always had a connection. If the accident hadn't happened, I think they would've stayed together and got married. But after Mistle . . . We all wanted distance from each other. It was hard to see the others without thinking about what we'd done.

'Ivy knew that he'd respond if she made a move on him, even after all these years. So she resurrected their relationship. She hoped by keeping James close to her she could have some sort of influence over him. Or that she would at least know what was going on in his mind.'

'So what did Ivy discover?' Danny said. 'Was James ready to come clean?'

Lorcan nodded. 'James' nerve had started to go. He

said that he would go to the police and say that none of us had any part in the accident. That he would take full responsibility and that he should have done it years ago. Ivy couldn't allow that to happen. She knew that the police would most likely discover that the girl had been bludgeoned to death, so he had to be stopped by whatever means necessary.'

He shook his head. 'I've always known how steely Ivy is, but this was something else. She was relentless in her planning.'

'How did she do it?' Danny asked.

'With sex. What I didn't know was that they were into tying each other up.'

CHAPTER 79

'Why am I still here?' Ivy Duffy's expression was one of outrage.

They had left her to stew while they interviewed Lorcan and Emer and the hours alone in the interrogation room had clearly made Ivy furious.

'I'm sure you will appreciate that we are running a murder inquiry here and that your patience and cooperation is appreciated.' Danny tilted his head and smiled.

Her composure was nowhere near as cool and collected as she had been in her home.

'Your friends have been most helpful today. They've filled us in on your history with James.'

She looked startled, as if she had been caught out.

Danny continued. 'You and James were childhood sweethearts. Isn't that romantic?'

Rose said nothing.

'We tracked down your old teacher, Mr Bradley. He'd fond memories of the four of you. Told us all about you and James and how the pair of you were inseparable.

That got us thinking about all sorts of things, like how close you four were. Thick as thieves.'

Her hands played at the buttons on her silk shirt. 'James and I had a brief relationship in our teens. So what?'

'Young love's pretty powerful, wouldn't you say? I'm sure you'd have done anything for each other. Aren't I right?' Danny said.

She tutted. 'Where are you going with this? Honestly, I really don't have time to sit here listening to your nonsense.'

'There's one thing that bothered us though, as we just couldn't figure out how you persuaded James to place a noose around his own neck. That really got me for a while, there. But then a good friend of mine over in state pathology, Dr Lyons, got back on to me. Seems the rope marks weren't the same as the marks of the item that had caused the strangulation. And I can tell you Dr Lyons doesn't let something go easily. If he isn't one hundred per cent certain he goes at it like a dog with a bone. The good news is he came up trumps. Isn't that right, Dr Lainey?'

Rose turned over a photograph of James' neck and pushed it across the table to Ivy. She looked at it dispassionately.

'Right at this moment my colleagues are searching your home. We expect to find DNA evidence that James was in your house on the night he was murdered.'

For the first time she flinched. And then she started to speak.

'It's not what it looks like. When he lost consciousness and slumped to the floor, I thought he was messing around. I thought he'd laugh. He was into strangulation, or "breath-play", as he called it. On this occasion we both got a bit carried away.'

Danny placed his elbows on the table. 'We've asked James' wife and she said this is not something that was part of their marriage. Further questioning has also revealed that erotic asphyxiation wasn't something that James had expressed interest in with previous sexual partners. So why was it something he did with you?'

Her head jerked back as if she had been struck by an invisible force.

'I don't know.'

'One thing you might like to know is that your friends have had enough; they've been talking.'

She pushed a stray strand of hair behind her ear and jutted her chin in a haughty gesture of defiance. 'You can't keep me here. I know my rights.'

'Oh please, we are playing this by the book. You can continue having this conversation and get your say or we can arrest you right now based on what your friends have told us.'

She placed her elbows on the table, joined her hands together, and leaned forward. 'I would like to assert my right to have my solicitor here.'

'Fine. One last thing though. We believe that James McCallum was responding to what *you* wanted in the relationship and you instigated the asphyxiation play because you intended to kill him.'

Ivy Duffy stared straight ahead, her face contorted in anger. 'As I said, anything further will involve my solicitor.'

CHAPTER 80

Rose slept fitfully and when she woke it was with a certainty that the four friends had not acted without some help. She showered, blow-dried her hair, took some time to put on a little make-up, and dressed in one of her best suits.

When she arrived at the station Danny was waiting for her.

'You look well,' he said. 'No sign of the end of a drawn-out case for some.'

She shrugged. 'Thought I'd make a bit of an effort this morning. I think we've a bit more work to do before this is wrapped up.'

'Can you imagine how desperate James must have felt? To have lived with the guilt all those years . . . A sense of shame would also add up for the choking fascination. It could have be a form of self-flagellation with Ivy taking on the role of the one in control. We do know she seems to have no problem inflicting pain.'

Further questioning last night had revealed that

Lorcan's beating had been organised by Ivy. She'd paid some hoods to ensure he kept his mouth shut and it had almost worked.

Rose and Danny now had to unravel the final threads of the investigation.

'I can't help thinking that there's something we're missing. Maybe James' father dying was the catalyst for him no longer being able to live with what he had done. Also, his daughter, Grace, had just turned eight, the same age that Maeve was when she died. That was bound to have affected him in a profound way.'

Danny nodded.

'I'm certain that the friends didn't act alone. Four teens, even bright ones like them, couldn't have kept this to themselves without some orchestration. Remember how I said that it was possible there were actually two cars with Northern Ireland plates seen in Mistle at the time of the disappearance? What if James' parents were in on it somehow? Tidying up after their children. Making sure that they stuck to the story all these years.'

'Shit! You're right,' Danny said. 'Let's pay Rhea McCallum a visit as soon as possible. Maybe she'll be more inclined to talk to us if she thinks we have something on her involvement. Play it as if we're responding to new information.'

An hour later they were sitting in Rhea McCallum's living room.

The woman looked down at her hands, fiddling with her gold rings.

'Do you remember what car your husband drove in 2001?' Danny asked.

'How would I remember that? Why would you ask me something like that?'

'Mrs McCallum, we know your husband was in Mistle after Maeve Lunn went missing. His car was seen. James had the accident, panicked, and called his father. Your son was a grade A student, never in any trouble. This would ruin his chances of university, would be a blight on his life. So, you and your husband went about cleaning up his mess, eradicating the evidence of the accident so you could all pretend it never happened and go back to the way life had been.' They watched as Rhea McCallum pulled herself up straighter in the chair, visibly gathering her strength.

'Except James couldn't forget so easily, could he? He was tormented by what he had done. He begged you and your husband to come clean. To help him make amends. But it was too late for that. There was no way you could go to the Gardaí and explain away your involvement.'

Rhea lifted her head, defiant now. 'He did what any father would do if his child was in trouble – he tried to sort it out. He covered up his son's mistake.'

'Except we aren't talking about a pranged fender or cheating in an exam. This involved the life of a little girl.'

'It wasn't like that. It wasn't as if we could bring the child back. The worst had happened. We couldn't do anything for her.' She shut her eyes, as if trying to shut them out.

'Even if it was an accident her family deserved to know the truth. To give her a proper burial,' Rose said. 'Your actions and those of your son and husband have given that family a lifetime of pain.'

357

'What good would it do anyone for James' life to have been ruined too?' she cried out, her voice hoarse. 'He had his whole life ahead of him. He didn't deserve to have it ruined by one reckless mistake. He was so young.'

Danny looked to Rose and then back to Rhea. 'But James didn't kill Maeve,' he said.

The colour drained from Rhea McCallum's face. 'What do you mean?'

'When Maeve was hit by the car, she was knocked unconscious. James panicked, placed her in the boot and returned to the house. He thought she was dead and Ivy, Emer, and Lorcan took it upon themselves to hide her body. Except when they moved her, Maeve began to wake up. They killed her to cover up the accident and avoid detection.'

Rhea's head shot up. 'No. That isn't what happened. Is it? Was James innocent all along?'

Rose looked straight at Rhea McCallum. 'Your son thought he had killed her and he sought to conceal his crime. The fact that the others finished the deed does not make him any less guilty.'

'When his friends had gone to hide the body, James phoned his father and told him what had happened. Your husband arrived at first light the next day and ensured that all loose ends were tidied up,' Danny said.

The woman's face crumpled in anguish. 'He was our son. What were we supposed to do? Hand him in to the police? Ruin his life over one terrible mistake? He was a good lad.'

'You know,' Danny said after a moment. 'I do have some sympathy for your son. With the proper guidance he might have done the decent thing. But you and your husband chose to make the whole sorry mess disappear for him.'

Rhea McCallum looked up, her eyes bloodshot and puffy. 'I've thought about this a lot over the years. We didn't do what we did lightly. Do you have children, Detective?'

Danny shook his head.

'If you do, one day you'll remember this case and you'll understand that you'd do anything – anything – for your child.'

They were gathered in the conference room for a run-through of the most recent findings, specifically the involvement of James' parents.

'It's the parents that I can't understand. How could they have gone along with it all these years? Surely they must have felt some crisis of conscience,' Malachy said.

Rose fiddled with a paperclip, bending it out of shape. 'It's called cognitive dissonance. The facts clash with their pre-existing convictions and beliefs about their son and themselves so they refuse to acknowledge or believe the truth.'

'At the end of the day, they were trying to protect their son in some sort of vain attempt of ensuring his life wouldn't be fucked up,' Danny said from where he was leaning against the wall.

'It didn't exactly go according to plan,' Mal said.

'No, it most certainly didn't,' Rose said. 'And all that damage and suppressed emotion culminated in his murder.'

'I'll ring through to the Gardaí and have them update

Maeve's family but first we need to make the arrests official,' Danny said.

The work and long hours had paid off. They weren't finished yet but the end was in sight.

CHAPTER 81

Finding Maeve Lunn's body turned out to not be so difficult in the end. The crypt, partially sunken into the bogland, revealed its secrets during the first proper search. Danny and Rose watched from a live video link. Lyons had joined them, wanting to see the case through to its sorrowful end.

'Death is nothing more than a chemical process. A chain of reactions involving gases and autolysis, bloat, decay, and skeletonization,' Lyons said. He was enjoying his day away from the morgue and the opportunity to make a show of his expertise.

Thanks to the videographer in Mistle, the three of them watched as an investigator climbed into the sunken glen of the crypt, a red rope tied around his waist for safety. It wasn't far down but the bogland was precarious, soft and squelchy, and the ancient brick crypt was subsiding. They didn't want anyone getting stuck. Peering at the screen Danny saw the others off to the side of the crypt take samples of moss and lichen while the forensic anthropologist on site, Siofra O'Leary, stood back and waited to be called on.

'Entering the cavern. Looks like there are four old coffins,' the voice of the unseen investigator called out. The camera panned around the dark space. 'Looks like there's something in the back.'

'Here, look at that,' Danny said, pointing to the corner of the screen where a bundled mass was illuminated by the floodlight.

'I bet that will be her.'

They fell silent, thinking of the child hidden in the damp chamber of death. How painful the finding would be for her family; the long years of wondering about what had become of her arriving at this sad end. They watched as the crime scene investigators, dressed in their white plastic suits, went about their work, lit up by the huge overhead lamps.

The camera person climbed out of the crypt well to allow the forensic anthropologist and the Gardaí team to take over and the exhumation work began. Danny felt frustrated to not be there overseeing the final details, but he accepted that the case of Maeve Lunn's disappearance wasn't in his jurisdiction. The removal of Maeve's remains and the pathology report would be completed by their southern counterparts in due course.

Lyons watched the screen intently. 'They should be able to roughly date the bones in the first few hours, but more extensive forensic tests could take two to three months.'

Suddenly they heard a shout out of sight of the videographer. 'Yes, looks like it's her.'

Danny sighed. He hadn't realised that he had been holding his breath while watching.

Now that the case was almost concluded the previous long weeks had caught up with him. He longed to go home and see his parents. Spend a few days on the farm and not think about anything to do with work.

CHAPTER 82

There was a strange quiet in the office the following day. Danny sat staring at his computer screen, trying to gather his thoughts. He hoped that whatever came his way next would involve working with Rose again. She may have only just got her feet under the table, but he was certain Battle saw her as being a permanent fixture. He just hoped HR wouldn't spirit her away to work with them on a permanent basis.

Ivy Duffy had been charged with James' murder along with the murder and unlawful burial of Maeve Lunn. Emer and Lorcan faced charges of murder and the unlawful burial of a child, with Lorcan also being found as an accessory to James' murder. Rhea McCallum would also be charged with withholding information. They may never know which of the friends delivered the deadly blow to Maeve, but they were all guilty as sin in one way or another.

* * *

Danny called Garda Cillian Leahy for an update. 'So, Maeve was in that crypt all along.'

'It's terrible to think she was there right under our noses and never found,' Leahy said.

'Some places don't give up their secrets so easily.'

'Or some people don't want them to be found out. I'd say there was a sense of "don't look too hard" for fear of what else might turn up. It wasn't as though someone bent had obstructed the investigation, I think it was more a matter of no one wanted to find something incriminating. There's a few of the old boys round here had more clout and power than they should have. Pockets were lined in those days as matter of course. I'm not saying the force was corrupt, but there were definitely a few bad apples.'

'Makes you wonder, doesn't it? At least the family have some answers now,' Danny said.

'In those days it seemed inconceivable that a child could disappear into thin air. Mistle was a safe wee town, despite the odd problem. Or so we all thought. There was no CCTV beyond that on the pub. No investigation into mobile phone records the way you would do now. Christ, kids these days leave the house with a GPS system in their pockets. I had a word with some of the boys on the original investigation. They kept thinking they'd get a break, someone would remember something, or somebody would talk. But that break never came.'

'What about formal identification?' Danny asked.

'That will come from DNA and dental records but we're pretty certain it's her. The clothes Maeve had been wearing when she went missing were more or less disintegrated but there was enough of a partial match to the description of the outfit she was wearing the day she vanished. And her red bike, it was also found in the crypt.'

CHAPTER 83

Danny sought out Rose to tell her about Garda Leahy's update.

'There's considerable damage to the skull,' Danny said. 'They can't say for certain how long she's been dead yet, but it all adds up to being Maeve. The family have been notified and are on standby for more information.'

'God, after all those years of not knowing. I can't imagine . . .' Rose trailed off. 'And the crypt, was it not searched when Maeve went missing?'

'Apparently the site was given a cursory once over. The metal gate on the crypt entrance looked secure so they didn't challenge it. It was no longer in use, and the keys had been lost long ago. The lock was intact when it was checked by the Guards last week but the gate itself could be lifted back with enough effort.'

'All those people out looking for the child and she was lying in that dark, damp hole all this time.'

James McCallum's death was the final act in a performance of death reaching back into the past to little Maeve Lunn.

Now, all that was left for her family was the funeral they had been denied for so many years.

'I know, but we've solved her case and hopefully provided the family with the closure they deserve,' Danny said.

'Looks like it's wrapping up nicely.'

'We're good at this,' he said.

'At what?'

'Working together. Hanging out. Me and you; it works.'

'We don't have to try too hard to get on, so that's a bonus.' She smiled.

'I can think of other bonuses.'

She looked serious. 'Jesus, you're in dangerous territory there, Danny boy.'

He smirked. 'Steady on, I was only—'

Battle arrived at the door before he had time to finish his sentence.

'Lainey and Stowe, I was looking for you both. Another win for the good guys. Well done.'

'Thanks, sir. It was a team effort,' Danny said, looking at Rose.

He still hated to think of her as part of internal affairs – cop watching – waiting for one of his team to slip up and make some fundamental mistake that he should have foreseen. Not all cases go your way – not out of bad policing, but out of sheer bad luck – and you have to watch the guilty party walk off into the sunset with not so much as a dent to their reputation. In those moments, few and far between as they thankfully were, you know you'd be prepared to do anything even if it meant bending the rules a little. He had made it clear that he wanted Rose working closely with him, but something had made her hold back. Having a foot in two departments appeared to suit her.

'I need to get some air,' Danny said to Rose after Battle had gone. He grabbed his coat, left the station and headed out to the car park. The rain was spitting down in sharp, cold daggers. He was grateful for his thick North Face jacket and pulled it tightly around himself. The amber glow of the streetlights emanated a noir vibe that Danny could appreciate. More often than not his job was dull, dry paperwork and phone calls, but every now and then a case came along that knocked the ennui out of the park. This one did that. The stakes felt high and the intrigue at the heart of it was compelling for even the most world-weary cop.

He had not reckoned on feeling so captivated by it though. The long hours, working so closely with Rose, and the nature of the case itself had created a strange alchemy that had enraptured him. It was as if when it was all over, done and dusted, he would be transformed. That this case would change who he was as a person.

He looked up at the night sky and felt the rain tingle against his skin. What remained was paperwork, the orderly side of the job, which at times felt a lifetime away from the crime scene. But he felt it all deep within him. The theories, the stories, the lies, the dead-end leads were like papercuts, barely visible but stinging nonetheless. At the end of the day though, the little girl couldn't be brought back to life. The futility of it hummed through him.

'Are you okay?' He turned to see Rose standing beside him.

'Sure.' He shrugged. 'I guess so.'

'It's okay to feel angry.'

'Yeah, the whole lot of them have made me want to punch something very hard.'

'You care. That's why it hurts so much.'

'Rose, have you ever thought of having kids?' It was a deep, out of the blue question but Danny was in that kind of mood.

'I've thought about it in an abstract way but never had to make a choice as such. Why?'

'Amy appeared on the scene a few weeks ago. Arrived at my house, wanting to talk.'

Rose turned to him. 'Wow. How did that make you feel?'

'Please don't psychoanalyse me. How do you think it made me feel? Pissed off, angry, sad. Take your pick.'

'How was she?'

'She looked well.' He thought he caught a flicker of something cross Rose's face – curiosity? Jealousy? – but he couldn't be sure.

'I mean healthy looking. She looked like she's doing everything she needs to do to get in better shape.'

'Did you work anything out with her?'

'If you mean, did we patch things up, then no. I think she was looking for some sort of closure. She said she didn't want bad feelings between us. That's rich. I wasn't going to say I forgive her or that it didn't matter that she had aborted our child.'

'Life's complicated.'

He shrugged. 'It's only as complicated as you want to make it. She could've had the child. We could have had a good life together.'

'You could try forgiving her like we discussed. Maybe giving the relationship a second chance.'

He turned and looked straight at Rose. 'I definitely don't want to do that.'

'Do you still miss her?'

'No, not anymore. Not with you here.' They were both quiet. Letting the words hang between them.

'Rosie?'

'Yeah?'

'When this case is over the line can we do something nice?'

'Like what?'

'Like go for dinner or spend the day walking in the Mournes.'

'As long as we don't talk work.'

'That's a promise I'm not sure I can make. But I promise to try.'

'I'll take what I can get,' she said, slumping against his arm in a friendly gesture. They watched the rain fall, illuminated by the orange streetlights, while Belfast's traffic rumbled around them.

THE END

ACKNOWLEDGEMENTS

This book was largely written during lockdown, and I am sure I am not alone in being relieved that we can once again see family and friends. I am so fortunate to have a tight-knit group of friends who have been with me through the good times and the bad: Deborah, Zoe, Joan, Tracey, Andrea, Katie, Roma, Carmel, Donna, Joanne, thanks for always being exactly what I need, when I need it.

The NI crime writing community are without doubt the most supportive bunch around. Special thanks to Claire Allan, Steve Cavanagh, Kelly Creighton, Gerard Brennan, Simon Maltman, James Murphy, Catriona King, Anthony Quinn, Brian McGilloway, Tracy Means, Stuart Neville. If I ever need to hide a body, I know who to call. Thanks also to my PhD supervisors Prof Andrew Pepper and Dr Dominique Jeannerod.

Writers are dependent on booksellers, bloggers, readers and other writers to champion our books. I want to thank Dave Torrans, from No Alibis in Belfast, Lesley

Price from Bridge Books in Dromore, Jo Zebedee and Deborah Small from the Secret Bookshelf in Carrick, Cara Finnegan, Aìne Doran (PR supremo) and Vanessa O' Loughlin aka Sam Blake, and Marie O'Halloran aka Casey King (my tequila sister).

I'm so grateful to my agent extraordinaire Lina Langlee and the North Literary Agency, as well as the entire Avon team, especially editors Katie Loughnane, Lucy Frederick and publicists Becci Mansell and Patricia McVeigh. You have worked your alchemy to make this book as good as it is. Thank you!

Thanks also to my brilliant family: Liam, Kate, Owen, Sarah and Daisy the duchess cat. Thanks for putting up with my obsession for weird dolls, typewriters and Led Zeppelin.

Don't miss Sharon's first mysterious, twisty crime thriller

'Gripping and pacy'
Steve Cavanagh,
author of the Eddie Flynn series